DAN FLETCHER

DAWN OF DECEPTION

PART I of THE DAVID NBEKE SERIES

DAWN OF DECEPTION
PART I of THE DAVID NBEKE SERIES

First Printed in Great Britain in 2015

FOR MY WONDERFUL CHILDREN,
JOSHUA, KIMBERLEY, OLIVER AND
ABIGAIL

Acknowledgements

Thanks must go to my parents, friends and family for their support in more than just this book and giving me the experiences to draw from and the time to write.

Special thanks to Clare for her unquestioning support, to Charlie Brotherstone for giving me the belief to really get going on the book, and to Andrew Papaconstantinou for doing such an excellent job on the cover.

PROLOGUE
Masai Mara Game Reserve, Kenya
August 8th, 1961

Maliki grimaced as the laces holding the leather straps were pulled tight. There for protection, they covered most of his sinewy arms.

"Why can't I go? I have every right to hate them as much as he does!" Maliki was referring to the raid that his father was planning on a British settler's farm. The attack was set for the early hours of the following morning.

"You heard him, not until you're a man." His younger brother shook his head, "You should be concentrating on today. If you don't...well, you might never get the chance."

"Don't worry, I'll be fine." He puffed out his chest, "Nothing scares me." Maliki avoided looking back into his brother' eyes and tried to keep his breathing regular. Both of them knew that many young warriors had failed the test with fatal consequences.

"Come on, let's go. They're waiting for us." His brother pulled back the hide covering the entrance and stepped outside.

The sun announced its approach by reflecting on a thin layer of stratus high in the atmosphere. The clouds glowed orange, golden, red and yellow rays bursting through their sides.

Maliki headed for the men huddled around the smouldering campfire. The group's animated discussion ceased as he approached. They watched him closely, searching for any sign of nerves. Maliki strode confidently towards their leader.

"A good day to go hunting," he looked up at his six foot five inch father. Maliki would probably exceed that height when he stopped growing. Even now at thirteen he was just a couple of inches shorter.

Chief Zuberi shook his head, "Remember, this is not a normal hunt."

"Don't worry, I will," Maliki smiled. He embraced his father with the arm holding his spear and their ebony chests touched. The other held his four-foot tall shield, slightly wider than his toned body. He'd removed his brightly coloured shuka and jewellery to avoid spooking his prey. He had even taken off his most prized possession, a gold medallion with the two-headed figure of the Maasai God Engai Narok etched into the face. It was a gift from his mother, meant to bring good luck and wisdom. Maliki felt naked without it.

The older warriors scrutinising him were also dressed for battle. Their hair and cheeks dyed red to give them a more fearsome appearance.

"I'm not worried about your ability. If you weren't ready I would not have permitted it. What I worry about is your over-confidence." The Chief put his hand on Maliki's shoulder, "Now make me proud!"

"They will have left if we don't hurry up. As soon as the grass is dry they'll be gone." His brother turned towards the gap in the bush that marked the beginning of the track. It led east, away from the clearing that the temporary settlement was built in.

They were being forced to move so often to escape the authorities' resettlement programmes that there wasn't enough time to build the usual defences. Normally they would surround the village in a boma, a ring of acacia bushes wound together tightly to form a sturdy fence. The steely spikes acting as a serious deterrent to predators and other intruders. As it was they only had a sentry and the fire to ward of any nightly visitors. Although laid out in the traditional way, the rondavels were hastily built. Some were hardly round at all and had patches of dung missing from the rattan frames that formed the walls.

The group were in high spirits as they filed down the track. Maliki joined in with their chatter, anticipating the celebrations that they would be enjoying later that day. As the bush grew denser the men became quiet. They picked their way through the long undergrowth with graceful strides.

He heard the sound of a warthog grunting near to them as it searched the forest for grubs. An orchestra of birds occupied the canopy above them, singing in symphony to the sunlight breaking through the leaves.

His brother's hand went up, signalling them to stop. He beckoned Maliki to join him at the front of the line. They had reached the edge of the forest.

"Over there," he pointed to the base of a gigantic boulder, a lump of granite fifty feet high, dumped there when the glazier carved its way through the rift valley millions of years ago.

"Where?" Maliki squinted. The crimson slither of sun was growing rapidly.

"By those two smaller rocks near the end...look, one of them's moving now!"

His brother had found the pride's den the previous day. There were eight of them in total. Two of them were females, four young cubs and one an adolescent male. But it was their elder leader that Maliki was interested in.

"I see them."

The pride was sheltering under an overhang of rock that wasn't quite deep enough to be considered a cave. He moved out from the trees, into the open field of corn-like grass that separated them from the rock. Dew covered the long stalks in large teardrops that soaked Maliki's skin up to his waist. He welcomed the feeling. Like all cats lions hated water. They would wait for the sun to dry out the field before leaving. In the twilight hours they could often be seen using the dirt roads that crossed the park to avoid getting wet.

The men appeared from the bush behind him. Moving like silent spectres in their red war paint they formed a bullhorn shape, with Maliki at the centre. Once they were in position he started walking slowly towards the pride. They were downwind from the lions, using the light breeze to mask their scent as they approached. The other warriors followed suit, keeping their formation, treading slowly and deliberately. They gradually increased the space between them to spread the reach of their human net.

At some thirty meters away one of the lionesses heard their approach. She jumped onto a rock and let out a low rumbling growl to alert the rest of the pride.

The battle-scarred male rose up from its haunches. Shaking a dark and matted mane it let out a tremendous roar. The lion focussed on Maliki and padded towards him, making grunting noises that seemed to come from its belly. For a moment he thought it was going to charge straight away. But the giant cat stopped a few meters from him, tilted its head to one side and snarled, displaying four-inch canines to warn him off. Maliki had to admit he was a magnificent specimen, a worthy opponent for a future Chief.

The men banged spears against their shields and chanted. They took turns to bait and distract the lion, causing it to circle between them.

Maliki overcame the urge to turn and flee. Even though his legs and heart were telling him to run like he had never run before. The lion was pacing from left to right, blocking them from the rest of the pride. He snapped and growled at the men either side but kept his eyes fixed on Maliki. The unblinking amber globes burnt into his soul.

Maliki took a deep breath and let out a guttural scream. The beast stopped prowling. Head dipped to the ground it let out a low growl. Its haunches heaved and the lion's claws dug into the ground as it searched for purchase. Maliki screamed again and took a step forward. He rammed the wooden spike on the bottom of his shield into the ground and prepared to spear the lion from his fixed position.

Instead of charging and leaping at him the scarred veteran wriggled backwards. Maliki pulled the spike from the ground and moved a step closer. His father shouted for him to stop. But it was too late. Sensing his opportunity the huge male rushed forward and attacked. Using one enormous paw it knocked Maliki's leg from underneath him and sent him crashing to the ground.

The beast pounced on top of him, biting into his arm and clawing at his face. Razor sharp teeth passed through his flimsy leather armour as if it were paper and latched on to Maliki's forearm. Canines drove through flesh and hit solid bone. He cried out as red-hot pokers of pain were messaged to his brain. Maliki let go of the shield and struggled with his attacker. He grabbed its mane with his free hand. The pain ripped through him and his primeval screams intensified as the huge cat worried at his arm, tearing flesh and muscle apart.

Suddenly the animal cried out, a short sharp yelp, and went limp, crushing him with its weight. He felt the chest deflate and with one last twitch of its legs the lion went still. Maliki tried to move but his back was pinned to the ground.

"Help me get it off."

The carcass was dragged away and Maliki could see his younger brother looking down at him spear in hand, blood dripping from the tip.

"No!" Maliki screamed, realising that the worst shame possible for a Maasai had befallen him. By killing the lion his brother had effectively exiled Maliki from the family and tribe forever.

CHAPTER ONE
South of Kisii, Western Rift Valley, Kenya
October 21st, 1991

David was desperately fighting the need to urinate. They had arrived in the midday heat, using the animal's resting time to find a suitable hiding spot. The five hours since then had passed slowly as they waited and watched the waterhole. He couldn't feel his feet and wondered how his father managed to look so comfortable.

"We might as well just give up," David whispered. Fidgeting as his urge to pee overcame his desire to shoot his first buffalo. He had hunted smaller animals before. But having just turned sixteen, this was the first time his father had allowed him to test his skills on more dangerous game.

"I thought you were the one who wanted to do this?" Sefu smiled, "Be patient, they'll be along soon. They're always the last to come, just before dark."

The waterhole was the only one for miles, enticing a small herd of impala, some zebra and a few giraffes to drink the brackish water. They were thirsty enough to risk being attacked by the handful of hungry crocodiles lying in wait. The giraffes splayed their front legs to reach the prized liquid. Gazelle and zebra took brief sips before flicking their heads up, ears turning and eyes twitching as they scanned their surroundings for predators.

All the time keeping a beady eye on the stationary crocodiles submerged in the water, the bony ridges of their prehistoric backs visible above the surface.

It was the height of the dry season and the receding waters were very low, their retreat marked by stains on the shallow banks. The long grass had been scorched tinder crisp by the fierce African sun and the season of bush fires would soon be upon them. David could taste the dust between his teeth, carried on the hot breeze hitting his face. Dusk approached, and the light was starting to fade.

"But..." David spotted a familiar dark shape emerge from the shrubbery to their right. The buffalo stopped a few meters out into the clearing and raised its nostrils, sniffing for danger before it proceeded towards the water's edge. The other animals moved out of its ambling path. A pair of resident tickbirds rode the buffalo's back, tolerated for the service they provided. It was the perfect target. Replaced by younger males the old bull would have left the herd to live out his final years alone, wandering around in an endless nomadic search for food.

David's hand trembled slightly as he aimed down the beaded scope of the Lee Enfield .303.

"Breathing," Sefu instructed him quietly.

David took a deep breath, and held it for a second. Allowing for the distance, light breeze and slight drop, he exhaled slowly and gently squeezed the trigger. He aimed for the heart, above and behind the beast's front haunches.

Just as the shot rang out and the rifle recoiled into David's shoulder the bull lurched forward. Searching for clearer water having stirred up the mud with its own hoofs. The bullet missed David's intended target by a few inches and deflected off the bull's rib cage, tearing into its lung. The tickbirds fled in a flutter of tiny wings. The other animals scattered in a flash of hooves and haunches, leaving the injured prey to stagger back into the bush and disappear from sight.

They rose slowly to their feet, muscles cramped and legs unsteady after being immobile for so long. David shot his father a worried look as he slung the rifle strap over his shoulder. They both knew that a wounded buffalo was extremely dangerous. Many a hunter was mauled to death by their fierce horns and trampling hoofs, sometimes just for startling them as their paths crossed in the night.

David followed his father into the forest and the circulation slowly returned to his aching legs. They picked their way along the track between the acacia bushes. The two-inch needles caught him occasionally, digging into his flesh. Nerves on edge they headed west towards the LandRover, constantly scanning the bush for any sign of the buffalo.

Eventually the trees started to thin out and they reached the edge of the veldt where the jeep was parked. David relaxed and loosened his grip on the rifle.

There was a loud crack as a branch was snapped under the buffalo's weight. Hidden in the last of the bushes to their left it ambushed them. David's father shouldered him out of the way, his rifle pointed towards the charging mass he pulled the trigger.

The .303 slug shattered the buffalo's skull and exploded into its brain, killing it instantly. Weighing over half a tonne, the dead animal's momentum meant that it didn't stop. It ploughed through the earth and slid to a halt inches from their feet. The huge nostrils flared and David felt the heat of the bull's last breath on his toes.

"That was pretty close," Sefu shouldered the rifle and wiped the sweat from his brow with the back of his hand.

"Close? I think I wet myself," David replied and they burst into fits of relieved laughter.

"I'll get the jeep," Sefu said, once the adrenalin and laughter subsided. The twilight was dwindling and it was getting dark.

They gutted the beast under the glare of the headlights and Sefu hacked it into quarters using his machete. Between them they struggled to lift the pieces onto the back of the vehicle, their chests heaved and arms swelled as they got covered in blood.

"You can drive," Sefu tossed David the keys and closed the tailgate.

"Thanks," David grinned.

They left the entrails on the ground for the scavengers and headed off over the bumpy terrain, the suspension straining under the enormous load it was carrying.

*****

"That was delicious," Waseme licked the grease from her long delicate fingers. "Well done you two."

"Father killed it, not me. If it wasn't for him we'd probably both be dead," David's reply was muffled by the piece of meat he rammed into his mouth.

"I'm sure you would have reacted if I hadn't," Sefu smiled. "You did well to hit it from that range in the first place. Tomorrow we'll salt the rest of the meat. We're going to be eating it for months."

"Can we give some to Aunty Farisi?" David looked at his mother.

"You can take some over to her tomorrow on the way to school. Now finish your food, it's late," Waseme cast Sefu a nervous glance.

They were sat around the blazing campfire, carving the meat off the leg as it cooked on the spit. The smell as the fat sizzled and spat was almost as delicious as the taste.

"You heard your mother, it's time for bed so eat up," instructed Sefu.

David knew better than to argue. It would only mean more chores if he did, and there were enough of those to go around already.

His Aunty Farisi was his mother's older sister and the only relative he had. Well the only one he was allowed to have anything to do with. At twelve years old Aunty Farisi had helped his mother run away from their clan. She wanted Waseme to escape the genital mutilation that she had suffered. By chance they stumbled across the catholic mission outside town and the sisters welcomed them in. His Aunty Farisi had been there ever since. She had become one of the nuns, caring for other misfortunate girls.

His father's parents were Kikuyu and wouldn't accept Sefu marrying outside their tribe. They and the rest of his family refused to come to the wedding and his father never forgave them. Sefu never spoke of his parents and David had no idea who his grandparents were or where they lived. He thought that by now there might have been some form of acceptance and he would have been allowed to meet them. There wasn't, the tribal rift between the families was as wide as the great valley itself, timeless and unmoving.

Like his Aunty, Waseme rejected Maasai traditions and turned to the Christian faith. She too would no doubt have become a nun if not for meeting his father.

"Don't forget to read a page of your bible tonight," she said, as if reading his thoughts.

"But you said, it's late," pleaded David.

"I suppose just once won't hurt, but make sure that you say your prayers." Waseme smiled, "Now off you go, we'll see you in the morning. Have you put the hens away?"

"Don't worry they're safe, I locked them in earlier," David sighed dramatically. He got up and dusted the bits of food from his lap. "Good night then," he bent down and kissed his mother on the forehead.

"Sleep well," she moved closer to Sefu.

"Good night," David nodded to his father, turned and headed for the wooden barn.

David crossed the patch of earth that separated the barn from the bush surrounding it. Every year they burnt back a large area around the farm. Forming a barrier against the natural fires that raged the savannah in the dry season. He pushed the roughly hewn door open and stepped over the piece of timber that both held the frame together and represented the threshold to their home.

Although they were close to the town they were still not connected to the national grid. The electric poles not venturing out from the main road that led into Kisii. A gas lamp flickered on the rickety table that acted as the kitchen surface. The light it produced was unstable and shifting, not quite able to fill the room.

David walked over to the bed and kicked off his sandals before kneeling next to it. He put them underneath the bed and clasped his hands together.

*****

He sat up, wondering what had woken him from his deep slumber, and why the usually dark room was bathed in light. There was another loud blast from the horn of a vehicle outside and David's brain groggily put two and two together.

He squinted blindly around the room. When his eyes adjusted David could make out his father, crouched next to the door with his rifle held in front of him.

"Who is it?" he peeled back the blanket and swung his legs over the edge of the squeaky metal bed.

"Stay still and keep quiet!" Sefu glared at him briefly before turning his attention back to the door.

"Listen to your father," whispered Waseme, seeing David look towards his rifle. It was propped up in the corner opposite his bed. David stayed where he was, trembling as the adrenalin pumped through his veins. The silence was broken by another long blast on the horn.

"Come out now and you won't be hurt," was the loud cry that followed.

"How do I know that?" Sefu shouted through the door. He beckoned them to move onto the floor at the foot of his parents' bed. David crawled across the room as instructed and joined his mother. He could feel her arm trembling as she pulled him close to her. They crouched together, arms looped around one another's back. David pulled back the hessian bag covering the window and peeked outside.

"You have my word," replied the man wearing a red and white chequered shemagh. The scarf was wrapped around his head so just a slit was left for his eyes. He nodded to the man holding an AK47 machine gun standing beside him. The man smiled and nodded back, but kept his finger on the trigger.

David swallowed. Something wasn't right about the way the man smiled. He could feel the hairs on the back of his neck standing up, the way they did just before a kill shot. Behind the group of six men, including the one who appeared to be their leader, there were two more men in the cab of an old Bedford truck. He could hear another three or four of them stumbling around in the maize patch behind the barn. David guessed that there were twelve of them altogether, dressed in un-matching t-shirts, combat trousers and black leather boots. The men that he could see were tall, probably Maasai, and despite the t-shirts they moved with military precision.

"We have the building surrounded, if you don't come out in sixty seconds then we'll burn the place down. With you in it."

The movement behind the house confirmed that the unseen intruder was telling the truth. His father stood and leant his Lee Enfield against the wall next to the door.

"Hold on, I'm coming out," said Sefu.

"No," David shook his head, "I don't trust them."

"Quiet!" Sefu put his finger to his mouth.

His father opened the door and stepped out into the glare of the headlights, keeping a hand on the doorframe next to his rifle.

"Step forward, away from the door."

Sefu must have realised that to disobey would result in a barrage of bullets. He let his hand slip from the door and moved a pace towards them.

"What do you want?" David's father was shielding his eyes with his hand.

"Somewhere to stay for the night, that's all. Who else is in there with you?" the man lowered his machine gun so it pointed at the ground.

Sefu hesitated for a second before replying, "Just my wife and son...you're welcome to stay the night if you want. We don't have much, but I can offer you some food and shelter."

"See, I told you they were hospitable in these parts." The leader turned to his entourage, "You can relax. We won't find any trouble here."

David watched his father walk over to the group with his hand outstretched, "I'm Sefu..."

The man standing next to the one doing the talking cut his greeting short. He struck David's father viciously on the temple with the stock of his gun, dropping him to the ground. Sefu lifted his hands to protect himself from further blows and was thrust face down in the dirt.

The leader and three of his men rushed into the building. David stood up to confront them, putting himself between Waseme and the gang of men.

"Leave us alone!" spittle flew from his mouth.

The man wearing the headscarf lunged forward and grabbed him by the throat. He squeezed hard and David could feel his windpipe being crushed.

He grabbed hold of the hand on his throat and tried feebly to prise it off. The man's grip was like a vice. David spluttered in protest as he was dragged into the middle of the room.

"Shut up," the man let go and struck him across the face with the back of his hand, his maniacal eyes gleaming behind the shemagh.

He caught hold of David's arm, twisted it behind his back, and pushed his hand up between his shoulder blades. The pain shot through his arm. David bit his lip to stop himself crying out. He was thrust towards the doorway and felt a heavy boot connect. It sent him sprawling in the dirt beside his father.

"Bring her outside!" the madman shouted.

Two of the men shouldered their weapons and moved to the corner. They picked Waseme up by her elbows and carried her outside to join the others.

"Good, I want this bitch to see what happens to Kikuyu bastards, especially ones that steal our women and land. Get them to their knees!" he snarled. "And make sure that she watches."

One of the men pushed his mother to the floor and used both hands to hold her head fixed towards David and his father. She closed her eyes, tears running down her cheeks. The man in the headscarf stepped in front of Sefu and aimed the machine gun at his kneeling father's head.

"No!" David screamed as he pulled the trigger.

The bullet burst through Sefu's head, spraying bits of bone and flesh over David's face. His father fell backwards, legs trapped underneath him.

Waseme broke free from her captor and scrambled to her feet. She launched herself forward and attacked the masked man with her nails, scratching at the scarf, trying to get at his eyes. The neck of his t-shirt was torn open and revealed a gold medallion surrounded by an ivory lattice. It glowed like a small fiery sun in the truck's headlights. Etched in the centre was the figure of a man with two heads, it was an image that David would never forget.

The murderer grabbed hold of her hands and laughed, his face only inches from his mother's, "I think we'll have some fun with this one before we kill her. Keep the boy alive until I've finished with her. I want him to hear how she screams with pleasure."

"You bastard!" David struggled to his feet, hoping the man could feel the hatred in his eyes. Wanting to strangle him with his bare hands.

It was the last thing he remembered before the butt of the AK47 smashed into the back of his head and the lights went out.

CHAPTER TWO
Maasai Mara, Near the Tanzanian Border
August 9th, 1996

David woke with a start and the soaked sleeping bag fell away from him as he sat up. His chest glistened with sweat and he stared blankly at the canvas, struggling to come out of his recurring nightmare. It always seemed so real, like the five years that had passed since didn't exist.

He waited for his eyes to adjust to the light filtering through the olive green material. He glanced over at Damo, worried that he might have screamed and woken him up. Thankfully his friend seemed to be asleep, Damo's back was to him but he could hear his slow rhythmical breathing.

David lay back down on the bedroll and stared up at the point where the sides of the Government Issue two-man tent met in the middle. The canvas started to blur and then melted away, he found himself being transported back through time to that night. The rumbling bellows of a lion down in the valley snapped him back to the present. David shook his head, dream or daydream? He wasn't sure. At times his conscious and subconscious overlapped, and reality and fiction became blurred. In some of his dreams he managed to save his father. Only to awake and have to undergo the painful realisation that Sefu was really dead and never coming back.

David sighed, sat up and swung his legs out of the sleeping bag. He scratched his itchy scalp, feeling along the ragged line where the bone had grown back together to form a pronounced ridge. The doctor in Kisii had told him that he was lucky to survive the blow that fractured his skull, David wasn't so sure. Death would have at least meant an end to witnessing the daily torment and suffering that his mother went through.

The raid on their farm and his father's murder was not an isolated incident. It was part of a widespread campaign of terror and ethnic cleansing, designed to keep the Kikuyu away from the ballot polls and Moi in power. Reports emerged over the years that tens of thousands of Kikuyu lucky enough not to be slaughtered were held in detention centres to prevent them from voting.

Most of the land returned to Kikuyu ownership by President Kenyatta after the British withdrew was now being contested by Moi's regime. The Kikuyu farmers were being driven out and the title deeds signed over to people from Moi's tribe, the Kalenjin. Their farm was just one of thousands taken from its owners by force.

"Are you OK David?"

Damo's voice startled him for a second. He had forgotten where he was again. "Just tired, I didn't sleep very well with all the commotion that the pride was making down by the river."

Damo nodded, as if accepting his excuse, but after camping together hundreds of times he knew

David as well as any man ever would. One drunken night in Narok he had told Damo about his father's murder and the all too real nightmares. That was when any lingering reservations he had about working with a Maasai were extinguished. Damo had tears in his eyes when he hugged him and apologised for what another member of his tribe had done. A bond was formed between them that day, made stronger by their experiences in the bush. They had become like brothers, relying on each other for survival on a daily basis in their campaign against the poachers.

What David hadn't told Damo was that joining the Kenyan Wildlife Service gave him the opportunity to travel and explore different parts of the country. Improve his chances of finding the monster responsible for destroying his family.

He looked over at Damo, "Go and wake the others. I'll get the fire going and the water on."

"OK boss!" joked Damo. "Right away!" He gave a mock salute before pulling on his combat trousers. Although Damo always followed his orders without question David occasionally wondered whether he resented taking them from someone almost half his age.

At forty-six Damo was as a fit as any member of the squad and could outrun him easily, his extra height and longer limbs giving him a distinct advantage. David noticed that he too had lost a lot of weight, his sinewy muscles more defined. The whole squad were leaner and harder after three weeks of trekking through the bush. They were covering up to thirty miles a day through unforgiving landscape just to keep up with the herd.

They got dressed into their camouflage fatigues and packed away their equipment in silence. A two-minute routine they had completed together countless times before, never leaving the tent until they were fully kitted out. When they were done David picked up his rifle and binoculars before following Damo outside.

They had spent the night in a camp not far from their base, the Purungat Outpost on the western edge of the Maasai Mara Reserve. David had thought about going back to the crumbling outpost for the night but there seemed little point. With broken windows, collapsed ceilings and no running water or sanitation they might as well stay closer to the elephants. Lack of funding was crippling their efforts to maintain the Park, half of the time staff weren't paid and didn't bother turning up for work. David's team were one of the few still fully operational.

There was still a General Service Unit base near to Oloolola Gate, the paramilitary wing of the Kenyan police. The place was usually deserted and they didn't venture out. Crime was on the increase and the roads and Parks facilities had fallen into a state of disrepair, but nobody seemed to care. No matter how many requests he sent through to headquarters for new equipment or staff, they didn't arrive. David was beating his head against a brick wall and knew that they were fighting a losing battle. These days only one third of the Mara Triangle was safe for tourists. The rest was a no-go zone that most of the rangers avoided. He couldn't blame them they were outnumbered and outgunned. Most of his time was spent policing the Park, arresting petty criminals and cattle rustlers instead of protecting the wildlife.

The camp they were staying in was one of many dotted along the Tanzanian border. A clearing surrounded by a thick boma of acacia bushes, sat on a rocky escarpment that overlooked the Serengeti and the limit of David's jurisdiction. He threw some kindling onto the smouldering ashes of the campfire before adding a couple of thinner logs from the stockpile. The seasoned wood was light and crisp after a couple of years drying in the sun. Within seconds the fire burst into life and flames engulfed the branches.

David walked over to the barrier of thorns and pulled the sleeve of his jacket over his hand to protect it. He grabbed hold of one of the branches and dragged out a three-foot wide section not interwoven with the rest of the boma. He walked through the gap that acted as the entrance, his rifle held loosely in front of him as a precaution. It would be unusual for any predators to be this close to the camp with daylight approaching, but not unheard of.

He wandered over the edge of the rocks and looked down. A thin blanket of grey mist shimmered over the veldt below, heaving and rolling between the trees as if the land itself was taking shallow breaths.

David shouldered his Heckler & Koch sniper rifle and lifted his field glasses from his chest. He scanned along the dried up riverbed to the east, hoping that the elephants were heading back into the relative sanctuary of the park. But they weren't. It took him a while to find them, just their backs poking through the mist. Moving like boats on water, leaving wispy trails in their wake. They must have gone left at the fork in the river during the night and were heading southwest in the worst possible direction. Along the meandering Mara River that loosely marked the border and the edge of the National Park. Half of the loops in the river belonged to the Kenyan side, the rest to Tanzania.

At points it was difficult even for David to be a hundred percent certain which country he was in. It was a favourite killing ground for the poachers at this time of year. When the waters were low and the riverbed easy to cross. A short dash and they were in the safety of the Serengeti where David and the other Rangers weren't allowed to follow.

He put down the binoculars. They had better get moving. The herd was already a few miles away and getting further with every minute he wasted. By the time he got back to the fire Damo had already boiled the water and was making the maize meal porridge. He was adding honey from a jar to the pan, sweetening the mixture.

He looked up as David approached and raised an eyebrow, "I thought that you were going to put the water on?"

"I went to check on the herd, they're moving south along the river." David sat down next to Chege, the radio operator, and greeted him with a nod. A beast of a man with legs like tree trunks and a ready smile who seemed not to notice the extra weight he carried.

Damo's expression changed and the men's chatter died out as the mood turned serious. After wolfing down the porridge they packed away the tents and left the boma.

Dawn came in pastel shades of pink and blue as David led the six-man team along the rim of the escarpment to the track going down to the river. The rest of his squad were carrying AK47s, even Chege who was keeping up the rear. Russian bought machine guns to match the poachers' firepower. It also meant that they could use most of the ammunition recovered, as the Kalashnikovs were their enemy's favoured weapon.

A group of rock dassie had emerged to bask in the morning sun. David knew them by their Swahili name 'pimbi'. Fat rodents the size of a rabbit. Like mongoose they posted a lookout to guard against attacks from eagles, caracals and puff adders. Apparently scientists had proven that their closest living relatives were actually elephants. Something to do with the proportion of their limbs to their body and snout, but looking at them David found it difficult to believe. They looked more like oversized rats. The tawny grey sentry let out a trill whistle as they approached and then started barking to alert the others. In a heartbeat they disappeared under rocks and into crevices.

Once they negotiated the treacherous slope and made it down to the riverbed David increased the pace to a steady trot. What was left of the river, a ribbon of water about twelve feet wide and knee deep, snaked its way through the sand and shingle from one side to the other. He followed the left hand bank, keeping an eye out for crocodiles and hippos. Most of the water was too shallow except in the bends of the river where it collected to form deeper pools. They passed a family of five hippos, just their backs, the pinks of their ears and flaring nostrils showing above the surface. As they got closer a turtle riding the back of one of the adults slipped into the water. The large bull with yellow rotten teeth yawned lazily, snapping its tremendous jaws together like a steel trap and sending a spray of water in their direction.

Tall trees lined the banks of the river, a mixture of cedar, juniper and the odd weeping willow. White-bellied Go-away-birds made repeated calls of 'gwa, gwa' as they flew from tree to tree.

Suddenly the rat-a-tat of machine guns firing in the distance sent the birds squawking from the canopy. David stopped and held his arm up, waiting for another volley so he could get a bearing. Seconds later there was another burst, the familiar sound of an AK47, it confirmed his fears that it was coming from further down the river.

He threw Damo a worried look. "Tell Chege to radio it in and catch us up, sounds like they're four or five miles south of here. Tell them we need the spotter plane." He guessed that the shots were coming from about two miles further southwest than he had seen the elephants earlier. Near the point where a large sweeping bend took the river into Tanzania for a few miles before turning back across the border. David didn't wait for the order to be passed on. He started running towards the gunfire.

Although only five miles as the crow flies the twisting route they were forced to take along the river was almost triple that. David checked over his shoulder at regular intervals to make sure that the men following him were keeping up. He needn't have worried. They were conditioned to running with their twenty-five kilogram loads and took on water from the flasks in their webbing as they went. His legs were burning and a patch of sweat covered his back by the time they found them. Almost three hours after the shots were fired.

He saw the vultures first, circling above a clearing next to the banks. Then he rounded the bend and could see the carnage spread out before him.

They had left the calf alive, barely six months old she still had her milk teeth. Her tusks wouldn't start to grow and replace them until she was twelve months old so they had saved their bullets. She nudged the butchered carcass of her mother with her trunk, trying to get her to wake up.

David had seen dead bulls a few days after their tusks were removed, deflated skin and bones once the scavengers were finished. But never a whole family freshly slaughtered like this. Even the foot long stumps of the two-year old calves had been cut from their bullet-ridden corpses. As he got closer the stench of death got worse, the bloated bodies emitting foul smelling gasses as they quickly expanded in the heat. The earth around them was stained with blood, pools of the stuff collecting around trunks. Bellies covered in urine and excrement where the great mammals had defecated for the last time.

The legs of the younger elephants were sticking up in the air where the poachers had rolled them onto their backs to get at the ivory more easily. In order to save time they had mutilated them, hacking back half their faces with machetes and axes to get at the roots of the tusks. One of the elder cows' trunks had been sliced off completely. Presumably it had been in the way, hanging over the overgrown incisor that was both the elephant's greatest asset and her Achilles' heel.

Nature's opportunists had beaten them to it. A pack of black-backed jackals and dozens of vultures were already tearing at the carcasses. Snapping and pecking at each other to get their heads and necks into the gaping wounds and soft grey underbellies of the elephants.

David swallowed the excess saliva his mouth was producing and the urge to vomit. He fired a single round into the air that sent the jackals scampering for cover and the vultures into flight.

He turned to face the others. Chege, usually the most jovial of the group, was openly crying, silent tears running down his flat cheeks. David felt a lump in his throat and realised that his eyes were also threatening to overflow. He wiped at them with his sleeve.

"Chege call in the location and ask them where the hell the spotter plane is. Damo you come with me. The rest of you spread out and find the trail, they can't have got far."

Weighing over sixty kilos each the matriarch's tusks would need two strong men to carry them. David walked with Damo along the bank near to the killing ground. It didn't take them long to find the tracks. As he feared they headed across the river. Around twenty men carrying heavy loads, their feet had sunk deep into the sand. Two of the men had dragged a large tusk behind them as they struggled through the mud on the other side of the shallow water.

David stared across the bank and then made up his mind. He took a step forward but felt Damo's hand on his shoulder holding him back.

"Don't even think about it David."

He pulled away from his friend's grip, "I can't just let them go, not this time."

"You have to," said Damo softly. "Orders are orders. If we get caught it'll start an international incident. Besides, there's just too many of them."

He knew that Damo was right but that didn't make it any easier. David could feel the tightness in his chest, the bile rising up from his stomach. He fell to his knees and was violently sick.

CHAPTER THREE
Kilindini Port, Mombasa
August 10th, 1996

Maliki turned his back to the cargo ships and peered up at the industrial estate behind the port. He smiled to himself, thinking how much the landscape had changed and how different his life was since the first time he arrived in Mombasa over thirty years ago. The fields and the shepherd's hut he had sheltered in after jumping from the train were long gone. The land between Kilindini Harbour and the town was now filled with row upon row of new warehouses, even the abandoned kerosene store that he lived in with Jozi for over a year had been torn down and replaced.

His smile evaporated as he checked the time on his gold Rolex, Gupta was late. The corner of his mouth twitched where the scar met his lip. A sure sign that he was irritated. He looked at his reflection in the window of the Mercedes saloon. The welts on his face were pronounced purple lines that stretched the skin around them making it itch constantly. He rubbed his cheek to relieve the sensation, the scar tissue dead to his touch. The three parallel ridges of puckered darker flesh that marked the passage of the lion's claws ran from above his right ear down to his chin. The top one only just missed his eye and ended level with his nose, the bottom one passed where the tip of his ear used to be.

As if on cue the first of the Bedford trucks appeared at the top of the causeway and headed down towards the docks. Gupta waved as they drove past him into the open warehouse. Maliki nodded to Lembui, one of his personal bodyguards, and then followed them in. Lembui stayed a few dutiful paces behind him, his right hand resting on the Glock hidden under his undersized sports jacket.

'EAST AFRICA TIMBER COMPANY', one of his many legitimate enterprises, was emblazoned in bold red letters on a yellow background. Both on the sides of the trucks and above the roller shutter doors. Deepak Gupta jumped down from the cab of the last truck and dusted of his dirty white robes. The electric motors whirred into action as the doors were shut behind him, the strobe lights flickered before illuminated the huge warehouse in a harsh glow.

Gupta smiled, tobacco stained teeth above a straggly grey beard that tapered off to a point where it touched his chest. Yellowed around his mouth from excessive smoking. "Peace be with you my friend."

"You're late!" grunted Maliki. "Where the hell have you been?" Maliki didn't trust the turbaned fool as far as he could throw him. Their relationship was based on mutual greed and fear, Gupta's fear. He was pleased to see the man flinch and shrink away from him.

"The rains have washed away some of the roads near Moshi. One of the trucks got stuck and it took us hours to find another way around."

Maliki knew the roads south of Mt Kilimanjaro better than anyone having made the trip many times himself in the early years. The foothills of crumbling volcanic rocks were treacherous during the rainy season, landslides commonplace. But it avoided the busier route through Nairobi and was the quickest and safest way to get their precious cargo to Mombasa. He could have used the port in Dar-es-Salaam but that would have meant employing a third party and losing a good chunk of the profits. As well as control, which was something Maliki cherished. He preferred to keep their operations based in Kenya where his influence extended deep into the government.

"Any problem with the border guards in Holili?"

"No they were expecting us as you said."

Maliki nodded. Fifty thousand shillings, just under one thousand US dollars, was a small price to pay for safe passage across the border. A fortune to the two guards it was split between, the cash equivalent to three months regular wages.

"Good." Maliki gestured towards the trucks, "How was the hunting?"

"Plenty of ivory." Gupta looked at his feet nervously, "But we didn't see any rhino this time."

Maliki's lip started to twitch, "I told you what I needed? What the buyer wants?"

"Yes," his pupils dilated and Gupta started to tremble. "You also told me that there would be no

Rangers in the area. Otherwise we would have stayed longer."

"Rangers...did you see them?" The news surprised Maliki. According to his sources the nearest member of the Kenyan Wildlife Service should have been twenty miles further north, at their base camp in the middle of the Masai Mara triangle.

Gupta shook his head slowly, "No but we heard them fire a shot less than an hour after we left the elephants. We were only a couple of miles away."

That was too close for comfort, the last thing Maliki needed was for Gupta to get caught. The man would probably sing like a canary to save his own skin. Maliki made a mental note to ensure that it never happened again. He would speak to his informant when he got back to Nairobi in the morning.

"What were they shooting at?

Gupta shrugged, "Who knows? At least it wasn't us."

Maliki was suspicious but he let it go for the moment, they needed to get the shipment inspected before loading it on to the container. "Tell your men to hurry up, the ship starts taking on cargo in six hours."

"Chop, chop!" Gupta clapped his hands and shouted, "Or nobody gets paid."

The seven men were working as fast as they could, the first pallet already being unloaded by a forklift from the back of a truck. Nevertheless the men undoing the canvas seemed to move quicker with the ropes and another scurried across the loading area to start the other forklift.

Maliki walked around to the other side of the trucks. Aisles of timber where stacked out on pallets before him disappearing off into the warehouse, a bounty of hardwood ready for export to China, including iroko and bubinga but mostly mahogany.

Next to them an empty container sat on an eighteen-wheeler ready to be driven out into the port once it was full. The first pallet of six by two inch timber planks was put down for inspection. Maliki waited for the men to cut the steel straps and remove the top few layers of planks before walking over.

One of them used a crowbar to open the crate that was hidden inside. What looked like a full pallet of stacked timber really consisted of two rows of planks either side of the crate and short cut pieces at the ends.

The crate inside the pallet was filled with ivory. Each one was a different size and shape, a mixture of creamy alabasters and pearlescent whites. Patches of blood bore evidence of the violent way in which they had been removed from their owners. Nearly all of them measured less than a meter, taken from females or young males, a few just over a foot in length that once belonged to calves. Only one pair of scimitar shaped shafts belonged to an older bull, worn with age and stained dark with vegetable juices.

Maliki nodded and the crate was re-sealed and placed into the container whilst the next one was dropped onto the ground and made ready to be checked.

Each truck carried four pallets. In all but one there was around half a ton of ivory. The last one contained thirty-three rhino horns. The buyer had asked for thirty-five. Maliki would have to make it up in the next shipment, there were none left in their stockpile in Karatu.

Since branching out into the pharmaceutical business Wei's lust for rhino seemed insatiable. Maliki allowed himself the briefest of smiles. A bit like the horny little bugger's appetite for sex, the market for Viagra was expanding at an exponential rate. Rhino horn was the key ingredient.

"Everything OK, boss?"

He turned to face Gupta, "So far."

Maliki remained poker faced, hiding his excitement well. The price would be comparatively low because of the amount of poor grade immature ivory but he should still get $120 per kilo. Nine hundred thousand US dollars, but the rhino horn was where the real money was. One crate of the black gold was worth more than the fifteen crates of ivory put together. Taking an average price of $30,000 per horn he would get $990,000. He smiled, why not call it a cool million, he was sure that Wei wouldn't protest. He knew the greedy little bugger would get as much as ten times that on the black market in Guangdong. Where it would be sold to one of the many carving factories owned and run by the Chinese government.

Minus his costs, which included Gupta and his gang's $80,000 fee, he should make a tidy profit of

1.75 million dollars. Maliki rubbed his hands together, not bad for one shipment. Wei would transfer half the money to his Swiss bank account once Maliki confirmed that the 'VENTURA' had left port, a Spanish registered ship out of Barcelona. The remaining half would be wired to him once the cargo reached the docks in Hong Kong, by way of Singapore.

After three hours of going through the inventory they resealed the final crate and the pallet was loaded with the others into the front part of the container. The empty space was then filled with normal pallets of wooden planks. Any Customs officer outside either his or Wei's payroll who decided to inspect the container would probably give up before reaching the hidden treasure.

Maliki watched the steel doors get bolted shut and the padlock put in place before he turned to Gupta.

"I guess you want paying?" Maliki reached inside his Brioni suit jacket. The Italian cerruti cloth was tailored to fit his long sinewy arms and legs perfectly. Gupta cowered and took a step backwards. Maliki grinned with pleasure. He could feel himself getting hard. "Don't worry it's only your money."

He produced the thick manila envelope containing forty thousand dollars in hundred dollar bills and held it out towards Gupta. The man's eyes lit up and he held his palms together as if in prayer.

"Thank you boss," Gupta put both hands on the packet and tried to take it. Maliki didn't let go.

He stared into the man's eyes, "Next time make sure that you bring me more rhino horn or I won't be happy." He spoke slowly and softly to emphasise his words, Gupta's arms started to tremble. "Do you understand?"

The idiot bobbed his head repeatedly and Maliki let go of the envelope. Gupta had better deliver next time or his body would be dumped into Kilindini Harbour and one of the other men promoted to fill his boots. They both knew that rhino were scarcer and harder to find than elephants. Gupta was concentrating on ivory, as it was quicker and easier for him to fill the crates.

Maliki nodded towards the door, "Now get lost and move those trucks out the way." Gupta was counting the money. "I said get lost!"

Gupta stuffed the money back inside the envelope and it magically disappeared inside the folds of his robes. He put two fingers in his mouth and made a loud wolf whistle.

Most of the men were already waiting in the trucks but the ones that weren't put out their cigarettes and jumped inside. Engines sparked into life, exhausts coughed and spluttered. Gupta hurried over to join them.

Lembui opened the doors and within minutes they were gone, nothing but diesel fumes in the warehouse to mark their presence. Maliki walked over to the doors and took one last look back at the container. A pair of the factory's regular employees would be along in a couple of hours to drive the trailer out onto the docks, completely unaware of the more precious cargo hidden inside.

Maliki glanced out across Kilindini Harbour to Mtongwe where the ferry was docking, a mixture of a dozen cars and small trucks on its open deck ready to disembark. Dancing lights reflected on the water from the expensive villas that occupied the shoreline on the other side of the half-mile expanse of the water. Behind them the lighter coloured tin roofs of the shantytown glowed brighter than their neighbours. The rusty red and grey-white buildings were squeezed so close together that they appeared to be one continuous patchwork quilt stretching off into the distance.

Without warning the wind suddenly picked up and the taller palm trees began to sway back and forth above the port. Clinging on to rocky slopes for dear life. Maliki could feel the change in pressure and smell the rain on the air before the monsoon hit. Within seconds thick black clouds covered the moon and the heavens opened up. Huge globules of water the size of his thumbnail combined in such numbers that they formed an impenetrable wall, pelting the pavement with rapid-fire.

Sabore, his other Maasai bodyguard and driver, appeared through the downpour with an umbrella. He held it above Maliki's head and escorted him back to the car. He felt safer once he was shut inside the bulletproof glass and armour plating. The S500 was kitted out with a 5.0L V8 engine to pull the extra thousand kilograms of weight. The modifications had cost Maliki $120,000 but they were worth every cent. A close range assassination attempt by the Kiambu Mafia earlier in the year would have succeeded if it weren't for his shrewd investment.

A bright flash lit up the sky as lightning struck land somewhere beyond Mtongwe, followed by a long rolling rumble of thunder seconds later. The cannon-like explosion and raindrops beat out a staccato rhythm on the roof of the Mercedes as it accelerated along the dockside. The loading of food and supplies for the crew of the VENTURA was already under way. Spanish deckhands in their Sou'westers and locals dressed in robes leaning against the wind in the torrential rain to get the job done. The cargo ships at anchor and dhows unlucky enough to be caught out in the storm had disappeared from view. Swallowed up by a black shroud of water.

He could make out the huge cylindrical storage tanks at the Changamwe Oil Refinery on his right but that was about all. They sped over the bridge onto the mainland. Maliki lay back in the leather seat as they left the port behind them and prepared himself for the long drive back to Nairobi.

CHAPTER FOUR
Sheldrick Animal Orphanage, Nairobi
August 10th, 1996

David slowed the truck to a gentle stop in front of Mbagathi Gate on Magadi Road. The side entrance to Nairobi National Park was a smaller imitation of the main park gates. A pair of male lions, cast from sheets of black metal, faced each other to declare that the park was closed to the general public. The walls that supported the gates on either side were covered in what looked like crazy paving.

A Ranger in combat fatigues with a machine gun hanging from his shoulder appeared from behind the guardhouse. He was zipping up his flies.

The guard smiled and waved, recognising both David and the converted Nissan truck. The vehicle rocked as Ella moved her weight from one side to the other. The sedative must have worn off. He could see the pink tip of her trunk poking between the bars in his side-view mirror, sniffing out the strange environment. David pulled forward once the gates were opened.

"Jambo," the guard greeted him. "They are waiting for you over in the orphanage. I'll radio ahead to say that you've arrived."

"Thanks Joseph." David leant out the window, "But don't let Tanui catch you doing that or he'll have your balls."

Joseph's smile widened into a conspiratorial grin, he flicked a look over his shoulder to make sure that the Deputy Director wasn't anywhere in sight before waving them through. David drove slowly, trying to make the ride as comfortable as possible for Ella and the two keepers nursing her.

Julias and Mishak had been flown in the day before to the Mara Serena airstrip, near the Lodge and Conservancy HQ. They had brought half a dozen bottles of substitute milk with them, the life saving formula that took Dame Daphne Sheldrick twenty-eight years to develop. Early trials using cow's milk were unsuccessful, the lactose like poison to the young calves. Eventually Dame Daphne found the key ingredient, coconut oil, using it to replace the high fat content found in elephant milk.

Mishak managed to coax Ella away from her dead mother with a bottle and had spent the night sleeping with the tiny elephant in a stable at the lodge. Ella was in distress, mourning the death of her family, and wouldn't stop crying for hours. To David her wails of anguish sounded unnervingly like an amplified human baby. He was impressed by Mishak's devotion, constantly whispering to Ella and stroking her, letting her suck on his finger until she calmed down. If the little orphan survived it would be largely due to his care and the bond forming between them.

Mishak gave her a mild sedative in the morning and she was loaded onto the truck between eight of them using a blanket. The two keepers on board fed and doused Ella in water during the journey to keep her hydrated.

Traffic in Nairobi these days was horrendous and it had taken hours longer than David anticipated crossing the city. Ella's activity in the back was a good sign but he needed to get her out before she injured herself or one of the keepers trying to stand up in the moving vehicle. Weighing around a quarter of a tonne she could easily crush one of them.

He drove past the driveway belonging to Dame Daphne Sheldrick's house and stopped in front of another set of gates. Benjamin, one of the elephant keepers, was already opening them. Like all the keepers that David had met he had a ready smile and a friendly nature. The ability to radiate calm was a core skill that they all seemed to possess and was essential to each orphan's survival.

"So you've got another one for us," he peered into the side of the truck. "Go straight through to the stalls." He pointed past the row of parked cars to a collection of buildings that looked like horse stables.

David stopped in front of them and killed the engine. He was in a courtyard broken by a cluster of trees and a stone well in the middle. A door opened and Dame Daphne emerged from the building on the opposite side of the dirt patch. Followed by a younger woman with curly auburn hair that fell like a mane past her shoulders.

She ignored David getting out of the cab and marched straight to the back of the truck, moving surprisingly quickly for someone in their sixties.

"How's she doing Mishak?" Dame Daphne stood with one hand on her ample hip and brushed a few curly grey locks away from her face. He knew not to let the floral patterned dress and pearl necklace fool him into thinking she was on the way to a garden party. David had met her briefly once before but only really knew her by reputation. Dame Daphne was a legend in the world of conservation. A tough, formidable, woman who had helped with and then carried on the work of her departed husband. David Sheldrick had been the first warden of Tsavo National Park and a pioneer in wildlife preservation. With his wife, one truck and a handful of rangers he had transformed a five thousand square mile patch of desert into a wildlife sanctuary the size of Michigan State, Israel or Wales.

"Not so good," replied Mishak. "She has diarrhoea and is very weak."

"Let's get her in the shade quickly," she waved at Benjamin and another keeper who had appeared from the stables. "Come on get the tail-gate open."

She turned to David whilst they were unbolting and letting down the ramp. Her piercing eyes reflected the intelligent mind behind them, "Captain Nbeke, isn't it? Where did you find the poor thing?"

"Near the Mara River," he stopped himself from scratching his itching scalp. Somehow standing in front of this Kenyan institution it didn't seem like the right moment. "Her mother and the rest of the herd were killed by poachers."

"Did you catch them?" she raised an eyebrow.

David shook his head, "Unfortunately not. They had escaped across the river into Tanzania by the time we got there."

"How very convenient!" she snorted before turning her attention to the commotion in the back of the truck.

"Sorry?" David was taken aback. "What exactly do you mean by that?"

The redhead spoke for the first time, almond shaped eyes and a pointed chin that she thrust in his direction, "Perhaps what Dame Daphne is suggesting is that you aren't doing your job properly." There was the soft lilt of an Irish accent.

David turned so that he was facing her and held her gaze. He spoke through gritted teeth, "That's one hell of an assumption. Do you have any idea what we are up against out there?"

"So how do you explain that the number of animals being poached has risen dramatically since the Kenyan Wildlife Service came into existence? Surely it should be going down not up?"

"And you are?" David realised that his fists were clenched tight. He relaxed his fingers.

"Dr Caitlyn Brennan, I'm the new vet." She didn't offer her hand and David wouldn't have taken it if she had.

"Well Dr Brennan, can I suggest that before you go running your mouth off in the future that you should know what you're talking about. That kind of wild accusation could get you into a lot of trouble."

Her cheeks glowed red to match her hair, "Are you threatening me Captain Nbeke?"

They were interrupted as the keepers lead Ella down the ramp. Differences momentarily forgotten as everyone helped to shepherd the baby calve into the stable, Mishak leading her with a bottle of the magic formula.

"We'll take it from here," Dr Brennan gave him a dismissive wave once the stable door was shut. "You've done quite enough already." She knelt down beside Ella and started prodding her swollen stomach.

David bit his tongue for the moment. He needed to know something before he left.

"Is she going to make it?"

Dr Brennan looked up from her examination, disbelief on her face, "Do you really care Captain?"

David was too angry to speak, afraid of what he might say if he opened his mouth. He glared at her for what seemed like ages before she relented.

"Fifty-fifty at best." She shook her head and pursed her lips, "If she makes it through the next forty-eight hours she's got a good chance, but then she'll have to be accepted by the surrogate herd. That doesn't always happen."

"And if it doesn't?"

Dr Brennan shrugged her shoulders, "Then she'll die Captain Nbeke, like the rest of her family."

*****

50

David was still thinking about it when he reached the main gates. He didn't know what type of reception he was expecting but it certainly wasn't to be accused of being in league with poachers. He barely noticed the Ranger on duty as he drove under the strip of peaked tiled roof marking the entrance.

The reserve had closed to the public for the day and the lot was almost deserted. Only a handful of cars and a couple of jeeps parked near to the buildings. Tall trees grew from islands between the rows of parking spaces. The whole site was set in an ancient forest. Huge trees surrounded and hung over the roofs of the buildings, some almost enveloped by the canopy that had grown over them. After the chaos that was the streets of Nairobi it was like entering an oasis.

Ahead of him were a couple of two-storey buildings that housed the main offices and reception. Behind them was a secure compound and another set of wooden gates that led into the Park itself, a sanctuary to over eighty species of mammal and more than four hundred resident and migratory birds. Elephants were the only members of the big five not represented in the park. Covering around forty-five square miles it simply wasn't big enough. Only seven kilometres from the centre of Nairobi and boasting lions, buffalo, leopards and rhino it was the only park of its kind in the world.

David pulled up close to reception and went inside. He felt his spirits deflate further. Idi Tikolo was manning the front desk. Managing to look over-worked between stacks of paperwork even though he had very little to do other than man the phones and point visitors in the right direction.

"Ah Nbeke," Tikolo looked up from the ledger he was writing in and produced a wry smile, "What brings you to civilisation?"

If Idi Tikolo represented civilisation then there really was little hope for humanity. The over-zealous snake in the grass would sell his own mother if he thought it would benefit his career.

"Where's Tanui?"

Tikolo sneered, "If you mean the Deputy Director then I assume you have an appointment?"

"Just tell Deputy Director Tanui that I'm here and that I need to speak with him urgently."

"Someone like you can't just come barging in here to see the Deputy Director unannounced." Tikolo reached for a leather-bound ledger, "I'll check his schedule but it will be next week at the earliest."

David reached over the desk and placed his hand on the agenda, "Look Tikolo I've had a bad couple of days. Now are you going to call Tanui and let him know that I'm here, or do you want to end up wearing that precious diary of yours?"

"There's no need to be so melodramatic," Tikolo tried to pull the book away but David maintained enough downward pressure to stop him. "He already knows all about your little elephant, it's been causing quite a stir. Although I can't see what all the fuss is about, saving one animal after losing so many."

David let go of the ledger, "Never mind, I'll find him myself." He stormed outside, slamming the door shut behind him, leaving Tikolo protesting and reaching for the telephone.

He couldn't remember saying or doing anything to offend him, but for some reason Idi Tikolo had taken an instant dislike to David. Perhaps it was because they were complete opposites. Although they were roughly the same age, Idi was short and overweight, the paunch of his belly overhanging the belt of his trousers. He had struggled with the physical elements of recruitment and marksmanship, whereas David excelled. Unfortunately they had both opted for additional courses in 'Intelligence' and 'Investigation' after passing basic training. Idi was the annoying member of the group who always had a string of questions to ask at the end of each lecture or seminar.

That was two years ago at the Manyani Training School in Tsavo West. The Rangers' facility was situated in the heart of the National Park established by Dame Daphne's deceased husband. Fortunately David only had to put up with Idi on his rare visits headquarters.

What Idi was good at was politics, treating the job as a way to climb the social ladder rather than a professional calling. He seemed to be more worried about promotion than wildlife. No doubt believing that he was destined for far greater things Tikolo hadn't spent a single night in the field. A Kalenjin and out-spoken supporter of President Moi's brutal regime Idi would have been equally at home in the Gestapo.

David realised that he was angry with himself as well as annoyed by Idi's ignorance. The reason he over-reacted with Dr Brennan earlier was that she had struck a chord. Despite the number of elephants being poached they hadn't managed to catch many of the perpetrators.

The ones they did catch were usually small fry, pairs of men working on their own to try and scrape a living. Not capable of devastating the herds like the organised gangs that they were looking for. He began to wonder if the poachers were being tipped off, the most likely conclusion was by someone within the KWS. David headed towards the main building wondering exactly what he was going to say to Tanui.

CHAPTER FIVE
KWS Headquarters, Nairobi
August 10th, 1996

Tanui wasn't in his office. His personal secretary, a veteran ranger called Ngozi, was more amenable than Idi Tikolo had been.

"The Deputy Director is out at the Ivory Memorial with some kind of freelance journalist. Claims to be a reporter writing an article on poaching for the National Geographic. Not a very well paid reporter judging by the way he's dressed." Ngozi smoothed the ends of his perfectly clipped moustache, "You can either wait for them to come back or try again in the morning."

David considered driving out into the park to speed things up but then thought better of it. Knowing Tanui's methods he would have taken the journalist there for dramatic effect. Twelve tonnes of reclaimed ivory had been symbolically burnt on the site. David wasn't going to interrupt. Besides which trying to discuss his suspicions in front of a reporter wasn't a good idea.

"I'll wait, if that's OK sergeant?"

"Of course," he indicated a couple of chairs against the wall, underneath a photograph of President Moi in full military regalia. "Take a seat and I'll get you a cup of coffee. You must need one after your long drive and such a dreadful business."

Ngozi shuffled off down the corridor towards the kitchen before David had the chance to respond. One of Ngozi's legs had been badly mangled by the steel jaws of a poacher's trap and it dragged behind him.

David glanced at the picture of the President before collapsing into the chair below it. The photo was obviously taken in the President's plumper days when the jacket still fitted his shoulders.

The short conversation with Ngozi concerned him. Everybody at headquarters seemed to know about the incident with the poachers already. Trying to find out who was leaking information wasn't going to be easy. Assuming it was someone in the Service. But if his theory about the spotter plane was correct then it had to be one of his colleagues.

Luckily he didn't have to wait long for the Deputy Director and managed to avoid dozing off in the chair. The bitter tasting coffee helped to keep him awake.

Tanui came striding down the oak-panelled corridor with the reporter scurrying behind him struggling to keep up. A ferret-faced man who was scribbling into a pocketsize notebook as the Deputy Director answered questions.

"So you don't think that there's any truth in the rumours then?"

Tanui stopped in his tracks. It looked like the blood vessels on his temples might burst. He turned and stared at the reporter for a few seconds before continuing walking. "They are as you said just rumours. I can assure you that all of the Kenyan Wildlife Service's employees are highly vetted and extremely dedicated professionals. The idea that any of them would be involved is both ludicrous and offensive."

"So how do you explain the rise in numbers?"

"It's an almost impossible task for our rangers. There's a huge economic demand for the product. The poachers we face are well organised, highly motivated and heavily armed. On top of that the borders are hundreds of miles long and unmarked for vast sections. We simply don't have the resources to be everywhere all of the time."

Tanui stopped in front of Ngozi's workstation and turned to face the reporter. He tapped the face of his watch and smiled, "Speaking of time I'm afraid that we have run out of it for today. If you have any further questions then please don't hesitate to get in touch. Ngozi here will see you to the door."

The sergeant was standing stiffly beside his chair and must have been waiting for the order. His limp disappeared as he rounded the desk and took hold of the reporter's elbow.

"I know my way out thank-you," the nasal twang was American, thin shoulder-length hair that seemed to stick to the reporter's head as he shook it. He pulled his elbow free from Ngozi's fingers, "And can I take this opportunity to thank you for your candidness and kind hospitality. Rest assured that it will all be in my article." He tipped an imaginary hat, "Now, good-day to you."

Tanui watched him walk off shadowed by Ngozi. He remained silent until they disappeared around the corner towards the stairwell.

"Good to see you again Captain Nbeke," he turned to face David. His steely gaze was intense and his brow hooded like that of an eagle intent on its prey. "Sorry it's not under happier circumstances. How is the orphaned elephant doing?"

David shrugged, "It's too early to tell by all accounts sir, could go either way. The new vet said that the first few days are crucial."

"Ah yes, Dr Brennan," the Deputy Director smiled and David thought he saw a twinkle in his eye. "She's quite something isn't she Nbeke?"

"She certainly is, sir," David nodded, pretty sure that they weren't on the same wavelength.

"Keep me informed of how it goes, won't you?"

"Yes sir," David noticed that there were more grey hairs sprouting from Tanui's temples than the last time they had met.

"Now, what was so important that you needed to see me in person?"

After hearing the tail end of Tanui's conversation with the reporter David decided to keep his theories to himself until he had a few more facts.

"Nothing specific sir," David hoped that what he was attempting looked something like a smile. "I just wanted to give you my account in person while I was in town."

Tanui raised an eyebrow, "As far as I understand it a large group of poachers, some twenty in number, came across the border and slaughtered a family of eleven elephants. They hacked off the tusks and made good their escape into Tanzania before you could catch them. Is that about the size of it Captain?"

"Yes, sir." David studied his bootlaces, "Apart from the fact that ten elephants were killed, the calf was the eleventh member of the herd."

"Ten, eleven, what difference does it make?"

"Not a lot I guess, sir." Unless of course you happen to be number eleven, David thought. "I just wanted to make sure that you knew the facts."

"Ah yes, the facts Captain Nbeke. Can you tell me what you were doing so far off the beaten track?"

"We were following the herd."

"And on whose orders was that?"

"Mine sir," David frowned. Why did he get the feeling that there was nothing spontaneous in Tanui's questioning? "It's usually the best way to spot the poachers, sir, it's worked for us before."

"Well it didn't this time did it Captain?"

David held Tanui's stare, "No sir, I'm afraid it didn't." The imprint of the bloodbath was still fresh on his mind.

The Deputy Director turned swiftly on his heel and walked over to his office. He paused with one hand on the door handle and looked over his shoulder, "I'm assuming that all of this will be in your official report?"

"Yes sir."

Tanui's smile was forced and didn't reach his eyes, "Good, then I'll look forward to reading it, but in future make sure that you let Base Camp know of any change in your patrol. We need to know where you are for your own safety. Now if there really is nothing else Captain, I've got work to do."

Then the Deputy Director was gone and the door closed. Leaving David feeling sure he had made the right decision not to say anything.

He bumped into Ngozi on the way out, an awkward moment as they rubbed shoulders in the stairwell. David went out through the fire escape and breathed in the cool night air. He couldn't shake the feeling that the darkness enveloping the city had somehow seeped into the very fabric of the building and its occupants.

Tanui's behaviour was out of character to say the least, far from the passionate and dedicated ranger that had convinced him to join the Service. David shrugged, probably just the pressure of the job.

The lights in the reception building were off, Tikolo nowhere to be seen and the parking lot even emptier than before. Although he would be staying on site David decided not to eat in Maggie's Restaurant, the staff canteen. The food was passable but he needed time to think and didn't want to be interrupted, especially not by the likes of Idi Tikolo. David walked over to the truck and fished in his pockets for the keys. He knew just the place.

*****

David took the longer route to avoid Kibera slum. Only the residents and lost tourists went there at night. The ghetto was a no-go zone for the police, run by street gangs and drug lords. Anyone unlucky enough to live there was pretty much left to their own fate by the authorities. Not a place that you wanted to break down in or have an accident. The detour, combined with the seemingly endless stream of traffic, meant that it was over half an hour before he pulled up outside the restaurant. He almost regretted the decision to eat there.

The Hankook Garden was a bamboo structure tucked away in a quiet residential suburb on Kindaruma Road not far from the hospital. A Korean BBQ serving the best food David had tasted in Nairobi. A place he stumbled upon by chance when he was a recruit exploring the city's nightlife.

His visits to the restaurant weren't often enough for him to be considered a regular. But the menu never changed and neither did the décor. David felt at home in the familiar surroundings and his stomach managed to lead him there whenever he was in town.

The bi-fold doors were wide open, adorned with snow-white linen that flapped gently in the breeze. The potted palms inside the building and exotic plants filling the garden gave the impression that you were on a tropical island somewhere in the Pacific.

He looked up as he walked between the columns marking the entrance, admiring the subtle elegance of the tall bamboo pillars and vaulted ceiling. Four cooking stations were spaced around a spacious dining area. Chefs were busy preparing food at two of them, the other's empty. He joined the smaller of the groups and sat at the opposite end of the long steel griddle. Trying to put some distance between himself and the trio of Asian businessmen.

"What would you like to drink sir?" asked the waiter in immaculate whites who headed over to him from the central bar and kitchen area. A round structure built of grey stone blocks. The illuminated shelves built into the walls displayed bottles of wine and beers, both local and Korean.

"I'll have a bottle of Tusker please, make sure it's cold." With the power company struggling to keep up with the growing demand Nairobi's establishments and homes were running on generator half of the time, finding an ice-cold beer was becoming increasingly difficult.

The waiter nodded and glanced over at the obviously drunk businessmen before handing him the menu. David studied the badly typed list even though he already knew what he was having. The dishes were roughly translated into English below the alien Korean script. He went for his favourite. The thinly sliced beef with special sauce, although chilli was the only ingredient that David could positively identify, with some spicy noodles. He gave his order to the chef and sat back.

The diminutive Korean nodded and gave the sizzling pork he was cooking a quick flip. With amazing speed and dexterity the ninja-like chef mixed together his chosen ingredients from the bowls on the counter and threw them onto the hot plate. Everything looked fresh and the smells that were wafting over as the meat, vegetables and spices combined were out of this world. The waiter returned and David took a welcome sip of what turned out to be a well chilled beer, it trickled like nectar down the back of his throat.

"You're not a Muslim then?" The American's voice beside him almost made him spit out the mouthful he was trying to swallow. "At least not a practising one."

So much for not being interrupted, David turned his head towards the man he had seen talking to Tanui, "What the hell are you doing here?"

"If you're asking whether I followed you, then the answer is yes." The reporter perched on the adjacent stool and wriggled to get comfortable.

Sergeant Ngozi was right about the clothes. Although David guessed that the torn holes in the knees of the reporter's jeans were a fashion statement rather than a reflection of his financial status. Well-worn Doc Martin boots, faded brown and scuffed at the toes. His collarless white granddad shirt was open at the neck, exposing a hairless chest and silver crucifix hanging from a thin piece of leather. The reporter was in his late forties possibly early fifties, right-handed and a heavy smoker, judging by the lines on his face and the tobacco stained fingers of his right hand. Probably involved in the Summer of Love and been protesting against injustice ever since.

"If you don't mind I would prefer to eat alone."

"What is it with you KWS guys? Do they train you to be anti-social or something?"

David smiled despite himself, "Sorry it's been a bad day that's all. As you Americans would say I need some 'downtime'. Now what is it you want?"

"Sorry I should have introduced myself," he held out his hand. "Aaron Bernstein, I'm writing an article for the National Geographic."

That explained the slight hook to his nose and unkempt beard. "So I heard," the man's grip was firm and confident, "David Nbeke."

"I know," Bernstein's smile seemed genuine, his otherwise perfect teeth stained from smoking. "You're the one who brought in the baby elephant today."

David nodded. He didn't see the harm in confirming something that the reporter already knew and would no doubt be in the papers tomorrow. "That's right. Did the Deputy Director tell you that?" David knew that Tanui wouldn't have given out his name.

Bernstein shook his head, "No, let's just say that I've got my sources and leave it at that."

"This source of yours, she isn't Irish by any chance?"

Bernstein's momentary hesitation and the widening of his pupils gave him away.

"A good reporter never reveals his sources," Bernstein shrugged, "You know how it is."

"Not really. What else did she tell you?"

"*They* told me that you weren't far behind the poachers, and that the rest of Ella's herd were butchered."

"We counted over twenty different sets of tracks heading over the Mara River into Tanzania," David took a swig of his beer, "They were only about an hour ahead of us." Bernstein's pad was out and he was taking notes but David didn't care. He needed to tell somebody.

"The bastards should be hung for the way that they did it, those animals really suffered before they died. There wasn't one single kill shot. Some of them were still alive when their tusks were removed."

Bernstein looked appalled, "How do you know that?"

"By the amount of blood around some of them," David grimaced as he pictured the scene. "Their hearts were definitely still pumping."

They were interrupted as the chef presented David with steaming plates. His stomach churned just looking at the food. He remembered to thank him and the Korean gave a curt bow of his head before returning to the BBQ. There was an outburst of laughter from the other end of the island as one of the businessmen slipped off the edge of his stool. Fortunately the man was prevented from hitting the floor by one of his friend's surprisingly quick reactions. They were seriously drunk now and starting to get rowdy.

"Do you mind if I get a beer?"

David shrugged, "It's a free country."

"Not if you're Kikuyu," said Bernstein solemnly, he swivelled in his seat and beckoned the waiter.

There was definitely more to Bernstein than met the eye. David was beginning to think that his casual appearance might be a deliberate disguise.

He scooped up a spoonful of the beef and stared at it, trying to get rid of the sickening images in his head. David couldn't see the point in trying to use chopsticks. He spent more time dropping food than eating it when he did. David summoned up his courage and shoved the spoon into his mouth. The meat was so tender it seemed to melt on his tongue but he still had difficulty swallowing it down. Bernstein waited for his drink to arrive and took a swig from the bottle before continuing.

"I understand that you're one of the few rangers who have actually made an arrest?"

Three to be precise, all of this was common knowledge, covered by the national newspapers. Bernstein was fishing for something.

David put down his spoon. He didn't feel like eating anymore and might as well find out what the reporter wanted. "Why don't we cut to the chase? I heard you talking to the Deputy Director. You obviously think that someone in the Service is involved."

Bernstein looked nervous for the first time. He frowned and fiddled with the label on the bottle of beer as if struggling to reach a decision.

"Maybe there's more than one person. They might not even be in the Service, but they definitely seem to know where the patrols are going to be and when. The few poachers being caught are just the tip of the iceberg, a peace token to make the press think that something is being done and appease international pressure. Whoever is in charge it has to be someone high up."

"What makes you think that?"

"The sheer volume of ivory being poached, we are talking about hundreds of elephants every year. Chinese stockpiles have gone up from 20'000 tonnes to ten times that in the last three years when there's supposed to be an international ban. There's also been a massive increase in the quantity of rhino horn being poached. Only someone with connections could pull that off."

David nodded, it all made sense and confirmed a few things, including his suspicions as to why the spotter plane hadn't turned up. Most of the illegal ivory ended up in China, where a loophole in the law allowed traders to sell stockpiles they had 'forgotten' to declare prior to the 1989 embargo. Hiding the illegal goods and shipping them to Asia would not be easy, not on the scale it was being done. There would be customs officials to bribe and other palms to grease along the way.

"Supposing your theories are correct, where exactly do I come in to all of this?"

Bernstein took another sip of beer before replying. He turned to look at David. "I need someone on the inside with access to KWS records, somebody who's not afraid to tell the truth."

"What makes you think that I'm that person?"

"Like I said you are one of the few rangers with an actual arrest record. And you brought that baby elephant in, not everybody would have done that."

David shook his head, much as he liked Bernstein they had only just met, "You've got the wrong man. Your suspicions are based on rumour and conjecture yet you expect me to lay my career on the line? Sorry but no thanks." He picked up his spoon and used it to point at his plate, "My food's getting cold."

"All I'm asking is that you keep your eyes and ears open." Bernstein stroked his beard, "Let me know if you come across anything suspicious."

"You've got no evidence that someone in the KWS is actually involved and nothing to go on."

"That's why I need you."

"Not interested. Now are you going to leave or shall I have you arrested for harassment?"

"Can you really do that?"

"Try me!" David pushed the food around his plate and made an effort to ignore Bernstein.

"OK, I know when I'm not wanted." The reporter stood up and produced his wallet from the back pocket of his jeans. He took out a business card and put it on the counter next to David's beer, "Let me know if you change your mind."

David waited until he was sure that Bernstein was gone before picking up the card and slipping it into the breast pocket of his shirt.

CHAPTER SIX
Royal Nairobi Golf Club
August 11th, 1996

Wei's one wood connected cleanly, his style was textbook. A straight swing and perfect follow through. Swivelling his hips and turning his trailing leg so that his knee pointed in the direction of travel. The ball bounced neatly in the middle of the fairway. What Wei lacked was power. The shot barely travelled 150 yards.

Maliki smiled behind the Counsellor's back, it would be a more even match if he used the women's tee. Why he insisted on betting on every game was a mystery to Maliki. Wei hadn't won since the very first time they played by claiming that he had a 28 Handicap. The cheating little bugger ended up sixteen strokes under par and took the thousand dollars without batting an eyelid. Maliki soon put a stop to that. The next time he insisted that they play on a level pegging or all bets were off. Wei accepted, his love of gambling outweighing his common sense.

The sun was still low in the sky and they were already on the fifth hole. An Imam chanting the Morning Prayer was being blasted over a cheap tannoy, the tinny sound coming from behind the trees to their left. Hard to believe that Kibera slum was on the other side, tens of thousands of people living in squalor without electricity or running water. A thin line of cedars and an electric fence separated the residents from the freshwater streams that belonged to the course.

Maliki secretly hated golf. Not so much the game, although there seemed little point trying to hit a ball into a hole on the other side of a field. What he really didn't like were the pompous attitudes and gaudy outfits worn by most of the members. Including Wei. The matching trousers and cap were offensive. Made from a yellow and purple tartan that was almost painful to look at. Thankfully Maliki was wearing sunglasses.

But golf was a rich man's game and a nice quiet place to do business. Maliki had natural talent and he practiced hard to lower his handicap and mingle with Nairobi's elite. He was first introduced to Wei at the clubhouse bar.

Not that it was a chance meeting. Maliki planned it for months and had Counsellor Wei followed to find out his weaknesses. It didn't take long to discover something he could use, Wei's addiction to gambling and his ability to lose made him an easy target. Maliki bought Wei's fifty thousand dollar debt from a local casino and had owned him ever since. Although Wei seemed to be forgetting that lately, he hadn't even mentioned the transfer.

He waited until Wei pulled back his arms to take his second shot, "Where's my money?"

The Counsellor's shoulders tensed up and he hooked the shot badly. The ball flew over the trees and Maliki smiled as he heard it hit a tin roof behind them.

Wei said something that sounded abusive in Mandarin and then turned to face Maliki. His pencil-line moustache quivered, "It will be transferred today as agreed. All in due course." He smiled weakly and flicked the fringe of his jet-black hair to one side. For some reason it was styled to fall over his right eye and covered a good portion of his face. A few strands of grey hair suggested that the colour came out of a bottle.

"This isn't a joke Counsellor. You better not be holding out on me."

Wei waited for his caddy to place another ball in front of him and move away before replying, "There is nothing to worry about. I spoke to the buyer this morning. Everything is in hand." He lined himself up for the shot and took a practise swing, "Although he wasn't happy to hear about the two missing items."

He allowed Wei to take the second attempt without interruption and the ball landed just beyond Maliki's drive. The Counsellor held the club out to be taken and they set off down the fairway with the caddies trailing some way behind.

"They will be made up in the next shipment." Maliki's lip twitched, "I already have my man working on it."

Wei glanced over his shoulder and then spoke quietly, "I take it that this is the same man that let the baby elephant live?"

"What elephant?"

"The one with her picture on the front page of this morning's newspaper." Wei raised his eyebrows, a smug look on his face, "The one that was rescued in the Maasai Mara and brought to the orphanage yesterday. According to the report poachers killed the other ten members of the herd and then fled into Tanzania with the ivory. Your man must be getting sloppy, leaving the calf alive has brought a lot of unwanted attention."

Bloody Gupta, Maliki had known that there was something he wasn't telling him. Maybe it was time for the old fool to retire after all.

He maintained his composure, "What makes you think that it has anything to do with us? We were in Mombasa yesterday."

"I just thought…"

Maliki cut him short, "Well don't! It's my job to do the thinking around here. If there's ever a problem then I'll deal with it. You just make sure that I get paid or it will be you that the papers are writing about."

Wei opened his mouth as if to say something but must have thought better of it. Maliki lengthened his stride and headed towards his ball. Distracted by the story about the elephant he scuffed his shot and it fell well short of the green.

*****

Maliki barged past the sergeant into Deputy Director Tanui's office. He slammed a copy of the 'Daily Nation' onto the desk in front of Tanui. A picture of the baby elephant being fed milk by her keeper with Dame Daphne occupied most of the front page. The caption at the top in bold capitals read 'LEFT TO DIE BY POACHERS'.

Maliki gripped the edge of the desk with both hands and leant towards him, "What's all this about an orphaned elephant?"

Tanui nodded to Ngozi, "That will be all Sergeant. Please close the door on your way out."

"Yes sir."

Maliki caught the Sergeant's perplexed expression as he left the room. The door closed softly behind him and he turned his attention back to Tanui.

"Tell me why I have to read this in the paper instead of hearing about it from you?"

"I tried to call but your secretary told me that you were unavailable. You should check your messages." He looked Maliki up and down and raised an eyebrow, "But I guess that you were too busy playing golf."

Maliki cursed himself for not stopping to get changed before going to see the Deputy Director. The wily old fox must have noticed the grass stains on his trousers.

Tanui stood up and walked over to the bureaux next to his desk. He poured a cup of filtered coffee from the jug being kept warm on a hot plate and returned to his seat. Tanui nursed the cup in both hands and slurped the filthy liquid. The fact that none was offered to Maliki didn't go unnoticed. His lip twitched, the Kikuyu bastard was trying to wind him up.

Maliki gripped the desk and his knuckles turned white. Forcing himself to relax he released his hold. He walked over to the coffee machine and helped himself before occupying one of the seats in front of Tanui. Like the rest of the office it was bought on a budget and about as uncomfortable as it looked. The metal frame dug into his shoulder blades through the thin foam padding.

Maliki swallowed, the coffee tasted like shit and was lukewarm. Pretending to drop the cup as he put it down Maliki spilled the contents over Tanui's paperwork.

"How very clumsy of me. What a mess," he picked up some of the papers and started using them to mop up the rest of the spillage. He locked eyes with Tanui, "But then accidents do tend to happen when you least expect them. Don't they?"

The Deputy Director pretended not to notice the threat. But Maliki could tell by the short intake of breath that his words had the desired effect.

Tanui's tone was more respectful this time when he spoke, "Why is the baby elephant so important?"

"The elephant is irrelevant. What I'm concerned about is the press snooping around the place, twisting the facts and stirring up trouble for us. How did they get hold of the story so quickly?"

"The reporter happened to be here when the orphan was brought in."

"And you let him in?"

"What else was I supposed to do? If I had denied him access then it would have fuelled his suspicions." Tanui gave him a strange look, "He

74

already thinks that someone in the department is working with the poachers."

"Does he now?" Maliki's lip twitched and he scratched at the scars on his face, "Is this the same reporter who wrote this rubbish? I'm guessing he's freelance."

Tanui nodded, "Aaron Bernstein, he's writing an article for the National Geographic."

"Did you check his credentials?" There was every chance that this Bernstein wasn't who he claimed to be. The American Ambassador was putting serious pressure on President Moi's government to clamp down on poaching. On top of that the CIA had hired reporters before to investigate the election fixing.

"Of course I did," Tanui took another noisy sip of coffee. The tasteless fool actually looked like he might be enjoying it. "He checks out, the New York office told me that he was on assignment for them."

"And they gave you a description?"

"Yes, they even faxed over the photograph page of his passport." Tanui pointed to a file that had somehow escaped the onslaught of coffee.

"Good," the twitch wasn't so bad this time. "Get me a copy and I'll have my people do some digging. You can never be too careful these days."

Tanui shook his head, "I don't think that's necessary."

"Do I really have to remind you who you are talking to?" He said the words through gritted teeth.

"I guess not." Tanui shrugged, "It doesn't matter anyway. You won't find out any more than I've already told you."

"For your sake you'd better hope not," Maliki thought about the pain he would like to inflict on the Deputy Director. "Now hurry up with that file."

"Give me a minute," grunted Tanui. He picked up the document, "The photocopier is out in the corridor."

Maliki remembered something else that he wanted to ask. It would save him from reading the official report. He stopped Tanui before he went out the door.

"In the article it says that Rangers who were tracking the herd found the elephant and brought her in but it doesn't mention any names. Who was in charge?"

The Deputy Director frowned before speaking, "Nbeke, Captain David Nbeke."

CHAPTER SEVEN
Sheldrick Animal Orphanage, Nairobi
August 11th, 1996

David followed Benjamin along a wide path that cut through the dense forest surrounding them. The ground was churned up to mark the recent passing of the herd and a few of the trees along the route also showed signs of their attention. The bark stripped off the lower part of the trunks where they had stopped to sharpen their tusks and feed. He had come to check on how Ella was doing before he left, but she was on an outing with the rest of the orphans. The keeper was kind enough to show him where they were. On the way he explained that the daily treks were a vital part of the integration process for the elephants, both with nature and each other. Learning social skills as well as their way around the different plants.

After a short walk they came to a point where the trees opened up and the track entered a clearing, a dusty patch of red soil. The twenty-something orphans were playing and cavorting about, chasing and blowing dust at one another, all except Ella. She was clinging to Mishak's side for dear life, nuzzling him with her trunk. A chequered blanket covered her back, large brightly coloured squares roughly stitched together. Mishak was trying to steer her towards the others but she was having none of it and kept pushing him in the opposite direction. Six other keepers were in attendance, shepherding their flock. Including Julias, the other keeper who had escorted Ella from the Mara.

"I'll leave you to it then."

"Thanks Ben."

Benjamin was one of those names that always got shortened whether the owner wanted it to be or not, there were just too many syllables.

David watched Benjamin disappear back down the track before heading over towards Mishak and Ella. He stopped about twenty yards away, not wanting to spook her any more than she already appeared to be.

Mishak beckoned him to come closer, "Come and help me get her nearer to the others. Go around the other side and spread your arms, make yourself big."

David followed Mishak's instructions but Ella was being stubborn. He soon realised that trying to make the two hundred and fifty kilo animal move when it didn't want to was futile. Fortunately so did Mishak.

"That's enough for today, we'll try again tomorrow," Mishak was puffing and panting from the effort.

"Why's she wearing the blanket?"

"We give them the blanket as a reward for good behaviour. Normally the others respect the one wearing it and give them special attention." He sighed, "But not today, some of them have even been trying to take it off her. I've never seen them do that before."

"How's she doing generally?"

Mishak tipped his head towards her and stroked Ella's back, she rumbled appreciatively, "She's feeding well enough but every time she goes near the others they try to chase her away. Her fear frightens them and they can still smell the death of the others, even though we have washed her many times."

"When will you know if she's going to be OK?"

"She needs to be accepted in the next few days, a week at the most or she will stop feeding." Mishak shook his head and looked pitiful, "I've seen it happen before. Elephants are even more social than humans. If Ella doesn't find affection soon, someone to replace her mother, then she will lose the will to live and there will be nothing we can do except pray for her."

He bid Mishak and Ella well before leaving the keeper with his charge and heading back towards the orphanage. There seemed little point getting into a theological debate with Mishak but praying didn't seem to do much good.

He was so lost in thought that Dr Brennan startled him. "Captain Nbeke," she rushed out of one of the stable doors with a syringe in her hand. "I was hoping to catch you."

David spread his arms in mock surrender, "Is that some kind of truth serum?"

"This?" Dr Brennan held up the thick two-inch needle and looked at it. Her smile was wicked, "No this one will only knock you out, it's just an elephant tranquilizer." She hid the scary looking syringe behind her back, "Seriously though, I wanted to apologise for what I said to you yesterday. It was bang out of order."

David found himself wondering what kind of figure lay beneath the over-sized lab coat. Her prominent cheekbones, graceful neckline and slender wrists suggested that it was slim and athletic, but it was hard to tell. She was wearing dark blue jeans, a small portion of them visible between her white coattails and green wellingtons. Her thick auburn hair was tied back in a bun and she didn't appear to be wearing any make-up. Her rose coloured lips and striking emerald eyes didn't need the enhancement of cosmetics, she looked stunning.

He didn't say anything so she continued, "I'm really sorry. Sometimes I forget to engage my brain before opening my mouth, it's a terrible habit." She pleaded with her eyes, "No hard feelings?"

He shrugged as if it didn't matter, "What made you change your mind?" He guessed that it was as a result of speaking to Bernstein.

"I was talking to Mishak and few of the other keepers. Apparently you're one of the good guys." She frowned, more to herself than at him, "I just get so angry, you know?"

David nodded but felt little empathy. She hadn't seen the corpse of Ella's butchered mother or watched her own father being murdered.

He decided to be polite, "It's good to be passionate Dr Brennan. Too many people simply don't care. Let's just pretend it never happened."

"Thanks for being so understanding." Her face widened into a smile and her eyes seemed to sparkle, "And please call me Caitlyn." Maybe it was his imagination but David got the impression that she was flirting with him. He liked this Dr Brennan much better than the one from yesterday.

"OK, Caitlyn." He realised that his smile probably looked stupid and wiped it away, "Out of interest can you tell me where you got your figure from?"

"What figure?"

He raised an eyebrow, "The one about the levels of poaching?"

"Oh," her cheeks flushed red with embarrassment. She laughed nervously. "I should have remembered really shouldn't I? The statistics came from a friend of mine who works with the 'Friends of the Maasai Mara'. Have you heard of them?"

David nodded. They were a voluntary group who supported the rangers' efforts by keeping tabs on the numbers of rhino and elephant in the reserve. He had seen their vehicles a few times whilst out on patrol in the park.

"He told me that there are only twenty-three black rhino left in the country. All thanks to old men wanting to get a hard on," her cheeks flushed even redder. "Sorry there I go again getting carried away, but it's just ridiculous."

"Please stop apologising," he was smiling at her again. "And it's worse than ridiculous, it's barbaric."

Her eyes seemed to be searching his soul for something, "Do you think that someone in the KWS could actually be involved?"

"I hope not," he sighed. "But who knows? Some people will do anything for money."

Caitlyn glanced towards the stable door, "I'd better get back, there's a sedated patient in there that needs a bullet removing."

"Nothing life-threatening I hope?"

"No, it's been in there a while but the scar tissue building up around it might cause problems. So we're taking it out as a precaution." She made it sound easy.

"Before you go, would you mind telling me the name of your friend and where I might find them?"

"You mean the one that works for the 'Friends of the Maasai Mara?" She smiled, "You're not going to have them arrested are you?"

David grinned. That settled it then. She had definitely been talking to Bernstein. He found himself wondering what kind of relationship they had.

"I just want to talk to them about an idea I've had, see whether they might be able to help."

"Help with what?"

"I'd rather not say at the moment, not until I've spoken to them at least."

"How mysterious." Then she frowned, "Are you going to try and catch whoever's responsible?"

David had to think about it, "At this stage I'm not really sure but a lot will depend on what your friend has got to say."

"His name's Spencer, Spencer Scott. He's a great guy but a bit rough around the edges." She smiled briefly, "Thinking about it you two will probably get on like a house on fire."

The expression she used made him think about the barn, the heat of the flames and his father lying dead in the dirt. His face must have betrayed his emotions.

"Are you OK?" she touched his elbow. Her fingertips sent Goosebumps up his arm. "You look like you've seen a ghost or something."

"I'm fine," he forced a smile. "How can I get hold of him?"

"He's usually out in the bush, but the Fund own a lodge near Emurutoto, on the road leading to Oloolola Gate. Someone there will know where he is." She released his arm, "I really should get going. The sedative will have kicked in by now. Hopefully I'll see you again some time."

"I'll drop in the next time I'm in town," he promised. "And thanks for the contact."

Caitlyn was already heading for the stalls but she stopped and turned around to face him wearing a frown, "No problem, you just take care of yourself, I'd feel partly responsible if something bad were to happen to you."

"Don't worry I'll be fine," he replied, but her back was already turned. David wished that he really were that confident. The feeling of impending doom had been growing ever since finding little Ella.

*****

He slammed the door shut on the battered Nissan and headed across the busy car lot towards the main building. A busload of school children on a day trip was disembarking near the Veterinary Centre, kids of around five or six with backpacks. Wearing navy blue uniforms and white sunhats, all smiles and energy. One of the teachers, a bald headed man with horn-rimmed spectacles, was struggling to do a head count whilst two of his female colleagues tried to round up the rowdy rabble into some sort of line. It reminded David of the school trip he'd been on to Nairobi, the anticipation and excitement they all felt as they entered the city.

But that was before *it* happened. There hadn't been many happy times since then, apart from when he was accepted into the Service. Even that was tainted by the guilt he felt leaving his mother and sister behind at the Mission with Aunty Farisi. They were both well looked after and he visited them as often as possible but David still felt that in some way he had abandoned them. His experiences seemed to be divided into two distinct categories, before and after his father's death.

He crossed the space between the last two rows of parked cars, half of them jeeps painted in khaki green camouflage belonging to members of staff. One vehicle stood out from the others, a black Mercedes saloon with tinted out windows. Although by far the most expensive in the lot it wasn't the price tag or sleek lines which made the car noticeable. It was the burly gentleman standing next to the bonnet trying to act casual who seemed out of place. He looked like an over-dressed heavyweight prize-fighter with a squashed nose. David could see the bulge of a firearm under the tightly fitting sports jacket and his attention seemed to be fixed on the door to headquarters.

The man suddenly stiffened and became more alert, checking up and down the car park he moved to one of the rear doors of the Mercedes. Must be some bigwig's minder, it wasn't uncommon for Ministers to visit the Park. A photograph with a rescued animal and a bunch of school kids equalled good publicity. David joined the pathway that led to the entrance. A man dressed in dark slacks and a white sports shirt heading the other way seemed to be the centre of attention. Another grey suited bodyguard was following him, taller and thinner than his colleague waiting by the car. This one was almost as tall as his employer, who must be approaching seven feet.

Even from a distance he could tell that something was drastically wrong with the boss's features. They seemed lopsided. As he got closer, David could see that three scars running down the right hand side of his face were the cause of the distortion. The middle one crossed his cheek and pulled up the corner of his mouth into a permanent sneer. They might have been knife wounds. But something in the symmetry of their appearance told him that an animal's claws had caused them, possibly a large dog's. The good side of his face seemed vaguely familiar. Maybe David had seen him on television.

The man was staring right back. As they passed each other his eyes narrowed and the damaged side of his face twitched, turning the sneer into a menacing snarl. David almost bumped into his escort, only just sidestepping him at the last moment. The bodyguard looked edgy and had one hand under his suit jacket, no doubt on the handle of a semi-automatic.

David felt relieved when they went by and nothing happened. There was definitely something sinister about the three of them. He paused and glanced back before going inside. The larger of the two was holding the door to the Mercedes open for their boss whilst the other scanned the surrounding area. They were clearly drilled professionals. Maybe they were from the GSU or Secret Service? The GSU were responsible for setting up the KWS and their officers still ran the paramilitary part of training so they had every reason to be there. David shrugged, what did it have to do with him? They were obviously there on official business, yet he couldn't shake the feeling that the scar-faced man's presence was significant.

Deputy Director Tanui was in his office this time when he got there. "I'll just let him know that you are here Captain," Sergeant Ngozi reached for the intercom.

David's curiosity got the better of him. "Sergeant," Ngozi's finger hovered over the button, "I saw a man on the way in dressed like he was going to play golf or something. I don't suppose you know who it was?"

He took his hand away from the device, "Ugly gentleman with scars down one side of his face?" the sergeant dragged three fingers across his cheek to demonstrate.

"That's the one."

"Commander Peter Abasi, sir, he's head of the GSU."

"Any idea what he was doing here?"

"He came to see the Deputy Director." Ngozi flicked a nervous glance at Tanui's door, "It was something to do with that baby elephant you brought in. He had a copy of the newspaper with him and was waving it around."

David had read the article in the staff canteen whilst eating breakfast. Although it was aimed to tug at the reader's heartstrings he had to admit that it was well written. Bernstein managed to bring across his outrage in a good balance of fact and fiction.

The sergeant must have realised that he had said too much. His hand went back to the intercom, "What shall I say it's regarding?"

"On second thoughts don't bother, there's no point disturbing him." David held the file out holding his report. "I only wanted to give him this, could you do that for me?"

Ngozi smiled as if Tanui would appreciate the gesture of being left alone, "No problem sir, I'll make sure that he gets it."

"Thank you sergeant," David turned and walked away down the corridor.

CHAPTER EIGHT
The Mission, Kisii
August 11th, 1996

The decision to visit them had been made on the spur of the moment. Although it was a two hundred-kilometre detour, he would still be able to see Spencer Scott in the morning on his way back to the Mara. Besides it would have been dark by the time he reached the lodge and it was preferable to get there in daylight. It was easy to get lost on the tracks around the park. At least that's what he kept telling himself. The truth was he just needed to see them, make sure that they were OK.

By the time he arrived it was late afternoon and a golden hue covered the land, as if he was viewing it through a magical filter. Seen from the front, the Mission appeared to be a small single-storey building with whitewashed walls and a simple steeple above the protruding entrance. David knew that it was in fact built in the shape of a cross, the longest wing extending away from the road and out of sight. The parts he was looking at represented the crossbar and the entrance hall, the top of the upright. The sanctuary, home to around thirty women at any one time, was perched on top of a hill overlooking the town that was nestled down in the valley below.

He took hold of the plate-sized iron ring and knocked twice. By chance it was his Aunty who appeared to open the door a few minutes later.

"David, what are you doing here?" Her face broke into a broad grin and her head shook with excitement. "We weren't expecting you!"

Although not obese his Aunty was the only fat Maasai he had ever met. She spent most of her time at the Mission cooking and baking for the other nuns and their patients. He guessed that there must be a lot of tasting involved to make sure that the food was just right before it was served up to the others.

David smiled, "The opportunity just came up so I thought that I'd surprise you. Where are mum and Kiira?"

"Not until you give me a cuddle." She laughed, a deep and hearty chuckle, and squeezed her ample frame into the doorjamb. His Aunty dusted her hands on the white apron she was wearing over her navy blue habit and held them out to him.

David didn't argue, it was good to see a friendly face, she felt great and smelled of lavender.

"Are you here for long," she asked, holding him at arm's length and giving him the once over.

He shook his head. "I'm only in town for the night. I'm afraid it will be a while before I get any real time off."

She looked crestfallen, "And when will that be?"

"Probably end up being Christmas the way that things are going." Considering recent developments it might be even longer.

"Oh, that's months away."

David knew that there was nothing wrong with her memory. She knew that he didn't have any time off until then. Aunty Farisi just kept asking the same question until she got the answer that she wanted. She treated God in the same way, repeating her prayers until he gave up. Or so David imagined.

"Well?" He raised an eyebrow.

"What?"

"Are you going to let me in?"

She covered her mouth and giggled, bosom wobbling with mirth. When she pulled her hand away it left a floury imprint that covered her cheek and chin.

"You only had to ask," she stepped back to let him in, chuckling at her own humour.

"Now why didn't I think of that?" David rolled his eyes dramatically. "Where's Kiira?"

"She's with one of the patients."

It was cool and dark inside and smelt heavily of disinfectant. The double doors leading to the ward were straight ahead, the left wing housed the sanatorium and operating room, the right the toilets, shower and kitchen.

Men weren't allowed onto the ward due to the trauma the residents had suffered at the hands of the opposite sex. Like his mother most were victims of rape and had suffered severe sexual abuse, including genital mutilation. The sisters patched them up, both physically and mentally, but some of the scars would never heal.

The youngest girl there was only nine and hadn't spoken since she arrived almost a year ago. The sisters had taken to calling her Mary. Another unfortunate girl brought her in from a neighbouring village when she was found wandering aimlessly down the road. The girls had both been raped repeatedly by the same gang of Kalenjin youths until their genitalia became bloody pulps and they were left to die. The elder girl, who had since been found a place at the local orphanage, said that she overheard a couple of the Kalenjin warriors laughing. Boasting that they should thank President Moi for paying them to have so much fun.

David had seen Mary a few times in the garden behind the mission, tending to the vegetable patch. She was a waif of a thing with a permanent distant stare. David felt bad thinking it but she seemed vacant, as if her soul had left her body to seek solace from the world.

"You wait here. I'll get Kiira and your mother." She started to turn and then stopped, "Would you like something to eat? I've got some lovely stew on the stove."

Now that she mentioned it David caught a whiff of something delicious.

She saw the hesitation in his face. David had never felt comfortable being in the Mission, "Go on, get yourself in the kitchen, we'll be there in a minute."

She turned and went through the door. David caught a brief glimpse of the ward. Kiira's back was to him, she was sitting on the lap of a girl of about sixteen and being fussed over by a couple of the other women. The door swung shut and the snapshot was gone so he followed the smell through into the kitchen. Aunty Farisi once said that Kiira's visits to the ward were therapeutic for the residents, gave them hope for the future. He wished that she had the same effect on his mother.

David walked over to the stove and lifted the lid of the steaming pot. His mouth watered as he sucked in the vapours, he picked up the wooden spoon and gave it a stir. He couldn't resist trying it and spooned out some of the collards and onions. He blew on it but not enough. The stew tasted great but burnt the roof of his mouth.

"David!" Kiira squealed with joy when they came in the room.

"I told you to wait in the kitchen, not start without us!" Aunty Farisi's grin didn't match her words. "You take Kiira and sit down. I'll fetch your mother she's out in the garden." Kiira let go of his Aunt's hand and ran towards him with her arms open wide. The olive dress flapped behind her, held to her wiry frame by a thin black belt.

Her smile could brighten the darkest room, "I didn't know that you were coming! I missed you."

"I missed you too," David replied, wrapping her in his arms and lifting her off her feet until their faces met. Her teardrop eyes and prominent cheekbones made Kiira the spitting image of their mother in her younger days. "I'm sorry, I didn't know that I was coming myself until today."

David pulled Kiira closer and nuzzled his chin into her neck. He heard a noise and looked over her shoulder to see Waseme coming in the back door.

"And how are you mother?" he raised his voice so that she could hear him.

The attack had left Waseme deaf in one ear, as well as mentally scarred and pregnant with Kiira. She didn't speak for months afterwards and David chose his sister's name, hoping that its' meaning, Dawn, would help his mother to begin her life again. Waseme never talked about that night, not once, but he knew it affected her in ways that not even her devout faith could resolve. She hadn't touched David or shown affection to anyone since.

"I'm fine, how else would I be?" Waseme took a seat at the table and started rocking as if in a trance, staring blankly ahead.

His mother had refused to go anywhere near Kiira at first, acting as if the child didn't exist. Ignoring the baby's cries in the night and leaving David to change the nappies and feed her. Kiira rejected the formula milk and after nearly a week David began to accept the fact that she might not make it. But Kiira was a fighter and gained the weight rapidly when she finally did take to the bottle.

After the fire they were evicted and the land was taken over by a Kalenjin family. David and his mother moved into the house behind the Mission that served as the nuns' accommodation. His Aunt nursed them both until they were well enough to look after themselves.

Thankfully his Aunt carried the conversation forward, "Get the bowls David and whilst you're doing it you can tell us all what you've been up to.

We read about the baby elephant in the 'Daily Nation'. Were you involved in that?"

It seemed that everybody had read today's paper. Thankfully Bernstein had kept his name out of the article.

David nodded, "We found her and took her to the orphanage in Nairobi. She's doing well..." David told them briefly what had happened, leaving out the gory details for Kiira's sake.

"Is she going to be OK?" Kiira's sad face looked up at him, her eyes were misted over.

"I'm sure she'll be fine." What else could he say to a four year old? "She's in the best possible hands. The people working there really know what they're doing." Caitlyn's cat-like eyes popped into his head for a second and then disappeared.

Farisi but the pot of stew and a plate of Ugali onto the table, David reached for one of the doughy balls.

Waseme stopped him mid act, "Are you forgetting your manners? Put your hands together and let us say grace. Dear lord..."

David's mind wandered as his mother recited the familiar blessing, guilt troubling him as he thought about leaving them alone again in the morning.

"Amen," he repeated, hearing the prayer come to an end. Picking up a ball of Ugali he used it to scoop up some of the stew and stuffed the dumpling into his mouth.

"This really is delicious," he said, using the back of his hand to wipe away the gravy that escaped his mouth and dribbled down his chin.

"Hey, leave me some," cried Kiira in feigned protest, pushing David's hand out of the way as he reached for a second. "No need to be a pig about it!"

"Look who's talking," replied David, laughing as she tried unsuccessfully to push a whole piece into her mouth as he'd done. Eventually she gave up and bit through the ball, catching the half that fell with her hand. Kiira's eyes sparkled with mischief.

Waseme didn't join in and remained silent as Farisi and his sister talked about what had been going on at the Mission. She picked at the meal with little interest, pushing the food around on her plate. His mother's face seemed even gaunter to David than the last time he had seen her. Emphasised by her tight curls of prematurely white hair.

After they had done the stew justice Kiira leaned back in the chair and stretched her arms out. "I'm ready for bed," she yawned.

"Come on then." David stood up, "I'll tuck you in."

He scooped Kiira out of the chair, she seemed to weigh nothing, and carried her out of the kitchen door, across the yard to the nun's accommodation. It was a basic bungalow comprised of six bedrooms, a toilet and a shower block. He took her to the room that she shared with their mother and held her over his shoulder as he pulled back the blanket on one of the twin beds. She looked up at him adoringly as he placed her onto the mattress and pulled the covers up to her chin. Suddenly her face turned serious.

"Mummy does love me doesn't she?"

"Off course she does...she's just..." David struggled to find the right words.

"Sad?"

"I...guess...so," David choked back his emotions.

"Because Daddy died," Kiira's innocent question almost broke him down.

"That's right, you know we've got to be strong for her and stick together." David lay on the bed next to Kiira, pulled her head to his chest and stroked her hair.

"I know but she's so mean sometimes, I think she hates me," Kiira's voice trembled as she whispered the words.

"Don't be silly, she doesn't hate you, she's just a bit grumpy. Now come on, it's time to go to sleep. You've got lots to do in the morning. Goodnight," David kissed her on the cheek before pushing himself off the bed.

"Goodnight, I love you," Kiira said, as she rolled onto her side.

"Love you too," David replied softly. Glad that she turned away from him and couldn't see the tear that ran down his cheek.

CHAPTER NINE
GSU Headquarters, Nairobi
August 12th, 1996

Maliki should have been concentrating on the task in hand but he wasn't. He couldn't stop thinking about Gupta and the baby elephant. He'd left a message for the idiot to call him the day before, but so far nothing. Gupta was already out collecting rhino horn according to the man who answered, no doubt prompted to say so by his Indian master. He was taking all of his frustration out on the prisoner. Maliki's knuckles were bleeding and his shoulders ached with the effort.

The naked man strapped to the chair in front of him was nobody as far as Maliki was concerned, worse than that he was Kikuyu. Patrick Konde had been caught red-handed in the workshop behind the store he owned, printing anti-government leaflets that he was about to distribute. Mostly it contained the usual speculative crap about oppression and ethnic cleansing in the run-up to next year's election, although Moi still hadn't set the date. But it wasn't the greengrocer or the propaganda that Maliki was really interested in.

"Why don't you make this easy on yourself?" He looked down at Konde's bruised and swollen face, "We know that someone on the Committee has been supplying you with information. All you have to do is give me his name and the pain will stop."

Some of the details regarding specific cases cited in the leaflet were not public knowledge and could only have come from someone working on the Standing Committee on Human Rights. The Committee's members were mostly lawyers and lead by a professor in law, Onesimus Mutungi. Set up by President Moi earlier that year the committee was intended to have no real power. Any investigations that it carried out were hindered by the inability to subpoena witnesses or order the production of documents.

Even so it was the political equivalent of stirring the hornet's nest and Maliki opposed the idea from the start. The new American Ambassador was breathing down the President's neck and Moi insisted that it was a necessary measure to appease both internal and international pressure. Now it seemed that someone on the committee was frustrated at getting nowhere and trying to cause trouble.

Konde spat out a mouthful of phlegm and blood, "Fuck you, you bastard! How many times do I have to tell you that I don't know what you're talking about?"

"What a shame," Maliki pulled back his arm and delivered another blow to the right side of Konde's face. He felt the eyeball squish in its socket beneath the already closed eyelid.

The stubborn shopkeeper lost consciousness again. He was surprisingly resilient for someone in his fifties. To his credit they had been interviewing him on and off for nearly twenty-four hours and yet he still wouldn't tell them anything.

Maliki nodded towards the greengrocer, "Wake him up!"

Lembui picked up the bucket of water mixed with Konde's urine and poured it over the prisoner's head. He woke up coughing and spluttering for air.

Maliki waited for Konde to regain control of his breathing, although it was still short and raspy. Maliki was sure that a couple of the man's ribs had been broken with his earlier blows. He had heard them crack, "You know that I can have you executed for treason? His name Mr Konde?"

"Go fuck yourself!" Although faint the shopkeeper's words still carried a significant amount of venom.

Maliki face twitched, he sighed and stepped back from the puddle of water. "You leave me no choice." He looked at Lembui, "Increase the voltage and give him another dose. Maybe it will help to loosen his tongue."

"No!" Konde's expression turned to one of terror and he struggled to free himself from the gaffa tape binding his arms and legs to the metal chair. "Please, not that again! I don't know anything!"

"We both know that's not true Mr Konde." Maliki nodded to Lembui.

Two jump leads trailed across the floor to a control box set up on a table in the corner that was connected to the building's power supply. One of the crocodile clips was attached to Konde's penis and the other to the fingers of his right hand. It was a technique that Maliki had used successfully many times before. Inflicting excruciating pain whilst at the same time ensuring massive trauma as the current passed through the victim's heart. He was yet to meet a man, or woman, who could resist the treatment. Lembui turned up one of the dials and pressed the button.

Konde started jerking around in the chair, violent sporadic movements as his muscles went into spasm. The odour of burning flesh and hair entered his nostrils and Maliki grinned. The smell reminded him of setting Douglas Mason on fire. To him the smell represented freedom and the moment he had taken control of his life. Suddenly the wiry shopkeeper's whole body went rigid and he stopped moving.

"Shit!" Maliki shouldn't have allowed himself to be distracted. "Turn it off you idiot! Can't you see that he's dead already?"

The problem with muscle was that they couldn't seem to think for themselves. He waited for Lembui to kill the power and then checked Konde's neck for the pulse that he knew wasn't there.

"Go and get Sabore to help you clean this mess up!" he stopped at the door to the corridor and looked back, "And make sure that you dump the body somewhere that it won't be found." He'd learnt that it was better to be specific with Lembui. Otherwise the numbskull would probably throw the body out of the car on his way home.

He went upstairs and waited for the guard to come through and open the gate. The ground floor of the detention suite consisted of twelve cells, six on either side of the corridor, and a small anti-chamber. Two sets of security gates separated the cells from the basement and the anti-chamber, where two officers were always on duty. Unlike a normal jail there were no desk clerk or interview rooms. Nor were there any windows in the cells, barred or otherwise. There was also no official record of the prisoners that were dragged there from their beds in the middle of the night and beaten. Or of the torture inflicted in the dungeon beneath his feet. This was his world. Here Maliki was Engai Nanyokie, the angry red Maasai God, master of life and death.

"Is there someone there? Please, I need water."

The jangling of the guard's keys against the outer gate stirred one of the occupants and he started banging on the sliding hatch in the metal door. There were only two at the moment, both Kikuyu. A pair of radical students in their early twenties who had organised protest rallies at the university campus. Maliki still hadn't decided whether to have them shot or simply badly beaten and then released as an example.

"Shut up or I'll take you downstairs," snapped the guard on his way past. Fortunately for the student the banging stopped and he remained silent whilst Maliki was being shown out. Otherwise he might have ordered his execution there and then. Konde dying had put him in an even worse mood. Moi wasn't going to be happy when he found out that Maliki had failed to get any information. He wanted to know who was behind the latest attack on his presidency.

As Maliki strode across the gravel courtyard into the central building of GSU Headquarters the drill sergeant's barked command made him glance over. A company of officers were being put through their paces on the parade square, straight lines of shiny boots and red berets split by camouflage uniforms. Maliki burst through the double doors, ignoring the desk clerk's salute and the beeping metal detector he went up to his office on the first floor. He sat in the leather recliner behind his mahogany desk and checked the answer machine. But there were no new messages. He slammed his fist down on the desk.

Why did he get the feeling that unseen forces were at work? Maliki forced himself to relax and took a deep breath. He was being paranoid. Really there was nothing to worry about. It was not uncommon for Gupta to be away from base camp for long periods of time. Maliki would deal with him when he showed up. Letting the baby elephant live was a huge mistake, one that Gupta needed to be punished for. Maliki would have to start thinking about who would replace him.

The reporter had been easy to trace. A few phone calls revealed that he was checked in at the Kenya Comfort Hotel. A place that was popular with westerners travelling on a budget. Maliki had set up a team of four officers to follow Bernstein, the first pair should be reporting in soon after completing their twelve-hour shift.

Maliki picked up the phone and started dialling. In the meantime he might as well find out what he could about this Captain Nbeke. If either he or the

American continued to make waves then they would have to disappear.

CHAPTER TEN
Emurutoto, Edge of the Maasai Mara
August 12th, 1996

David was beginning to think that he must have missed the turning and was ready to head back toward Lolgorien when he saw it. 'FRIENDS OF THE MAASAI MARA' and an arrow messily painted onto a rock pointing to a dirt track. Judging by the numerous drips running down from the letters the not very skilled artist had used some kind of whitewash and a thick brush. The sun had faded the letters so that they were barely legible. David smiled to himself. He had made the right decision to come in daylight, at night he could have easily driven by the sign without noticing it.

Transporting Ella to Nairobi had proven to be the final straw for the Nissan's suspension and the shocks badly needed replacing. He turned off onto the track and slowed to a crawl, nursing the truck over the bumpy terrain. The Kawai Dam wasn't far off to his right, an oval roughly the size of a football field that was fed by a spring higher up in the hills. The damn was meant to supply the neighbouring village of Emurutoto but a group of four Maasai in bright red shukas had pushed over a section of the fence and were letting their cattle drink from the brackish water, stirring it up into a brown soup.

There was nothing David or the villagers could do about it. By reinstating their nomadic rite of passage Moi had given the Maasai carte blanche to go where they wanted and do what they liked.

A bit further up the track he passed a man-made water hole surrounded by a large boma, put there by one of the local farmers. There to protect the goats from predators or the water from the Maasai herdsmen, David wasn't sure which. After a couple of miles of crisp dry savannah, only broken by the odd acacia tree, the track ended at a cattle grid and gate set into a chain-link fence.

There were two very contradictory notices attached to the rusty crossbars. By the craftsmanship, David guessed that the artist was the same person responsible for the sign near the main road. The first read 'FRIENDS OF THE MAASAI MARA – PLEASE CLOSE THE GATE BEHIND YOU'. The second said simply 'TRESPASSERS WILL BE SHOT'.

David could see a shrivelled waterhole in the dip below, a few tin-roofed cabins surrounding it raised about a meter from the ground on wooden stilts. Smoke was coming from the chimney of the largest structure, rising up lazily into the hot stagnant air. He gave the truck's horn a blast and waited, eventually a figure emerged onto the porch of the building with the fire going inside. From this distance it was hard to tell whether they were male or female but whoever it was waved in his direction.

Guessing that it was probably safe he went through the rigmarole of opening and closing the gates before pulling up outside the cabin. The Nissan's engine rumbled to a grateful stop and emitted a large hiss as steam escaped from a hole in the bubbling radiator. David reminded himself to check the water level again before he left for base camp. Hopefully it could be repaired and didn't need replacing like the suspension. There wasn't much cash in the emergency slush fund and getting money from HQ was like getting blood out of a stone. Besides which the paperwork could take months as the requisition was passed from one department to another. As much as possible David and the other rangers did the repairs themselves to keep the vehicles on the road. Fortunately Chege wasn't a bad mechanic and could fix most things when he put his mind to it.

David let the dust settle and then climbed down from the cab. He put a hand up to shield his eyes from the fierce mid-morning sun and squinted up at the figure hidden in the shade of the veranda.

"Sorry to turn up unannounced but a mutual friend told me that I might be able to find Spencer Scott here." There was no reply from the shadows. "Dr Caitlyn Brennan from the orphanage in Nairobi."

"Caitlyn sent you did she?" The booming voice definitely belonged to a man, or at least David hoped so. The alternative didn't bear thinking about. By the way he pronounced his 'I's to make them sound more like 'Y's and emphasised his 'E's David knew that he was a white Kenyan before he stepped forward and put his bear-like hands on the wooden railing. "Now why would she do that?"

David was getting used to cold receptions, "She didn't exactly send me. I was hoping that he might be able to help me with something."

The man he guessed must be Spencer Scott eyed his uniform and glanced at the truck before speaking, "And why would the KWS want my help? You've been ignoring my reports for years." He wasn't the under-fed environmentalist that David somehow expected. Huge tanned biceps flexed below the sleeves of his khaki shirt as he gripped the railing. David wondered if the wood might break and crumble into splinters beneath his cigar-like fingers.

"I'm sorry I don't know which reports you're talking about and I'm not here on any kind of official business." David hesitated, "Well I guess I might be. It's difficult to explain really."

Spencer Scott raised a bushy eyebrow, obviously intrigued, "What's it to do with?"

"Poaching," said David simply.

"I suppose you better come inside," grunted Scott before turning and disappearing through the fly-screen door. David went up the three rickety steps and followed him inside. The roughly hewn floorboards creaked and groaned under their combined weight. He began to wonder whether Scott had built the place and painted the signs himself. There didn't seem to be anyone else around and everything bore signs of the same shoddy handiwork. The cabin itself was on a tilt, slanting towards the waterhole. David put it down to subsidence.

"Would you like something to drink?" said Scott, heading over towards the breakfast bar built from wooden pallets. The uneven worktop separated what could loosely be described as a kitchen from the lounge area. Six inch nails protruding from some of the planks threatened to snag passers-by. Somehow Scott found a quarter-full bottle of Jameson amongst the empties and other debris covering the worktop. He held it up in the air and gave the contents a shake, "Whisky?"

"No thanks," replied David. "Beer if you've got it or water." Looking at the stacks of dirty crockery and empty food cartons it was difficult to imagine where either of them might come from.

Surprisingly Scott ducked behind the counter and produced a familiar looking bottle, "Tusker OK? Now if I can just find an opener." He started rummaging around under the counter, presumably there was a shelf hidden away under there somewhere.

"That would be great."

David found himself salivating at the unlikely prospect. One thing his Aunt refused to stock at the Mission was alcohol.

"Here we go," said Scott triumphantly straightening up into view. He popped the lid off the bottle.

"Cheers," David was even more shocked to find that the beer was cold when Scott eventually handed it to him.

Scott must have read his expression. His laugh was a suitably deep bellow, "We've got solar panels and a wind turbine to keep the fridges going. The odd beer mixed in with the medical supplies doesn't hurt anybody."

David smiled back at him and then took a long swig. His throat was so dry and parched after the journey in the hot cab that he could feel the isotonic reaction as his body welcomed the beer's arrival.

"Thanks, I needed that."

Scott had returned to the kitchen and was searching for something amongst the pots and pans piled up in what must be the sink, presumably a glass. His voice was muffled, "No worries." There was some more clinking of bottles, "Sod it!"

Scott gave up his search and took the cork out with his teeth before spitting it onto the counter. He gulped down half of the contents and held the bottle towards David, "Are you sure you don't want some? It's good stuff."

"I'm alright thanks, you go ahead."

Scott's shrug suggested that he thought David must be crazy, "Suit yourself." He necked the rest of the bottle in one go and dropped it to the floor.

David noticed a slight limp as Scott went over to the wood burner and collapsed into a rattan armchair that had seen better days, it creaked in unison with the floorboards. Scott had obviously been hitting the bottle hard for some time. The clothes he was wearing were crumpled and creased, like he'd been sleeping in them for days. His face looked haggard, bloodshot eyes and pallor skin, bristly stubble covering his jutting jaw.

"I didn't catch your name?"

"David Nbeke, I'm a ranger in the KWS," he said it as if that explained him being there.

"Well don't just stand there David, take a seat," he waved his hand towards the other beaten armchair. Apart from the trestle table folded against the wall, littered with books on wildlife next to a CB radio, they were the room's only furnishings. "So how do you know Caitlyn?"

David tried to get comfortable but broken bits of cane dug into him when he leant back. He perched on the edge of the chair hoping that it didn't collapse.

"I met her at the orphanage in Nairobi a few days ago..." David told him about their brief encounters. Scott nodded as if satisfied with something.

"So how is she?" He opened the door and stirred the embers with a metal poker hanging from the side of the burner. "The place just hasn't been the same since she left."

That explained the state of the cabin and Scott's unkempt appearance.

"She seemed fine to me," for some reason David felt knots of tension in his stomach. "If you don't mind me asking. Why did she leave?"

Scott looked like he might get up out of the chair and hit him for a second, but his expression softened, "I suppose it's old news. Nothing that dramatic, we just couldn't live together."

David decided that he had pried enough into their relationship and changed the subject.

"Is that where the black rhino are at the moment?"

Scott glanced over his shoulder at the large map of the park and the surrounding area. Around twenty little red plastic triangles were dotted about the surface. He gave David a strange look, "That's right, as of 6pm yesterday. We've got eight volunteers keeping an eye on them as best they can. For what good it does. We carry on monitoring them between our other duties but nobody from Parks seems to give a shit."

Scott was obviously old school. He used the same name for the KWS as David's father.

"What exactly do you guys do here?"

"We do what we can in conservation terms, look after a few sick animals, rescue them from snares, mend broken limbs that kind of thing. We keep them here until they recuperate," Scott nodded towards the waterhole where a group of Impala were lying in the shade of a tree.

Something was boiling away furiously in a pot on top of the stove. The heat in the room was stifling. It would have been unbearable but for the open windows that allowed in what little breeze there was.

Scott poked the fire again, apparently unaffected by the heat, "But most of our work is preservation, looking after the habitats they live in, recording their behaviour so that we can understand them better."

David nodded. They were one of the dedicated field teams that the likes of David Attenborough got his research from. "You said there are eight volunteers, where do they come from?"

"America and the UK mostly, students looking for work experience. Apart from me there's only one other Kenyan on the team." Scott seemed to suddenly remember why they were there, "This is all very nice but I'm guessing that you didn't come all the way out here just for a chat. You mentioned something about poaching?"

David had been working his way around to it, "Caitlyn tells me you keep records on the numbers of elephants and rhino poached and that you've seen an increase since the KWS was formed?"

"Apart from the recent rise in the amount of rhino horn being taken it's not so much the increase that's alarming, the figures have been rising steadily since the seventies," he threw David an accusing look. "It's the fact that the numbers should have gone down or at least levelled off that's most worrying."

David nodded to show that he was in agreement before wording his next question carefully, "Are your statistics based solely on the team's findings?"

"No," Scott shook his head. "The information is collated from all the parks in the country on an annual basis and put onto a spreadsheet. We've been keeping a record since the late seventies. I always send a copy to your headquarters but they don't even bother to acknowledge receipt these days. Look David, what's all this about?"

"I was hoping that we could work together." David didn't want to tell Scott everything, "That you could help me and my rangers catch some of the poachers."

"I don't know, it all sounds a bit too dangerous for my lot, and I'm no use, not with my dodgy leg."

The limp didn't seem that bad, David began to wonder if Scott had deeper psychological issues.

"What's wrong with it?"

"Broke my kneecap playing rugby back in High School," Scott slapped his right leg. "I was good, would have gone pro if it wasn't for that one tackle. Their centres took me down from opposite directions, one of those things I guess." There was no bravado in his voice, only bitterness. His eyes glazed over as if he was reliving the moment of his downfall.

Despite his current appearance David guessed that the kind of school Spencer went to wouldn't have been on Kisii's fixture list but he still had to ask.

"Where did you go to?"

"Nairobi School, do you know it?" Scott's face lit up like he was part of some elite club.

David nodded, "I've heard of it." Only the colour of the students would have changed since Scott had been there. A school that was once reserved for privileged white children, now its pupils were the sons of Kenya's upper class, celebrities, ministers and business leaders. Scott must have fallen from grace to end up in this shack, or maybe he had become a recluse as a result of his injury.

David decided to get the meeting back on track, "I wouldn't be expecting you to do anything that you're not already doing. Just keep me posted of the rhino's locations and let me know if you spot anyone suspicious. If a member of your group does see anything they need to stay well clear and we'll do the rest."

"So my team won't be in any direct danger?"

"None that they're not already in." Most people would consider following wild rhino around dangerous enough. Added to the fact that armed men were trying to kill the endangered species with machine guns made it practically suicidal. "You can use the radio to contact me."

Scott stared at the fire for a while. Sweat was dripping down the middle of David's back and he desperately wanted to wrap things up.

"Look if you don't want to get involved then I more than understand," he stood and moved over to the window where it was relatively cooler.

"I suppose it wouldn't hurt." Scott grinned, "It will be nice to be doing something positive for a change. Standing by and recording Kenya's wildlife slowly but surely get depleted has become a bit disheartening."

"Thanks," said David. "I owe you one. If you ever need a favour then just let me know." He started thinking about call signs and logistics.

Scott's smile was devilish, "Just look after Caitlyn or you'll have me to answer to."

CHAPTER ELEVEN
KWS Base Camp, Maasai Mara
August 12th, 1996

David hoped that he wasn't too late for lunch. He was famished but it had already gone 2 o'clock and the canteen staff would probably have started clearing up. His worst fears were realised as he pulled up outside the Rangers Cafe. The shutters were down, a closed sign in the window.

"Shit!"

He gave the steering wheel a gentle thump, worried that it might break if he hit it any harder. He would just have to rough it over at the hotel. The buffet there was out of this world but it would cost him a weeks pay, even with his forty percent discount. Fortunately the Mission took care of David's mother and sister and his Aunt refused to take money from him. With no place of his own and living on rations most of the time he managed to save most of his pathetic salary. When it turned up, two months had passed without anything going into his bank account.

He slammed the door shut. Dented by an angry buffalo it was the only way to get the damn thing to close.

The Mara Serena Safari Lodge was hidden from the KWS facility by dense bush that covered the hill. He went through the cutting that connected the two and skipped around the side to the terrace, going in what was effectively the tradesman's entrance. Deliberately avoiding the few tourists who would be waiting in the foyer to take their afternoon safaris or rides in a hot air balloon over the park.

Those not put off by the murders. Or maybe they didn't know about them? Although David found it difficult to believe that they hadn't read or seen anything on TV. Julie Ward's death and the subsequent investigation spearheaded by her father had been well publicized. The twenty-eight year old photographer's dismembered body had been found burnt in the park, a week after Julie disappeared on a solo safari. Maasai were suspected because of the ritual way in which the body was disposed of but nobody was charged.

Unable to accept the bizarre theory put forward by the GSU, that his daughter had been mauled by lions and then struck by lightning, Julie's father wouldn't let it lie. John Ward had been campaigning for justice ever since, accusing the warden and his men of a cover up. The rangers were acquitted in 1992 but Ward was still going after the ex-warden, driven by his daughter's death. Every so often a new fact or angle on the case would appear in the press.

David walked along the terrace. The hotel was built to blend in with the northeast slope of the hill, overlooking the Mara River. The seventy-four bedrooms were a series of individual pods that would be equally at home on the moon if painted white instead of green. The rooms fanned out to create a wide funnel shape with the restaurant and pool at the centre. The main buildings were a series of larger pods. One of them housed the restaurant and dining room, the others conference rooms, lounges and the reception area.

Thankfully there were only a few stragglers having lunch and nobody at the buffet. He felt self-conscious in his sweat stained uniform. Most of the hot dishes on offer had been exhausted. David piled his plate high with cuts of meat, salmon and salad. He took a table next to the low stonewall at the edge of the terrace. Manicured shrubs and flowers were dotted between the trees and rocks on the slope going down to the pool area. Kidney shaped and crystal clear, the swimming pool was surrounded by unoccupied loungers, facing out towards the breathtaking view of the escarpment below.

David tucked into the thinly sliced venison. There was no label to say which antelope he was eating. But judging from the size of the joint the meat was carved from it was probably Kudu. Whatever it was, it was delicious, as was the salmon. A waiter appeared and he ordered a bottle of Tusker to wash it down with.

When he heard the footsteps behind him he assumed it was the waiter returning with his drink, "Do you always eat so much?" Bernstein sat down in the seat opposite him. He was wearing what looked like a disguise, khaki shirt and shorts. A Nikon camera with a huge zoom lens dangled against his chest.

"What the hell are you doing here?"

"Nice to see you too," Bernstein smiled sarcastically. "I'm following up on Ella's story, came up here to see where it all happened."

"I would have thought that this place was beyond a reporter's salary?" At over $250 dollars a night Bernstein's expenses must be seriously totting up.

"It is." He thumbed over his shoulder, "I'm staying at the campsite down the road, great facilities."

David wasn't sure whether the last part was meant to justify his staying there or a simple statement of fact. He guessed the latter. Bernstein probably owned a Winnebago back in the States.

The reporter had obviously come looking for him, "What do you want Bernstein? I told you I'm not interested in being your stool pigeon."

The American allowed the waiter to serve David his drink and ordered one himself before replying.

"I'm only here to take photographs and get a feel for the place," his worried expression and the outfit he had on said otherwise. "I was hoping that you might be able to show me around. Give me your version of what happened."

"Sorry I'm busy. You'll have to find another tour guide," David speared some of the salad with his fork.

"I've tried. All of your rangers gave me the cold shoulder. Told me that I needed to speak with you first. You've obviously got them well trained."

The waiter arrived with Bernstein's beer.

"Like I said, I've got things to do."

"Come on cut me some slack will you? I kept your name out of the piece in the Daily Nation didn't I?" Bernstein's eyes were glued to David's food, "You're not seriously going to eat all of that are you?"

David sighed. "Feel free," he indicated the spare set of cutlery.

Apart from the scenery the other advantage of the hotel's outrageous prices was that you could refill your plate as many times as you liked. As long as they didn't charge him for two meals, that might actually break the bank. Bernstein didn't waste any time, he unwrapped the fork from the spare napkin and started digging into David's meal.

Bernstein spoke with his mouth full, "You know, considering everything that's going on it wouldn't do any harm to put a positive slant on the Service."

"We've been through this, it's all just conjecture. You've got no real poof." David thought he saw something pass across Bernstein's eyes, "You're not thinking about publishing the story already?"

"The statistics alone merit comment don't you think? My editor agrees with me that the readers can make up their own minds."

If Bernstein broke the story now it could ruin any chance of catching the person or persons responsible. At the moment the only name he had on his list of potential suspects was Deputy Director Tanui. David couldn't bring himself to believe that his old mentor was involved. He was going to have to stall the reporter somehow.

"Hold on a minute," David held up his hand. "Now I'm not suggesting that what you're saying is true. But let's just say it is. Alerting whoever's involved is only going to send them underground. Don't you want to find out who it is?"

Bernstein scratched at his goatee, "So you're admitting that someone in the KWS is involved?"

"I didn't say anything like that, but I'd like you to give me the time to find out." David ate a forkful of salmon before Bernstein could finish it all off. "If someone from the KWS is involved I promise that you'll get the exclusive. Think about what a scoop that would be."

"And what if you don't find out anything? Where does that leave me?"

He watched in horror as the reporter picked up the last roll of meat with his fingers and bit into it. David glanced at the buffet. Two members of staff in white aprons and chef's hats were starting to clear away the silver trays.

"Release your article the way it is, no harm done."

"Apart from the fact that the editor is breathing down my neck and I need the money." Bernstein studied his beer bottle, "A week is the best I can do."

David was momentarily distracted by the men in suits that joined them on the terrace and took up a table near the entrance. The pair looked overdressed, possibly businessmen using the conferencing facilities, but instinct told David otherwise.

"A week isn't enough." His plan was shaky at best and might not even work. Who knew how long it would take? He carried on watching the men out of the corner of his eye. They dismissed the waiter without ordering anything.

"It's all I can promise and only on one condition."

David gave the reporter his full attention, "What condition?"

Bernstein smiled, "That you take me to the spot where Ella's family was slaughtered."

*****

After three days the great mammals' carcases had been stripped bare by scavengers, their skeletal frames partially draped in folds of ghostly grey skin.

David thought that returning to the scene of the crime wouldn't affect him, but he was filled with a mixture of emotions. Sorrow at the waste of life and anger against those who had caused it.

"So they went that way into Tanzania?"

David nodded and Bernstein took some shots of the river and the bank on the other side.

"And where did you guys come in from?"

"That way," David pointed down the river. "From the northwest. We camped near the Purungat Outpost and they wandered away from us during the night."

"Is following the herd standard practice?"

"No, but it ought to be. If it were down to me we'd track every single elephant and rhino."

"Why don't you?"

Bernstein wasn't taking notes but he might have a recorder hidden in one of his pockets. David decided to be careful about what he said.

"The KWS is overstretched, there's insufficient manpower and no funding to supply more."

Bernstein continued to ask questions and take photographs until the light started to fade.

"Come on we better not stay any longer," David waved his rifle in the direction of the LandRover. "The hyenas will be back once it gets dark."

Bernstein glanced at one of the skeletons, "But there's nothing left surely."

"Don't you believe it, they'll eat the skin and bones eventually."

"I think that I've got everything I need." Bernstein gulped, "Why don't we call it a day?"

David led the way up the path from the river and they headed back to the jeep. Besides the encroaching nightfall David wanted time to brief his squad on the changes he was making to tomorrow's schedule. He also needed Chege to find another radio set and train somebody how to use it.

A branch was broken by something hidden in the bush. David could tell by the sound that it was something heavy. He signalled Bernstein to be silent and they retraced their steps as quickly as possible.

"What the hell was that?" exclaimed Bernstein once they were safely inside the truck and David had the engine running.

"I'm not sure, something big, maybe a buffalo." He couldn't help thinking about his father and their last hunt together.

As they drove back to the campsite David pointed out the few zebra and giraffe that he spotted along the way.

"I thought that this was supposed to be a game reserve? Where the hell are all the animals?"

"Most of them have gone over into Tanzania, they'll be back when the rains come and there's something to graze on. That's when we get the huge herds of wildebeest and predators following them that you see on TV. During the migration the Mara River becomes a bloodbath between the crocodiles and the hippos."

"I thought that hippos are vegetarian?"

David nodded, "They're short tempered though and very territorial. Hippos are rare in that they are one of the few animals that will kill even though they have no intention of eating their victim."

"I'd like to see the migration, when does it happen?"

"Normally between August and September. But as long as there's a drought they won't come."

"Must be something to see," said Bernstein craning his neck back towards the river as if he might get lucky.

"There's nothing like it. Over a million animals risking life and limb to get to greener pastures. It's the greatest show on earth."

Bernstein gave him a sideways look, "Haven't I heard that line somewhere before?"

David grinned, "He stole it from me."

He pulled up outside the campsite but kept the motor running, "This is you I believe."

Bernstein held the door open so that David couldn't drive off, "You will keep me in the loop won't you?"

"I'll keep my side of the bargain, just don't forget to keep yours. I'll let you know as soon as there are any developments." David reached across and pulled the door shut before the reporter could reply.

Driving away he glanced in the rear-view mirror. Behind Bernstein a car pulled in at the roadside, the front seats occupied. Although he wasn't sure from this distance they looked like the two men he had seen on the terrace of the hotel. Maybe the noise that they heard down by the river didn't belong to an animal?

CHAPTER TWELVE
GSU Headquarters, Nairobi
August 12th, 1996

Maliki still didn't have the information he needed but the President wanted to see him anyway. He'd tried to get out of it. But Moi insisted that they needed to discuss what was happening with the human rights committee and the Ambassador. Prudence Bushnell had been making waves since she arrived in July, appointed by President Clinton to do just that. She was pushing for democratic reform and corruption to be rooted out from the government. If not for her the damn committee wouldn't even exist.

He wished that Moi would kick the interfering bitch out of Kenya altogether but since the fall of the Berlin Wall the President had been hell-bent on regaining favour with the Americans. More specifically Moi wanted them to bring back their money in the form of aid and investment. When the Cold War ended Moi's anti-communist policy was no longer useful to the States and they practically pulled out of Kenya over-night.

"Good day sir."

For the life of him Maliki couldn't remember the name of the nosy desk clerk standing to attention.

Maliki flicked a salute in his direction and hurried outside.

Lembui was waiting near the entrance to escort him to the car and Sabore was standing in front of the stretched Mercedes. Both were armed to the teeth, well prepared for the journey ahead. They were the best of his elite squad of handpicked GSU veterans but Maliki still felt naked travelling with so little protection. Since the attack on him the Kiambu Mafia had been more active, part of the run up to next year's election. President Moi should have let him wipe out every last stinking Kikuyu, but he was too soft, too worried about what the old American Ambassador Smith Hempstone would report back to Washington.

Maliki scanned the buildings surrounding the parade square nervously as Sabore scurried around to open the door for him.

"Take me to the airfield."

"Right away sir."

Gravel was sent flying as the wheels spun and the Mercedes roared down the driveway. Sabore gave the guard on duty at the gate just enough time to lift the barrier up as they shot through the checkpoint. Then they were racing towards the city. Maliki braced himself as they swerved in front of the oncoming traffic, turning left off Thika Highway onto Mathare North Road. The drive-in cinema flew past as the Mercedes accelerated south towards Moi Air Base. A few minutes later they went by the row of Hawk fighter jets and pulled up next to the Cessna.

Lembui and Sabore got out first to make sure it was safe and then they filed into the small plane. Maliki went first, stooping low to avoid hitting his head he clambered awkwardly into one of the back seats. Lembui accidentally bumped his thigh with the stock of his machine-gun as he sat down next to him.

"Sorry sir."

"You clumsy fool!" Maliki glared at him, "Do you even know which end to shoot with?"

"Yes sir...I mean sorry sir."

"Do it again and you will be, believe me!"

Lembui stared at something on the back of Sabore's seat. Maliki could feel his leg trembling against him. He grinned and turned to look out the window.

The pilot radioed the tower and soon they were taxiing to the end of the runway. The tiny 180hp Lycoming engine was pushed to maximum throttle before the pilot released the brakes. Trundling at first, the light aircraft slowly picked up speed until they lifted off, climbing steeply before banking left and heading northwest.

It would only take around fifty minutes to complete the 180km flight to Moi's farm in Kabarak, but still it was an inconvenience he could do without. Maliki's lip twitched to demonstrate his agitation. Bernstein had gone up to the Maasai Mara and he was waiting for an update from the officers that were following him. And he still hadn't heard from the idiot Gupta.

*****

Thousands of flamingos were sent flocking out of the way as they crossed Lake Nakuru. The pilot was forced to gain altitude to avoid them getting caught up in the propellers.

As they skirted the western limits of Nakuru City and the All Stars' stadium, Maliki could see a training session was in full swing, various groups of players going through different routines. Toy figures making zigzag patterns in orange and black shirts.

They left the stadium behind them and the rim of the Menengai Crater loomed ahead of them like a giant pimple. The vast cauldron was one of the largest volcanoes in the world, stretching twelve kilometres across and five hundred meters deep. The bottom was almost completely level. A green oasis covered in shrubbery and stunted trees.

Maliki could see fumaroles puffing up from one of the cracks as they got nearer, thin wisps of steam snaking skywards. Dormant since the last lava flow in 1991 it was a ticking time bomb waiting to erupt.

The city gave way to lush farmland and the pilot began a dogleg manoeuvre. Lining up with the thin strip of asphalt that cut through the fertile fields beside Moi's residence. Red-roofed buildings were clustered around the main house, including two reasonable size guesthouses and several wheat barns.

The President had become a recluse in recent years, rarely leaving the bloody place. Maliki spent half his time either discussing matters too sensitive for the telephone or travelling back and forth from

Nairobi. His life would be made much easier if Moi lived in State House like he was supposed to.

Maliki knew that Moi didn't stay there because it reminded him of the days when he was Kenyatta's lackey. Moi was scared of his predecessor and refused to let Maliki dispose of him. Saying that they needed the KANU party vote under Kenyatta's control. Moi let the Kikuyu pig slap him in public on two occasions when he was Minister for Home Affairs. Maliki was irate at the time and wanted blood for the loss of face but Moi talked him out of it.

There was a jolt and squeal of tires as they hit the runway. Maliki glanced out the window at the tree-lined avenue leading to the house.

Hopefully the seventy-four year old President wasn't taking a nap. His personal doctor could find no medical reason for Moi's ill health and was treating him for depression. Unfortunately the drugs made him drowsy. Only Maliki, the doctor and a few close family members knew of the president's condition. If the secret got out then Mwai Kibaki the leader of the opposition would use it to have Moi declared unfit and removed from office.

*****

Moi rested his elbows on the arms of the rattan chair and clasped his hands together, interlocking the bony fingers. Pausing as the crisply clad waiter served them ice tea from a jug on the polished silver tray he was carrying.

"Thank you Paul," said the President when he was finished pouring. "That will be all for now."

"Yes bwana," replied the beaming steward. "Just call me if you need anything."

"I will Paul, don't worry."

Moi waited for the man to disappear back into the house. They were sat in the shade of the covered veranda overlooking the President's prized vegetable garden.

The President waited for the patio doors to close, "So how are things going in Nairobi? Are we doing enough to keep the Americans happy?"

"If it was up to me they wouldn't be here at all," Maliki took a sip of his drink. His tongue recoiled from the bitterness. He added a spoonful of sugar from the pot on the glass coffee table.

"I know your views only too well," Moi sighed. "I've listened to you for years, let you sway my judgement. But not this time."

"My *views*, as you call them, have saved your ass more than once," Maliki reminded him. "Sometimes you are too naive."

"That may be true," the President nodded wearily. "But the violence must end. I have let it go on for far too long now."

"You question my methods but without them you wouldn't be where you are."

"Sometimes the ends do not justify the means," a tear formed in the President's eye. "We will burn in hell for what we've done."

"Nobody is going to hell." Maliki didn't believe in heaven either. "All we did was restore balance. Enk-ai Narok would be proud."

He was referring to the Maasai's black God, the good and benevolent deity. The reality was that Maliki secretly worshiped the other one, Enk-ai Na Nyoke, the angry red God, master of life and death.

"I wish that were true." Moi touched the corner of his eye with his finger. "But it is too late to change that now. What news do you have for me?"

"As you suggested we are letting the committee carry out limited investigations."

"Good." Moi was staring at something, or nothing, out in the garden. "And what of Konde? Did you learn anything from him?"

It was funny how the President seemed happy to turn a blind eye to his methods when it suited him yet still tried to maintain the moral high ground. Maliki had no such compunctions.

"He wouldn't talk."

Moi knew him too well, "Why did you use the past tense? Is he dead?"

"He had a weak heart." Maliki shrugged, "How was I supposed to know?" He took another sip of coffee.

"Christ!" when the President got angry he showed some of his former zeal, Maliki actually quite liked the revival, it was better than the apathy of late. "If the press get hold of this they'll have a field day!"

The only worry that Maliki had in that department at the moment was Bernstein, and he was a private matter, nothing to do with the President

"Relax will you? Nobody knows that he was in custody. His disappearance can't be linked to us in any way."

Maliki didn't think that the shopkeeper would be missed, at least not by anyone who would be willing to stir up trouble. Whoever he was working with on the committee would want to put as much distance as humanly possible between themselves and any official investigation.

"I'm not bothered about the messenger!" Moi slapped the table, a rare gesture these days. "We need to know who is leaking the information. They must be silenced and removed from the committee!"

"We're working on it. All of the committee members are being watched and their office and home phones have been tapped. It's only a matter of time before we find out who is responsible." In Maliki's experience most people slipped up eventually, it could be as simple as confiding in the wrong person.

"Be that as it may Peter, but Konde could have given us that information!"

It often amused Maliki that not even the President knew who he really was, but not today. "I agree that Konde's death was unfortunate but there's nothing that can be done about that now."

Moi obviously decided that pursuing the subject further was futile, "And what about Bushnell?"

"Don't worry we're keeping the Ambassador under constant watch. If she gets close to anything important I'll take care of it."

"You've always been there for me Peter. There's no denying that." The President's shoulders slumped and he stared out over the wooden balustrade.

"Is there anything else you would like to discuss?"

"No." Moi's outburst seemed to have weakened him, "I think that's enough for one day. I'm feeling tired. Could you send Paul out when you leave?"

"Of course," Maliki finished off the drink and stood up.

"And Peter?"

"Yes?"

"Don't forget to let me know if there are any developments."

Maliki nodded and turned away. He would tell the President what he thought the aging politician could handle and keep the rest to himself.

He checked his watch. There was still plenty of time to get back to Nairobi before tonight's meeting with Wei. There better be news from Gupta when he got there.

CHAPTER THIRTEEN
KWS Base Camp, Maasai Mara
August 13th, 1996

David's belly felt bloated after consuming a little too much scrambled egg, insisting that they all eat a big breakfast before leaving. He wasn't sure when they would be back at base camp but each man was carrying a week's worth of provisions. He spread the map out on the ground and the others gathered around.

He put his finger on a point between Keekorok and the border, "A pair of black rhino was spotted in this region yesterday, that's where we're heading." He traced the border north, "Chege, this is where you're going, a female with her calf should be somewhere in this region."

Rhino are territorial and normally stay within a twelve square mile patch. But they could have wandered a couple of miles in any direction from the locations Scott had given him. Finding them in the bush wasn't going to be easy and he couldn't use the spotter plane. David didn't want Tanui or anyone else finding out about the mission.

He had split his men into two groups so that they could cover more ground. David, Damo and Rashid formed one of them, designation 'Alpha'. Chege was leading the other. The two rangers with him were both veterans in their late thirties who worked together in the Park Service before it became the KWS. Haji, a Swahili from a village near Mombasa and Makori from David's hometown of Kisii were inseparable. Thick as thieves, even when they were off duty. Usually playing backgammon, cards or anything else they could bet their measly wages on. They made an odd pair, the short thickset fisherman's son from the south and the tall farmer's son from the north.

Chege managed to dig up an old radio set and show Rashid how to use it. He was the rookie having been in the Service just over a year, which was why David opted to have him in his group. A crack shot and the fastest member of his multi-racial squad Rashid was the only Luo. He was also the most devout Muslim that David had ever met. Not that he tried to ram religion down their throats, Rashid kept his beliefs to himself. But the prayer mat came out five times a day no matter where they were or what they were doing. In a way he was envious of Rashid.

"Is everybody clear on what our objective is?" there was a general nodding of heads. "Good, and remember to maintain radio silence unless you make contact."

David guessed that the poachers probably had their normal operating frequencies and would be listening in to their transmissions. He was using a different channel to keep in touch with Spencer Scott on a daily basis.

He checked his watch, "Do your final checks now, we leave at 08:00. That's five minutes gentleman."

He folded up the map of the park and shoved it into his webbing.

As he watched the men strip and reassemble their weapons David realised that he was looking at them in a new light. He found himself trying to spot anything out of the ordinary in their behaviour. A shaking hand, a nervous glance, wondering if any of them might be involved with the poachers. Someone was tipping them off, he started thinking about the Deputy Director's cold reception back at headquarters, David pushed the paranoid thoughts to the back of his mind. He needed to believe that they were on the same side if this was to succeed.

His plan was a simple one, start at the bottom and work his way up to the top. David figured that as there were far fewer black rhino and their horn seemed to be in increasing demand it made sense to follow them rather than elephants. It was slim at best but it was all that he had.

*****

David used the LandRover to get as close as possible to the co-ordinates supplied by Scott. He veered off the dirt track onto the flat grassland, now clinging to life in clumps. So short he didn't even need to slow down, the few rocks and other obstacles clearly visible. He could see a couple of eland in the distance, distinguishable by their long straight antlers. Otherwise the plain was devoid of wildlife. They passed the skull and bones of a wildebeest, bleached white by the sun. Would the rains ever come? If they failed again David wasn't sure how the few remaining animals would survive the summer months.

The landscape became uneven as they neared a small ravine, one of the tributaries that led down to the Mara River. Bushes and trees grew closer together between the rocks and the LandRover could go no further. David parked under the shade of large acacia tree and killed the engine.

"Looks like we're on foot from here on in." He pulled out the map and checked their location. "They should be about half a click in that direction," he pointed south towards the Mara Border Control, hidden from sight a couple of kilometres ahead of them.

They grabbed their backpacks and weapons from the back of the jeep and began the trek. The bed of the stream was bone dry but showed signs of something digging for water. David went closer and could see the familiar three-toed footprint. The hole the rhino had dug was partially caved in and dried out, telling David that it was probably made a couple of days ago. Still, it was encouraging.

"At least we know that they're definitely in the area."

A pair of tracks led away from the ravine in the direction that they were heading and disappeared into the bush on the other side.

David took the lead and used his machete to hack a path through the undergrowth. Fortunately the ribbon of vegetation following the banks wasn't very thick and they soon broke through into open veldt. Ten minutes later they found them. As usual it was Damo who saw the rhino first.

He whistled David to stop, "They are over there, down near the river."

David followed where his arm was pointing but couldn't see anything. But if Damo said the rhino were there then they were. He took his field glasses from his webbing and scanned the outcrop of rocks that Damo was indicating about two kilometres away. Even with the binoculars it took him a while to find them, two black shapes against the greyer stone. How Damo could see them from that distance he didn't know.

"Let's get a bit closer and then find somewhere to hole up." He grinned, "Damo, maybe you should take point."

*****

They kept close to the rhino during the day, making sure that they stayed downwind from the shortsighted throwbacks to a prehistoric age. It was their blindness that gave rhino a bad name. Often mistaken for aggression their defence mechanism was to charge whenever they felt threatened. An over-developed sense of smell compensated for their poor eyesight and they were remarkably agile. Reaching a top speed of over fifty kilometres an hour, and weighing in at around a ton, they were definitely not animals to be messed with.

For most of the day the rhino stayed near to the outcrop, foraging on the bushes and trees at its base. In the late afternoon they wandered down to the river for a cooling mud bath, rolling around and wading in the waist deep ooze until every inch of their hides were covered in red mud. Afterwards they returned to the same spot near the rocks and continued to feed.

Although fairly solitary animals it was a myth that rhino were completely unsociable. These were a pair of elder bulls who were obviously very comfortable with each other's company. It was written in the way they stayed close and mimicked one another's movements. Maybe that would change when the rains came and the mating season began. If they came at all, David scanned the horizon, not a single cloud could be seen in any direction.

Once it got dark they found a place to set up camp on top of the granite outcrop. A spot where the stone gave way to a patch of dirt a few meters across and almost level. They agreed to take the watch in three-hour stints so that each man would get a reasonable night's sleep. David agreed to do the graveyard shift, Rashid the first, leaving Damo with the early hours of the morning.

A fire would have given their position away so they were forced to eat cold rations under the moonlight. Damo was unusually quiet as they munched on corned beef sandwiches and bars of chocolate.

David waited until Rashid went to take a leak, "What's up?"

"Nothing," Damo dropped the hand holding the chocolate into his lap.

"Come on I know you better than that, you've hardly spoken a word all day."

"I didn't want to say anything in front of the others, but this is crazy." Damo looked over at him, "There are only three of us. What do you expect to happen if we find the poachers? We'll be heavily outnumbered."

David shook his head, "I don't think so. I'm guessing that they won't be using many men. The horns only weigh thirty kilos each and can be carried easily by one man. That's two men and possibly a couple of men for back up and to take turns carrying the load. I doubt there'll be more than four, whoever is running the show won't want to share the profits."

"What do you mean, *running the show*?"

"Just a figure of speech," he shrugged. "Someone's got to be in charge." The decision not to tell Damo about his suspicions regarding Deputy Director Tanui had been a difficult one.

"Why do I get the feeling that there's something you're not telling me?" Damo was still staring at him.

David met his friend's gaze, "Such as?"

"Like where you're getting the location of the rhino from for starters?"

"I'm sorry I can't tell you that," David had promised Scott the strictest confidence. "But as you can see it comes from a reliable source."

"OK then, play it your way," grunted Damo. "Do headquarters even know that we're out here?"

David looked away, "No, sorry we're on our own on this one."

"That's what I thought." Damo lowered his voice, "Don't you think the others deserve to know what they're letting themselves in for?"

He had considered telling them and giving them a choice, but only for a split second, it was far too risky. Even if none of them were involved 'loose lips sink ships', wasn't that Lord Kitchener's catchphrase? David couldn't take the chance that one of them might speak to the wrong person.

"They're not doing anything that they didn't sign up for." He could hear Rashid climbing back up the slope. "I'll let everybody know what's going on when the time is right but for now you're just going to have to trust me."

"I sure hope that you know what you're doing."

David lay back on his bedroll and stared up at the stars, "So do I Damo, so do I."

CHAPTER FOURTEEN
Near Keekorok, Maasai Mara
August 16th, 1996

Scott was ten minutes late but finally the constant hiss of static was broken.

"Crow's nest here, are you there, Eagle Scout? Over," Scott sounded flustered.

David pressed the button on the side of the handset wishing that he hadn't let Scott choose the call signs, "Eagle Scout here, I read you loud and clear Crow's Nest. What's the latest?"

"I've only got one new girl for you, co-ordinates are..." Spencer reeled off the latitude and longitude. "Crow's Nest over and out."

As agreed he kept the transmission short, only giving him details of rhino that were close to the border with Tanzania. Apart from tonight's delay in his broadcast David's fears about Scott's reliability seemed to have been unjustified. He and his team of environmentalists were proving to be quite an asset.

He handed the bulky headphones and square shaped microphone back to Rashid, "Thanks, it's all yours." David tried to stifle a yawn but couldn't, "I'm off to try and get some sleep. I'll see you in a few hours."

"Yes sir," always keen to impress the twenty-one year old seemed so young. David realised that taking over his father's responsibilities had aged him way beyond his years.

The drawback of sitting around waiting was that it gave him far too much time to think. Sometimes about his predicament or his family, but embarrassingly a lot of his thoughts seemed to focus on Caitlyn and what Scott had said to him back at the lodge. David shook his head and pushed the image of her soft red lips to the back of his mind.

Damo was already asleep when he got back to their natural hide in the rocks. David slipped into his sleeping bag as quietly as possible. He could hear the rhino foraging below the outcrop that they had returned to each evening. They were more active once it got dark and cooled down, spending a lot of the daytime sleeping. David found it amusing hearing them snore whilst standing up.

After three uncomfortable days and nights hiding and watching them David was beginning to realise that his plan might not work. Without knowing when and where the poachers were going to strike he probably had as much chance of winning the national sweepstakes. But as long as they carried on grazing near to the river the two bulls were prime targets. He decided to stay with them for now. If they moved away from the border he would think about switching to one of the other rhino. There had been no transmissions from Bravo squad so Chege must have found the female and her calf.

The broken sleep pattern and limited rations were taking their toll, David felt exhausted and the few pounds he'd put on with fine dining had quickly disappeared. He was also beginning to smell and in dire need of shower. The crocodiles swimming in the river had stopped him jumping in so far, but he was getting close.

He rolled onto his side and squirmed around until he found the small dip in the ground that fitted his hip. David wished that he could sleep like Damo, his friend's peaceful breathing drifted across to him.

Damo didn't speak about the clandestine nature of their mission again and had been back to his usual self over the past couple of days. Normally David enjoyed spending time with the good-natured Maasai. Especially out in the bush where Damo's knowledge of the native plants and wildlife far exceeded his own. He seemed to know the habits and minute detail of every animal and insect to be found in the Mara. But David was too on edge to relax. The longer they were away from base camp the more likely that Deputy Director Tanui would find out.

David lay there thinking about the consequences of his actions should he fail. The most likely result was that he would be out of a job and prosecuted for negligence for endangering his men. Eventually he drifted off into a fitful and troubled sleep.

*****

Someone was shaking his shoulder. David grabbed the hand instinctively, then realising that it was only Rashid, he let go.

"Sorry sir," Rashid looked shocked and nursed his knuckles. "You were having some sort of nightmare."

"Don't you know that you're not supposed to touch a person when they're dreaming? I could have hurt you by accident."

David had read about the case of a Vietnam vet who strangled his own mother to death when she woke him up sleepwalking. Rashid was lucky that it wasn't his throat David got hold of.

Rashid stopped rubbing his hand, "It won't happen again sir. It's time for your watch."

"Already?" David felt like he hadn't slept at all. The nightmares were so clear it was like being awake.

"I'm afraid so, sir," Rashid stepped back to give him more room. "The rhino have moved around to the south of the rocks."

"OK, thanks Rashid," David rubbed the sleep from his eyes with his knuckles. "Go and get some rest, I'll see you in the morning."

"Yes sir."

Rashid stepped over Damo and clambered into his temporary bed. David dragged himself out of the sleeping bag and stood up, stretching to ease the aching in his knees and shoulders. He picked up his rifle and slung it over his shoulder. The full moon made the climb to the top of the outcrop easy and David found the place he had sat on his previous watches.

He settled down on the ledge and took out his canteen. David took a short swig and then poured some over his face. The cold water helped to revive him and feel more alert. He swapped the canteen for his binoculars. Switching them to night vision David started to scan the dark foliage along the riverbanks searching for movement. After a few minutes he decided that there was nothing there and lowered the glasses.

By chance they were in a good position strategically speaking. Any poachers would be coming from the direction of the river and there was a wide expanse of open veldt between it and the outcrop. The moon was so bright he would have no difficulty seeing anyone crossing the grassland. Even without his state of the art binoculars.

The rhino were grazing quietly for such huge beasts. But he heard them occasionally as they ripped the leaves from branches and broke the odd twig underfoot.

Each minute passed painfully slowly with nothing to do but watch over the empty escarpment. His mind started to wander again. When Rashid had woken him he was in the middle of reliving the moment of his father's death in slow motion. He hadn't been kidding when he said the youngster could have been more seriously injured. The anger he felt always took a while to subside afterwards. Not that it ever went away, it just became bearable. But it was always there under the surface, threatening to boil over at any moment.

Something shone in the moonlight. David raised his binoculars, heart pounding against his ribcage as adrenalin surged through his veins.

They had emerged from between the bushes next to the river and began creeping towards him in single file. David waited for the last one to get well clear of the bushes to make sure that there was nobody else following. There were four of them, just as he'd predicted. They were either poachers or a group of militia taking their AK47s for a midnight stroll across the border. He could make out the curved stock that gave the weapon its nickname of 'banana gun' being carried by two of them.

Putting his weight on the balls of his feet and being careful not to make a sound, David got to his feet and slowly made his way down the slope to the others. He went to wake Damo first but somehow the Maasai had sensed his approach. His eyes were already open when David leant over him.

"We've got company," he whispered. "Four bogies heading this way from the river. I'm going back up top for a bird's eye view," his sniper rifle would be more use from there. "Take Rashid down to the north side of the outcrop and get ready to move on my signal. Remind him that we need at least one of them alive."

Maybe it was just youthful exuberance but Rashid had become a little too trigger happy when they stumbled across a similar group of poachers the year before. He laid waste to two of them, emptying a full magazine into their torsos. In Rashid's favour it was his first assignment and they did shoot at him first.

Damo was already up and waking Rashid as David left the relative safety of their hidden camp amongst the rocks and returned to the ledge. He didn't need the field glasses to find them this time. They were half way across the veldt, still heading straight towards him and the rhino below.

He knelt down to take the lens caps off and adjust the sights before lying in a prone position and lifting the stock of the Heckler & Koch to his shoulder. He twisted the zoom until they were in focus.

The poachers had stopped, one of them holding his hand up to the others. David panicked for a second, thinking that they must have been spotted. Then the man took the binoculars from his chest and lifted them to his face, he was scoping for the rhino. At least David hoped it was the rhino. He aimed for the man's thigh, ready to shoot if they made a run for it. A cool breeze was blowing up from the river but David felt a bead of sweat trickle down his forehead.

The leader lowered his glasses and turned towards the others. He thought he saw one of them nod and then they started to walk again. This time spreading out into a line with a gap of about twenty meters between each man. They looked well drilled and were dressed for the occasion, camouflage gear and combats. David wondered if he might be relying too heavily on the element of surprise.

As they got closer he realised that they were going to try and take the rhino in darkness. One of them was holding a huge flash lamp, the sort you get on the top of a pick-up truck. David adjusted his aim, prepared to take him down as soon as the light went on. There would be chaos when he did, blinding muzzle flashes and gunfire that would send the rhino stampeding through the bush. There was just as much chance of his men or the poachers being trampled to death as being shot.

But it was too late to think of anything else. David concentrated on his breathing and took up the slack with his trigger finger. Any moment now all hell was going to break loose.

CHAPTER FIFTEEN
American Ambassador's Residence, Nairobi
August 16th, 1996

Maliki hated wearing the damn tuxedo but it went with the territory. The shirt's starched collar bit into his neck and he felt claustrophobic in the suit. He caught a glimpse of himself in the huge gold-leafed mirror above the marble fireplace as he walked past and wished he hadn't. He looked like a giant bloody penguin, mind you so did most of the men there.

The Friday night function at the American Ambassador's residence in Muthaiga Road was the last place Maliki wanted to be right now. A very accommodating Russian girl was waiting for him in her apartment downtown expecting his weekly visit. On top of that he'd had to make a $2,500 donation, the cost of the ticket, for the privilege of being there. Not that he would dream of paying the money himself, as usual it was coming out of expenses. The President made sure that Maliki's budget was unlimited when it came to gathering information.

Restricted to a few hundred elite guests the gala was being held to raise money for 'ActionAid', one of the charities that Ambassador Bushnell supported. Something about empowering people in the community. Maliki had been forced to fight his way out of poverty and didn't see why anybody else deserved a handout.

The Ambassador was talking closely with three other people who were also high up on Maliki's political watch list. Huddled together with her underneath the crystal chandelier were the Kenyan Minister of Trade Joseph Kamotho, Professor Onesimus Mutungi from the Standing Committee on Human Rights, and Seymour Dewitt the Regional Safety Officer at the American Embassy.

There was something conspiratorial in the way the Professor was leaning towards Bushnell as he spoke. Red seemed to be the Ambassador's colour, the last few times he had seen her she was wearing it. Today it was the jacket over a flowing white ball gown that diplomatically hid her figure for the occasion. Although not pretty she was a handsome woman with thick wavy hair, full lips and an air of confidence that he guessed some men would find attractive. Not Maliki, he preferred his women to be far more subservient, and much younger. He could feel himself starting to get aroused thinking about what he would do to Katia later.

The Ambassador watched him approach. She said something to Professor Mutungi and the chubby academic backed away from her slightly. An almost imperceptible movement but the significance wasn't lost on Maliki. He could practically feel his ears burning.

"Ah, good evening Commander Abasi, how good of you to join us," Ambassador Bushnell smiled pleasantly. "We were just talking about security at

151

the embassy. I'm sure that you already know Minister Kamotho and Professor Mutungi." Maliki shook both of their hands, the professor's palm was hot and sweaty. "And this is Seymour Dewitt our RSO, he's in charge of security at the embassy."

"I've been hearing a lot about you Commander." The smile didn't reach Dewitt's grey hooded eyes, "it's a pleasure to finally meet you."

Unlike the others Dewitt's grip was firm and strong, his straight back, strong jaw line and shortly clipped grey hair betrayed his military background.

"And you, Colonel."

Dewitt raised an eyebrow at the use of his former title and Maliki smiled. Now they both knew where they stood.

According to the file Maliki had on him, Dewitt had completed two tours in Vietnam with the Marines and risen to the rank of Colonel before joining the Diplomatic Security Service. During his time as a Special Agent for the DSS he had served in Saudi Arabia and Angola before been given the job of security attaché at the embassy. Maliki knew that Dewitt's post was a cover. He was a spy, trained in counterintelligence.

"Maybe you can help us Commander," said Bushnell. "We've been discussing ways to increase security. Being so close to the street the embassy is a sitting duck as far as bomb attacks go. We were thinking that more of a police presence outside would act as a deterrent."

"I'm sorry, policing the streets doesn't really come under the GSU's remit unless there's an actual riot in progress," but then the Ambassador already knew that. "I can have a word with the Police Commissioner if you like and arrange a meeting?"

"Would you?" her eyes gave nothing away. "That would be appreciated, thank you."

"What exactly are the GSU's responsibilities?" there wasn't a trace of sarcasm in Dewitt's voice, even though he obviously knew the answer to the question.

Maliki stared at him, "Very similar to the DSS really, in that we are involved in counter terrorism and intelligence gathering. But we are a little bit more proactive." He glanced over at the professor who shrank visibly.

"In what way Commander?"

"We are essentially a paramilitary unit who respond to any threat on national security," Maliki smiled. "Be that from home or abroad."

"Isn't that a bit like combining the CIA with the Marines?" Dewitt raised an eyebrow as if the idea was preposterous.

"You've got it Colonel, we find that it makes more sense to keep everything under one roof. Cut out the middle man so to speak." Maliki turned to Professor Mutungi and adopted a serious expression, "And how are things going with the Committee Professor?"

Mutungi took off his spectacles and used a handkerchief to clean them. His hands were shaking and he was sweating profusely.

"I was just telling the Ambassador that we don't seem to be making any progress at all. Without the right to arrest people or seize records we're beating our heads against a brick wall."

Maliki shook his head, "So often our hands are tied by legislation Professor. If there's anything I can do to help then please let me know."

Professor Mutungi replaced his glasses, "I'm sure that you're already doing more than enough. But thanks for the offer, Commander."

"Have you heard anything about the baby elephant that was rescued in the Maasai Mara?"

The question came from Minister Kamotho. A short, stocky Kikuyu with a barrel chest, wide nose and brushed back white hair that had receded in the middle. One of the party's powerbrokers, the minister represented the provinces from outside the rift valley. Lately he had been stirring up trouble, calling for a free party system before the election. He was a great public speaker and people were starting to listen. As far as Maliki was concerned Kamotho was walking a fine line between life and death.

"Only what I've read in the paper Minister. By all accounts it seems like she had a lucky escape."

Kamotho looked surprised, "I thought you would know what was going on. Doesn't the GSU still run the KWS?"

"Not any more, Minister," Maliki's lip twitched. "We still supply instructors and help with training but the day to day operations were handed over to the Service a few years ago."

"I see." For a moment Maliki thought that he was going to be probed further but the Minister dismissed the subject with a wave of his hand and turned to Bushnell, "Getting back to the car park situation, Ambassador, I'll have a word with the President of the Cooperative Bank and see if they're willing to sell you the spaces."

Bushnell and the Minister continued to discuss what the going rate was in Nairobi for parking and how total ownership of the car park basement under the embassy would increase security. Apparently some of the bank employees using it were making life difficult for the Marines and local security personnel. Refusing to let them search their vehicles and driving through the checkpoint without stopping.

Maliki noticed that Dewitt was watching him the whole time, "Excuse me Ambassador, gentleman, there's someone I need to talk to. Enjoy the rest of your evening."

Maliki had learned all he needed to. It was obviously Professor Mutungi who was leaking information from the Committee. With Konde missing he was scared and seeking help from the Ambassador. The Professor probably thought that by bringing Bushnell into the loop he would be protected. He wouldn't, Maliki would take him down to the basement if and when the time was right. Maybe he would throw Mutungi and the Minister of Trade in the same cell.

Maliki had other business to take care of besides keeping tabs on the Professor and Ambassador Bushnell. He was hoping to catch Wei, who was attending the function as the Chinese representative. Maliki spotted him going out through the patio doors onto the terrace and followed him.

A few small groups and the odd couple were on the terrace, champagne and conversation flowing, the odd smoker taking advantage of the respite, including Wei. When Maliki got outside he was putting away a packet of Marlboros and lighting one up.

"Where's my $50,000!"

Wei spat the cigarette out as he spun around from the marble balustrade.

"I didn't know that you were going to be here," Wei glanced over Maliki's shoulder nervously as if looking for a way out.

"You didn't answer my question."

"I don't know what you're talking about."

Maliki could tell by the lack of hesitation that Wei was telling the truth, "The bloody transfer was short by fifty thousand."

Wei looked confused, "Must be something to do with the exchange rate. I'll check with the buyer."

Maliki glared at him. Did Wei really think he was that stupid? There was no way the rate could have dropped by that amount.

"Make sure you tell him that I expect the money in my account on Monday at the latest. Otherwise I'm holding you personally responsible."

Wei's hand was shaking as he took out another cigarette, "Don't worry, I'll make sure that you get your money."

Maliki's face started to spasm, "It's not me that should be worried Counsellor!"

He spun on his heel and headed for the front entrance. As Maliki made his way through the throng of people inside he felt the hairs go up on the back of his neck. He stopped and leant against the pillar next to the door. Maliki lifted his heel as if trying to remove something and glanced back. As he expected it was Dewitt that was watching him.

CHAPTER SIXTEEN
Near Keekorok, Maasai Mara
August 17th, 1996

The lamp shattered the darkness, illuminating the rhino and the base of the outcrop in an arc of white light. David reacted instantly and let off a single round. Amidst the noise of the retort there was the sound of breaking glass. The light went out before it hit the ground.

David switched his aim to the leader of the group and shot him through the thigh. The man went down clutching his leg, howling in agony. One of them started shooting wildly at David's position. He ducked for cover as the bullets ricocheted off the rocks around him. That was when Damo and Rashid opened up on them from the flank. The two poachers still standing dropped to the ground and started returning fire in short controlled bursts.

The flash of light and that many guns going off all around them sent the rhino into a blind panic. Knowing that they were trapped against the rocks the two bulls instinctively headed away from the outcrop. Two tonnes of angry bone and muscle was charging straight at the prostrate poachers.

There was a lot of shouting and flailing limbs as they tried to avoid the stampeding rhino. The poacher who David had shot in the leg dragged himself to his feet and hopped out of the way just in time before collapsing onto his side. The man who had been holding the lamp wasn't so lucky. He was on the ground and didn't seem to be moving at all. David guessed that the bullet must have passed through the glass and done him some serious damage. The larger rhino ran through the poacher like a bulldozer, lifting the man up with its horn and flicking him to one side as if he was a rag doll.

The two that were still mobile made a dash for the river, taking it in turns to crouch and give each other covering fire. They were good, concentrating their volleys to keep Damo and Rashid pinned down behind a boulder. Between bursts the rangers were shooting back at them from around the sides of the rock.

David aimed for the shoulder of the man on the left, who was now around four hundred meters away. He hesitated, from this distance there was a chance that the bullet would drop and hit a vital organ. There was a flash from the muzzle of his AK47 as the poacher fired at Damo and Rashid. David let out a long slow breath and squeezed the trigger gently.

There was a yelp as the man dropped his weapon and was thrown onto his back. Seconds later he scrambled to his feet holding the injured shoulder. He turned and ran for the riverbank, screaming at his colleague for help. The other poacher was well ahead and had no intention of stopping. He was gone, swallowed up by the bushes along the river.

David focussed the cross hairs between the injured man's shoulder blades and took up the slack with his finger. But it would have been an execution. He released the pressure on the trigger and watched as the poacher slipped away into the darkness.

He checked below him to make sure that the remaining poacher was no longer a threat, but Damo and Rashid had it covered. They were walking over to the unarmed man with their machine guns trained on him.

"Hands where I can see them!" he heard Damo shout.

"Don't shoot," the man waved his free arm feebly. The other was trapped under his body. His high pitched voice filled with pain, "Please, don't shoot."

David thumbed on the safety and pushed himself up to a kneeling position. His heart was beating ten to the dozen. Slowed down by his heightened senses, the firefight that had seemed to last for ages was actually over in less than a couple of minutes.

Climbing down the slope to the others, David's legs and arms started to tremble as the adrenalin began to decompose in his bloodstream. He felt drained, like he had just done ten rounds with Mike Tyson. By the time he got to the bottom the poacher was propped up against a rock with his hands handcuffed behind his back. He was a young Maasai in his late teens.

As David knelt in front of him Damo glanced up from the field dressing he was applying to the man's thigh and shook his head. The poacher's bloodstained trouser leg was slit open to allow access. Damo pulled the bandage tight and tied it in a knot. The teenager's scream threatened to burst David's eardrums.

"What kind of shape is he in?"

"Not good," Damo shook his head. "I've stemmed the flow but he's already lost a lot of blood. It looks like the bullet must have severed the femoral artery. If we don't get him to a hospital soon he'll lose the leg. He might not even make it."

"Have you given him anything for the pain?"

"I was just about to," Damo reached into the open backpack on the ground beside him.

"Don't," instructed David. "Not yet, I want to talk to him first."

Damo's raised his eyebrows in protest but he withdrew his hand from the bag.

"Do you speak English?" the youth didn't respond, he had his eyes closed and was whimpering to himself. David switched to Swahili, "Can you hear me?"

The boy's head rolled back and his eyelids flicked open. He was clearly in a lot of pain and it took a while for him to focus on David's face.

"Good," at least he was responsive. "You must know that you're seriously hurt. If we don't get you to a doctor soon then you're going to bleed to death." Being so skinny that probably wouldn't take very long. David waited for his words to sink in.

"Are you going to let me die?" the boy's voice was a hoarse whisper with what sounded like acceptance in his tone.

David needed him to believe that he was serious, "That depends on what you tell me and whether I think it's the truth or not. If you lie to me then I'll leave you here for the hyenas. Do you understand?"

The poacher's eyes widened at the prospect and then he nodded. David could feel Damo's accusing glare but ignored him.

"OK," David leant closer so that their faces were only a few inches apart. The boy's breathing was shallow and ragged.

"Let's start with your name. What is it?"

"Koinet," his eyes closed and then opened again, struggling to remain conscious.

"Who do you work for Koinet?"

"Nobody," he shook his head slowly. "I work for myself." He turned his head to the side and looked away.

"So you're in charge?"

No answer. David grabbed hold of his jaw and twisted the boy's head to face him.

"Listen Koinet I'm not messing around!" he spat the words. "If you lie to me again then I *will* leave you here to die. Now I'm only going to ask you this one more time. Who's your boss?"

Koinet tried to shake his head but David held it in place. He could see the fear in the boy's eyes.

"You don't understand! He'll kill me if he finds out that I said anything."

David released his hold, "You're going to die right here if you don't tell me."

Koinet looked scared but didn't speak.

David got to his feet, "It's your choice Koinet, don't try to say that I didn't warn you."

He turned away from the boy to face Damo. Rashid was stood a few meters behind his friend, watching the river in case any of the other poachers were stupid enough to come back.

"Come on, we better get going. This place stinks. It won't be long before the scavengers get here. Maybe even lions if they're hungry."

"The sooner the better."

Damo packed away the field kit, shouldered his backpack, and the three rangers set off without a word or a backward glance. It only took about twenty paces for Koinet to change his mind.

"Wait!"

David kept walking.

"Come back!" He started to sob, "Its Gupta you bastard! His name's Gupta! Just don't leave me here. *Please*!"

David touched Damo on the shoulder, "Sounds like he wants to tell us something." They went back and David crouched next to the whimpering teenager, "Does this Gupta have a first name?"

"Deepak," the effort of shouting had weakened him, his voice was barely audible. Either that or Koinet was thinking about the consequences of talking to him. "Deepak Gupta."

"Where can I find this Mr Gupta?"

Koinet made a feeble attempt at pushing himself up into a straighter position. But his arms didn't have the strength and David didn't try to give him any assistance. He gave up and collapsed against the rock. His eyes closed for a second and then opened.

"I asked you a question," David reminded him.

"He comes from Mombasa." Koinet grimaced in pain. "He's got a place down there."

"What's the address?"

Koinet must have realised that he was running out of bargaining chips, "Get me out of here first, then I'll tell you where it is."

"No deal Koinet," he shook his head. "I'm the one calling the shots here, not you." David pushed himself up with his rifle, "We're leaving. You've got thirty seconds to decide whether you're coming with us."

Defeated and getting closer to death with every passing minute Koinet gave David what he wanted, "It's on Diani Beach near to Tiwi."

David smiled, "Now that wasn't so hard was it?" He took a minute to assess the situation and then looked at Damo, "I guess that he's earned those painkillers."

He waited whilst Damo produced a syringe from its packet and injected Koinet. Then he made him drink water from the canteen.

"Give me a hand." David bent down and hooked his arm under Koinet's armpit. "It'll take too long to bring the jeep around. We'll be quicker on foot."

He would have to send someone back for the trampled body later. They would have to come soon or there would be nothing left to collect. The threats he'd made earlier to Koinet weren't completely idle, David could hear a pack of jackals coming their way. By the excited yapping he guessed that they must have already caught the dead poacher's scent.

Taking an arm each they hoisted Koinet to his feet, his injured leg hanging uselessly above the ground. The teenager held onto their shoulders and between them they half carried and half dragged him the kilometre back to the LandRover. They stopped a few times when he cried out in pain and to catch their breath. The ordeal lasted about thirty minutes and David was exhausted by the time they dropped Koinet onto the rear seat. The boy's eyes were closed and he didn't look good. As they packed their kit and weapons into the back of the vehicle David decided to break radio silence.

"Rashid, contact base camp and let them know that we're coming in with one casualty suffering shock and loss of blood from a bullet wound. We'll need to get him to the hospital in Narok. Tell them we want a plane to meet us at the airstrip in Keekarok ASAP. ETA ten minutes."

Koinet was his only witness. The last thing David wanted was the youngster dying on him.

"Do you want me to tell Chege what's going on?"

He thought about it for a moment, "No, let's leave them alone for now." The radio squawking into life at the wrong moment could spell disaster for the other team. David got into the jeep and looked over his shoulder, kicking himself for not asking the question earlier.

"Shit!"

Koinet had passed out from the morphine and loss of blood, his legs were propped up on Damo's lap.

Rashid jumped into the passenger seat and started fiddling with the radio. David gunned the engine and swung the jeep around so that they were facing the right way. Before Rashid could make the call to base camp the set came alive in a burst of static.

"Alpha this is Bravo, come in, over."

David hit the brakes and the jeep skidded to a stop. There was panic in Chege's voice and he could hear the sound of machine guns firing in the background.

"Give me that," he grabbed the handset out of Rashid's hand. "Bravo this is Alpha. What's your status?"

"We're outnumbered and taking heavy fire, Haji's dead." There was a pause as a weapon was discharged close to the microphone. "We need support and we need it fast, over."

"What are your coordinates," he snapped his fingers and indicated the glove box. Rashid handed him a pen and David scribbled the numbers down. "OK Bravo, help is on its way, just sit tight until it gets there, over."

He handed the microphone back to Rashid and checked the map using his pocket torch. The nearest support was the Anti-Poaching Unit in Ngiro-are about fifteen kilometres from Chege's position.

"Call Ngiro-are and tell them to get their most experienced squad down there ASAP."

David ground the gearstick and concentrated on driving hell for leather across the grassland whilst Rashid made the calls. All four wheels left the ground as they careered over the verge and landed with a thump on the dirt track. Koinet moaned loudly in the back seat and then was quiet again.

A few minutes later they reached the t-junction and David wrenched the wheel to the right. The back end of the LandRover slid out as he joined the main track heading east towards Keekorok. David floored the accelerator to correct the skid, metal groaning as the vehicle snaked back into a straight line.

There were going to be serious repercussions once Deputy Director Tanui found out but David didn't care about any of that right now. He'd screwed up and Haji was dead.

CHAPTER SEVENTEEN
Keekorok Airstrip, Maasai Mara
August 17th, 1996

Keekorok Airstrip was deserted when they got there, a levelled strip of red earth that cut through the bush around it like a knife. The only facilities were a four metre square stone building with a hatch that acted as the ticket booth and a covered waiting area open to the elements. Built for tourists staying at the nearby five star Lodge the airstrip was normally only visited by a few light aircraft each week. David slid the LandRover to a stop next to the shelter and killed the engine.

"Try and get hold of Chege for a sit rep and find out how long the damn plane's going to be." The radio operator was staring at the windscreen, mumbling something incoherent. "Rashid snap out of it! I need that sit-rep."

Everyone had different ways of dealing with death. Rashid's was to ask Allah for guidance.

He finished his prayers and twisted the dial on the set in his lap, "Yes sir, right away."

David's head was spinning as he got out and walked away from the jeep. He thrust his hands in his pockets and stood facing down the runway towards the sunrise. What the hell had he been thinking?

He heard the door open and shut and Damo's footsteps behind him. His friend stood next to him and shoulder-to-shoulder they stared at the rising sun.

It was Damo who spoke first, "This has turned into a bit of a mess."

"You could say that," David nodded, more to himself than at Damo. "Haji would still be here if it wasn't for me."

"That's true," his friend's honesty was just what he needed. "But you didn't pull the trigger, and if the poachers weren't here then none of us would be either."

"I still sent him to his death."

"No, you sent him to do a job. One that, as you said, he signed up for. Haji wasn't forced into anything." Damo shrugged, "It's the risk we all take."

David could have kissed Damo right then, but fortunately he didn't get the chance. Rashid shouted at him from the jeep, "I've got Chege, sir!"

David sprinted back to the LandRover and grabbed the handset from Rashid through the window.

"Alpha here Bravo, what's the latest?"

There was a ten second delay and David thought that he must have lost him. Then Chege's deep voice crackled over the speaker. Right then it sounded like the best thing he'd ever heard.

"Bravo here," no gunfire this time. "The poachers have retreated back across the border and we're waiting for the cavalry to arrive, over."

"Have you taken any more casualties? Over."

"No, Haji is the only one who didn't make it...sorry sir." Chege paused for a second, "I was hit in the arm but it's nothing serious. Makori is OK, over."

David forgot procedure, it didn't really matter now if the poachers were listening in, "Don't apologise Chege, you were following orders just like Haji. The unit from Ngiro-are should be with you soon. Just stay at the co-ordinates you gave me until they arrive. I'll see you back at base. This is Alpha over and out."

He gave the device back to Rashid. There was no point going up there, his main concern now was Koinet's survival and safety. David thought about going with him to the hospital but his time could be better spent elsewhere, time that he could feel rapidly becoming a precious commodity. Word would already have reached headquarters and maybe even the Deputy Director. If he was right then Koinet's life could be in serious danger, maybe even his own. David needed to find Gupta and fast.

Chege's transmission had helped him reach a difficult decision. He was going to have to put his men's lives at risk again or Haji's death would be for nothing.

"Damo, I want you and Rashid to escort Koinet to the hospital and stand guard until you hear from me. Nobody apart from medical staff is to go anywhere near him. I don't care if they're the Chief of Police don't let them in without speaking to me first. No matter what anybody says this comes under our jurisdiction. Is that understood?"

Damo nodded, "Nobody goes near him. I've got it. Where are you going to be? Just in case anybody asks."

"I'm heading back to base and then on to Nairobi. I'll call you at the hospital when I get there."

Damo frowned, "Nairobi?"

"There are a couple of people I need to see there." His friend's expression said that he was abandoning him. "Don't worry, I'll keep in touch and send someone along later to relieve you."

He turned to Rashid but his question was answered by the buzzing of an airplane in the distance. Sure enough a mosquito like speck was heading towards them getting bigger and louder with every second.

"Stash the radio and the rest of the gear in the back but take your weapons with you," the sight of Damo and Rashid armed with machine guns should be enough to put most people off. But then he guessed he wasn't dealing with most people.

The drone of the aircraft grew until it circled the airstrip before landing. The plane taxied over to them and the pitch of the engines dropped as it rolled to a stop.

"Damo," he leant towards him, shielding his face from the dust that the propellers were kicking up.

"Yes," Damo and Rashid were propping Koinet up, waiting for the gangway to be lowered so that they could board the six-seat Cessna. Koinet was out cold.

David shouted to be heard over the noise of the engines, "Watch your back!"

171

He sped through the park, only slowing down to pass the odd jeep of early bird tourists crawling along the tracks in search of the big five. David wished that he were one of the holidaymakers. Taking photographs of the wildlife, oblivious to what was really going on around him. But he wasn't.

David felt like he had the weight of the world on his shoulders. "Assumption is the mother of all fuck ups", wasn't that the expression? Haji was dead as a result of his guesswork and Damo was in great peril. Even Caitlyn might be in danger if the wrong person found out that he had been talking to her. He should warn her to stay away from the orphanage for a while.

When he arrived at the command post in Purungat there was nobody there. David started the small diesel generator and managed to get hold of Chege on the radio in his cubicle of an office. They had gone with Haji's body to the nearest mortuary in Kilgoris about thirty miles away and wouldn't be back for some time. The bullet had only grazed Chege's arm but it needed stitching. After dropping Haji off they were going to the clinic there to have it seen to. He thought about phoning the hospital in Narok to check on Koinet but they would only just be arriving.

David switched off the radio set and was writing a note for Chege when the telephone rang. He contemplated not picking it up but he would have to face the music sooner or later. The telephone was an ancient rotary dialler. David picked up the receiver and cradled it to his ear so that he could carry on writing.

"Purungat Outpost." Maybe it was a call about a missing tourist.

"Is that Captain Nbeke?" The voice on the other end belonged to none other than Deputy Director Tanui and he didn't sound happy. For a second David nearly changed his mind and put the phone down.

"Yes Deputy Director this is Nbeke."

"What the hell is going on up there? I was woken up by Idi Tikolo, he tells me that there's been some sort of firefight and that one of my rangers is dead?"

There was a pause where David was expected to say something but he didn't.

"Please tell me that it isn't true, Captain!"

Why wasn't he surprised that Tikolo was involved? The greasy bastard would have loved making the phone call to Tanui and dropping David in it, probably the highlight of his career so far.

"I'm afraid it is, sir." David took a deep breath before continuing. "Ranger Haji was shot by poachers earlier this morning near to Ngiro-Are and died at the scene. His body is being taken to the mortuary in Kilgoris as we speak."

"That's not even your territory, what were you doing so far north?"

He swallowed, "I wasn't there sir."

"For Christ's sake, Nbeke!" Tanui was shouting now, "What do you mean, you weren't there?"

173

David explained that he split the squad into two teams and what had happened, including Koinet's capture and being taken to the hospital in Narok. He left out the part about Gupta.

"I warned you about not following procedure and now Haji is dead because you didn't listen. What am I supposed to tell his family? That you took the law into your hands?"

There was another pause but David knew that this time the question was rhetorical so he stayed silent.

"Give me one good reason why I shouldn't have you kicked out of the Service and held up on charges, Captain."

Right then David couldn't think of one that Tanui would accept, "I don't know sir."

"You're damn right, you don't know Nbeke!" the Deputy Director sounded like he might choke on his own words he was so angry. "Consider yourself confined to barracks until further notice. You and your men are not to leave the outpost unless I authorise it personally. Is that totally clear, Captain Nbeke?"

"Yes sir," David had no intention of following the order but Tanui didn't need to know that.

"And Nbeke," the Deputy Director's voice dropped to a normal level. "Try not to get in anymore trouble will you!"

The line went dead in David's ear. He replaced the receiver and then yanked the cable out of the wall socket. Anybody who dialled the outpost would get an out of order tone. It wasn't uncommon for the line to be down for days thanks to the dilapidated phone service, so it should at least buy him some time.

He fetched the radio and weapons from the LandRover and stowed them away in the storeroom. He decided to keep his old Browning and grabbed some spare ammunition from the shelf before locking the metal door. David had a feeling that the handgun was going to come in useful before this was all over.

He left the building housing the office and stores and headed over to the accommodation block. A room with six beds and a latrine next door that hadn't been working for months, each man had his own spot in the bush to do their business. David stripped off his fatigues, realising as he did that the left hand side of him was smeared in Koinet's blood. He threw the soiled clothes into the corner and took a towel outside to their wash facilities. A bucket with holes in it suspended from a tree. After three nights in the bush David didn't care that the water was cold or that he had to keep filling the bucket.

He returned to his bunk feeling refreshed if not invigorated and got dressed into what could almost be considered civilian clothes. Tanned combats and a white t-shirt. David stuffed the ammunition and some spare clothes into his rucksack and took the Browning out of its holster before slipping it into his waistband. He put a sleeveless windbreaker over the top to conceal the bulge and then went out to the LandRover.

He threw his rucksack onto the passenger seat and climbed in. The gauge was reading around quarter of a tank but he could fill up at the post in

Serena on the way. David did a three-sixty and joined River Road, heading north towards Serena. He was going to find Gupta and get to the bottom of this if it was the last thing he did.

CHAPTER EIGHTEEN
GSU Headquarters, Nairobi
August 17th, 1996

"You're positive that he's in Narok?" Maliki listened to the voice on the other end and nodded, "Keep me posted of any developments."

He hung up and dialled a number but there was no answer. He tried another and got the same result. Maliki slammed the phone down and got up from behind the mahogany desk. He walked over to the window and stared out over the empty parade square. His lip started to twitch and he rubbed at the scars on autopilot. Where the hell was Gupta? Although he didn't recognise the name Maliki's gut instinct told him that this Koinet was one of Gupta's men. If he did work for the old fool then the boy would suffer a similar fate to the one he had in store for Gupta, a slit throat and a trip to the bottom of Kilindini Harbour.

Maliki was tempted to bring the poacher into custody and put him in the cells but decided to wait for confirmation. No point getting involved and making waves if it wasn't necessary. He needed to speak to Gupta first but the idiot must still be out in the bush.

Maliki's attention was drawn to the driveway next to the parade square. Tanui's battered Peugeot passed under the checkpoint barrier and headed towards him. Maliki resented having to come in to headquarters on a Saturday but Captain Nbeke had become a nuisance and needed to be dealt with immediately. The man's name had cropped up once too often. What was he trying to do, clean up the Maasai Mara single-handed?

He watched Tanui park in the shade of the carport before turning back to his desk. Maliki smiled to himself. The Deputy Director hated being summoned to his office, that's why he had insisted the meeting take place there.

A few minutes later his phone signalled an internal call, "Sergeant Jozi here sir, I've got Deputy Director Tanui with me at the desk. Shall I send him up?"

"Yes Sergeant." Maliki smiled to himself, "But take his gun and make sure that he goes through the metal detector."

"Sir?" the sergeant was put out, it wasn't normal for high-ranking officials to be screened.

"You heard me. Tell him its new procedure." His smile broadened into a wicked grin.

Maliki heard the Deputy Director stomping down the corridor and somehow managed to put on his poker face before he burst through the door. Tanui looked ruffled and his holster was unclipped and empty.

"First you call me in here for something we could have discussed on the phone and then I'm subjected to a search!" He stood in front of Maliki's desk with his fists clenched by his sides. "This better be something bloody important!"

Maliki indicated the seat in front of him, "I suggest that you calm down and take a seat Deputy Director. One more outburst in my office and I'll have you taken down to the cells."

"You wouldn't dare!"

"Try me." Maliki glared at him. "I'm sure I can think of something to charge you with. Negligence and dereliction of duty for starters."

"What the hell are you talking about?"

"I'm talking about this Ranger of yours, Captain Nbeke. I hear that he has been causing trouble again, something about gun battles in the Masai Mara and a dead ranger? Bodies everywhere and a poacher in the hospital. You told me that you had this Nbeke under control. What kind of fiasco are you running over there?"

Tanui looked like the wind had been knocked out of his sails, "You know about that already?"

"It's my business to know what's going on, to keep my finger on the nation's pulse. There isn't much that happens in this country that I don't get to hear about sooner or later."

He wasn't exaggerating. Maliki had an extensive network of spies throughout the government and its institutions feeding him information, including the KWS. The fear of being beaten, arrested and thrown in jail as a traitor was reason enough for most of them to agree to work for him. Not many refused to cooperate with the head of the GSU. Those that did would be brought in for a session in the basement. If the pain didn't convince a prisoner to co-operate then their families would be threatened, or tortured in front of them. Eventually they all confessed, or died in the basement the way Konde had.

There was also a growing list of people beyond his legal reach that Maliki bought information from, foreign embassy staff and diplomats who might be missed if they disappeared.

Tanui's brow furrowed, he was probably trying to work out who was the leak in his organisation. "KWS operations and what my rangers get up to is not really your concern Commander. Why the big interest?"

Maliki played it cool, "When a member of your staff keeps highlighting national problems and giving the KWS bad press then it becomes my business. The President is worried about the effect on tourism. And so he should be. Kenya needs to be seen by the international market as a safe place to travel. How many bookings do you think will be cancelled as a result of this bloodshed?"

"Right now I don't really care how many people's holiday plans are disrupted. Ranger Haji's death may be just an inconvenience for you but to the Service it is a great loss. His family need to be informed and funeral arrangements made."

"I understand all that and you have my sympathy of course." Maliki nodded. "But you have to see my point of view. President Moi has made the nation's security and well being my responsibility. That includes its international image, something that Captain Nbeke seems intent on wrecking. Now what are you doing about the situation?"

"I've already confined him to barracks until the shootings can be investigated."

"That's not good enough." Maliki put his elbows on the desk and clasped his fingers together. "I want him sacked and charged with manslaughter. It's much easier for the public to forget something like this when they've got someone to blame. Believe me, it will all blow over quickly once Captain Nbeke is locked up."

"Unless an investigation proves otherwise all Captain Nbeke is responsible for is trying to do his job. What's happened is regrettable but there's no way I'm going to have him arrested on some trumped up charges." The Deputy Director folded his arms and leant back in the chair. "By all accounts Captain Nbeke prevented four black rhino being slaughtered, killing one of the poachers and taking another into custody in the process. If it wasn't for the fact that he acted of his own accord Nbeke would probably be receiving a commendation."

"Yes." Maliki smiled briefly. "But he didn't have authorisation for the mission and men died. The President will want him to resign at the very least."

"We're talking about a man's career, his life. I won't do it. If the President wants somebody's resignation then he can have mine. Captain Nbeke is under my command and my responsibility." The Deputy Director stood up in front of the desk, "Now if there's nothing else I've got better places to be."

Maliki watched him walk towards the door, "You haven't heard the last of this. Somebody's head is going to roll, I would advise you not to let it be yours."

Tanui paused before opening the door but didn't turn around, "Good day, Commander."

Maliki waited a few minutes to make sure that Tanui had left the building before calling the front desk, "Sergeant go outside and send Lembui up here, and make it quick." He slammed the phone down for the second time that morning.

It was a shame for Captain Nbeke's sake that the Deputy Director hadn't agreed to his plans. Now Maliki would have to take matters into his own hands. A few minutes later there was a polite tap on the door.

"Come in!" shouted Maliki, his face twitching with irritation.

"You wanted to see me, sir?"

Lembui must have run up the stairs, his huge barrel chest heaved and he was short of breath.

"I've got a job for you Lembui." Maliki smiled, "One that you're really going to enjoy. His name's Captain Nbeke, I think he's earned himself a trip to the basement."

Lembui's face cracked into a wide grin and his eyes gleamed brightly at the prospect.

Before Nbeke died Maliki needed to know whether the pain in the ass captain knew anything, or was simply unfortunate enough to be in the wrong place at the wrong time.

CHAPTER NINETEEN
District Hospital, Narok
August 17th, 1996

David wanted to check on Koinet's condition. The hospital was almost exactly half way to Nairobi so it made sense to stop there. Before leaving he filled the LandRover's tank and all the spare jerry cans he could find at the ranger's depot in Serena.

David arrived in Narok a little under three hours later. He was surprised to find a queue of crawling traffic outside the usually quiet town when he got to the outskirts. The road ahead was partially blocked by crowds of people spilling onto it from a truck stop. As David got closer he could see why. Armed police with riot shields were trying to keep two opposing groups of demonstrators apart. On one side a group of Maasai warriors were chanting and shaking their spears at the Kikuyu opposite them. Most of them were young men under the age of thirty.

The police had formed a line facing the Kikuyu to keep them back. As David watched a pair of policemen dashed forward and grabbed a shouting youth from the crowd. He was dragged across the ground into the fold of waiting light blue uniforms and swallowed up as they converged around him. Truncheons wielded above the heads of the policemen rained blows down on the unfortunate protestor. A great cheer went up amongst the Maasai warriors and the chanting and dancing increased in tempo.

Policemen with angry faces were waving the cars forward. The whole scene was a volatile concoction of hatred and testosterone ready to explode at any moment. David kept his head down until he had gone through the bottleneck and breathed a sigh of relief.

He turned left onto the C57 that went up through the town and continued north to Lake Naivasha. The Saturday market at the junction was in full swing. People going about their business despite the riot taking place less than half a mile away. Streams of shoppers filed down the road between the brighter dressed street sellers and market traders. David slowed down and weaved his way through the throng of pedestrians, vehicles and the odd cyclist.

David slammed on the brakes to avoid being hit by a matatu, blasting its horn as it cut across the road in front of him. The dented mini-bus came to a jerky stop at the taxi rank beside the maze of stalls, selling everything from fruit to car spares. The conductor hanging from the open sliding door on the side jumped off and shouted at the occupants. Ushering them to disembark. Over twenty people piled out of the back of the fifteen-seat Toyota Hiace and three from the front. Once they were out a couple of the women helped each other strap babies to their backs using knitted shawls. The infants pressed so tightly against their mothers that their legs were bowed out like frogs.

David realised that the taxi driver had the right idea and started blasting the horn of the LandRover to clear people out of the way. Ten minutes later he pulled up outside the entrance. The hospital didn't look like much. A series of single storey buildings of various shapes and sizes connected by tin-covered walkways.

Inside it didn't get much better. The lights were out and a mixture of nervous patients and angry relatives were swamping the nurse on duty at the reception desk. At the front of the crowd a Maasai in loincloth and beads was arguing with her in Swahili.

"This is an outrage. I don't know how you can call this a hospital. How can you perform the operation on my father without electricity?"

"As I told you already Mr Wachira, mechanics are on their way to fix the generator. Until they arrive there is nothing I can do. Now please go back to the ward so I can deal with somebody else." She turned to an old lady leaning on the counter for support, "Next."

David pushed his way to the front and flashed his ID, "Excuse me, I'm looking for a patient called Koinet. He was brought in by two of my rangers."

The plump nurse in her early fifties gave him an appraising look before checking the register. A few loose sheets of paper stuck to a clipboard. Her layers of make-up threatened to crack as she smiled up at him.

"He's over in C-block." She pointed at a set of doors opposite to the one he came in, "Go through there and carry on down the path to the next building. It's where we keep the private patients." Her voice dropped a couple of octaves, "If there's anything else I can do for you just let me know."

David gave her his best smile, "I'll be sure to do that and thanks for your help." It didn't hurt to play the game occasionally. Having the nurse on his side might come in useful later.

He found Damo in the corridor outside Koinet's room, "How's the patient doing?"

Damo looked relieved to see him, "He's doing OK but still very weak. The surgeon managed to get the bullet out and stitch up the artery. Now they've got him on blood transfusions to replace what he's lost."

"Has he said anything? Asked for anyone?"

"No." Damo nodded towards the glass panel in the door, "He hasn't regained consciousness yet."

David glanced into the room. Koinet was hooked up to heart and respiratory monitors whose screens were blank.

"Where's Rashid?"

"He's gone to find something to eat." Damo lowered his voice, "What are you doing here? I thought that you were going to Nairobi?"

"I'm on my way," David went on to explain that Chege and Makori would be arriving soon and that they were to take turns guarding Koinet between them. David didn't mention his conversation with the Deputy Director, or the fact that he wasn't supposed to leave the outpost. "Ideally I want two of you outside his room at all times."

"You're expecting trouble then?"

"At this point I'm not really sure but I think that we should be prepared for the worst. Whoever this Gupta is he's not going to be happy when he finds out that Koinet is in custody."

"Who are you going to see in Nairobi?"

"I'd rather not say." By the way he turned away from him David could tell that he had insulted his friend. "Damo, it's for your own good. I'll tell you when the time is right and I've got something concrete to go on."

"Don't you think I deserve to know what's going on?"

"Yes," David nodded. "But unfortunately it's not that simple. I'll give you a call later when I'm settled."

David turned and walked away down the corridor before he had to tell his friend any more lies. Nairobi was only a pit stop, a chance to warn Caitlyn and an excuse to see her briefly. David was going to Mombasa in search of Gupta.

*****

David's back was covered in sweat by the time he got to the centre of Nairobi. It was mid-afternoon and sweltering inside the LandRover. There was no AC and the fans blew in hotter air when he tried them. The windows were down but with traffic at a standstill and not even the hint of a breeze all they did was let in exhaust fumes. David felt like he was being slowly cooked alive.

He couldn't help noticing that the city was declining rapidly, on a downwards spiral to rack and ruin. Money that should have been spent on infrastructure and keeping the streets clean was being filtered into a select few Swiss bank accounts. The streets had been much cleaner three years ago when he was there during training.

Many of the buildings looked rundown and in need of repair. On some of the walls graffiti displayed Moi and other politicians as vultures, feasting on the Kenyan public. Others showed the President's face behind bars, or slogans such as 'PEACE', or 'I WANT TO BE FREE'. But a lot of them bore the same repeated message in bold capitals that simply read 'MPs SCREWING KENYANS SINCE 1963'.

The people walked with their heads down, as if afraid to make eye contact with one another. Although officially speaking David wasn't supposed to know anything about Karl Marx he did. The term 'oppressed masses' came to mind. Moi had banned communism and any teaching related to it in 1982 when he made Kenya a one party state. But copies of Marx's books still existed. 'The Communist Manifesto' was available to read or hire from Kisii library. David had only leafed through the book and never risked signing it out, just in case it was some sort of trick to entrap socialists.

David began to feel paranoid. He wasn't sure whether it was the city's atmosphere or because he was nearing headquarters. He found himself looking in the rear view mirror constantly, checking to see if anybody was following him. He hadn't seen the two goons in suits or the dark sedan since dropping Bernstein off at the camping site. David's conscience told him that he should phone the reporter and let him know that he was being watched.

Finally he turned southwest towards the orphanage and the traffic started to ease up. David tried telling himself that he was going there simply to warn her, but he knew deep down that his motivation was more selfish.

On the way he spotted a large electrical wholesaler by the roadside and parked in the shade outside. The place was filled to the rafters with all manner of domestic appliances. It took him a while to rummage through the shelves and find the piece of equipment he wanted. A cheap pocket sized tape recorder. A basic model made by SANYO but it would serve its intended purpose well enough. At the counter he bought batteries and spares, as well as two rolls of gaffa tape. If everything went the way he expected it to David was going to need all of the items hastily stuffed into his rucksack.

Feeling better, his shirt dry and the jeep a more bearable temperature, he continued down Langata Road. The KWS offices were closed on Saturdays so there was little chance of bumping into Tanui, especially at the orphanage. But David still looked away as he passed the main gates to avoid being seen by the Deputy Director or anyone else that might recognise him. Idi Tikolo was the first name that sprung to mind. He would relish the opportunity to drop David in it.

To avoid having his visit being logged in the register David paid the admission of 300 shillings and drove in through Banda Gate with the tourists. Without markings his jeep blended in well with the locals and tour operators using the smaller side entrance to the park. He turned right onto the dirt track that skirted the edge of the forest, running parallel to the main road on the other side of the perimeter fence.

A few minutes later he found a gap between the cars parked outside the orphanage and killed the engine. The overheated LandRover wasn't used to doing long distances and would be grateful of the rest.

David spotted someone he recognised crossing the courtyard, going from one building to another.

"Ben," he shouted to stop him entering a wooden tool shed and jogged past the stone well towards the keeper.

He turned to face David, "Jambo." His smile changed into a confused frown, "I didn't know that anyone was being brought in today?"

"They're not," David shook his head. "I came to see how Ella is doing." He noticed that Ben referred to the orphans as people rather than animals.

"She's doing fine," he beamed enthusiastically. "One of the elder females took Ella under her wing a few days ago and has been looking after her. The change since then is quite something. They're down at the waterhole having a bath if you want to see for yourself."

David avoided eye contact, "Is Dr Brennan around?"

"Are you sure that you came to check on Ella?" Ben chuckled before pointing at the track next to the stables, "Just follow the signs, Dr Brennan is with the elephants."

"Thanks," David couldn't think of a reasonable excuse for wanting to see her so he didn't say anything and headed straight for the path.

The waterhole was closer than he expected, tucked away behind the buildings with just a small copse of trees separating them. A muddy red bowl with a tiny pool of churned up water in the centre. Although she stuck close to her matriarch Ella was playing with the younger elephants, spraying mud at them with her trunk and rolling around in the clay. She bore no resemblance to the dejected little soul he had brought into the orphanage.

Caitlyn was under the shade of an acacia tree next to the mud bath. Her back was to him, talking to one of the keepers as they examined the foot of a young elephant.

David called out to warn them of his approach.

"Hi, Ben told me I might find you here."

Caitlyn glanced over her shoulder and smiled before continuing what she was saying to the keeper, "It's healing nicely, just keep up the walks twice a day and he'll have full mobility in no time." She stood up and patted the elephant on the back.

"What happened to him?" David stroked the calf's leathery hide.

"Poachers of course," Caitlyn shook her head. "We found this poor thing in Voi caught in a snare.

I know that people are hungry but there are more humane ways of killing an animal." She gave the elephant a final pat and turned to look at him, "So what are you doing back here?"

David lowered his voice, "I came to warn you."

She tilted her head to one side, "Oh, what about?"

"I'd rather not talk about it here," he glanced at the keeper nearest to them.

"I see," she smiled nervously. "In that case you might as well walk with me back to the stables."

"Sounds good."

"So what's all this about?"

"Err...well..." David could feel his cheeks going red. "Like I said I just wanted to make sure that you were OK."

Caitlyn laughed, "So you're worried about me are you? Why's that"

"One of my Rangers was killed last night in a raid by poachers and other people's lives might be at risk," David paused. "Maybe even yours."

Her smile disappeared, "Oh God, I'm so sorry David. But what does his death have to do with me?"

"We were watching Rhino, waiting for the poachers, based on information given to us by Spencer." David swallowed, "I'm worried that whoever's behind this will put the connection between the three of us together."

"Do you have any suspects?"

"Maybe," knowing about Gupta would only put her in more danger. "I'm on my way to Mombasa to find out for certain."

"Oh," her eyes widened. "Will you be OK?"

David nodded, "I'll be fine, but I'd like you to keep away from the orphanage for a while. Stay somewhere safe, at least until this is all over."

She shook her head. "Nobody's scaring me away from my work, or telling me what to do for that matter. It's unlikely that anyone will make connect me to Spencer. We were only together for a few months, and nobody here knew anything about him. I'll take my chances."

David realised by the tone of her voice and the thrust of her chin that she wasn't going to change her mind. He shrugged, "I suppose you're right. Maybe I shouldn't have come. I just didn't know how else to contact you."

"Are you asking for my phone number?" Caitlyn smiled mischievously.

"If you're offering," he couldn't help but smile back.

"So what did you think of Spencer?"

He could see Caitlyn watching him out of the corner of his eye as they walked up the path.

"He's quite something," David wasn't sure what he was supposed to say about her ex-boyfriend. He felt like he was being tested.

"That's one way of putting it," Caitlyn smiled briefly. "I'm sorry that you lost one of your men," she slipped her arm through his and squeezed, the contact sent electrical pulses to his brain. "Were you close to him?"

"I suppose," David realised he didn't know Haji that well despite working with him for over two years. "We spent a lot of time together. He comes from a fishing village somewhere near Mombasa."

"I see."

There was an awkward silence, as neither knew what to say next. Funny how death does that, maybe it's the realisation that we're not immortal. Caitlyn finally spoke as they stopped next to the stables.

"What do you hope to find in Mombasa?"

"The guy we caught gave me an address for his boss so I'm going down there to check it out," David didn't know why he was confiding in her but it felt right.

Caitlyn turned to face him. Her eyes were misted over like she might cry. She took both of his hands in hers, "You will be careful won't you David? I'd hate for anything to happen to you."

"Don't worry." David forced a smile that he hoped looked convincing, "I'll be fine. I'm only going to see what I can find out about him for now."

"When will you be back?"

"I'm not sure, I'll be a couple of days at least."

Caitlyn glanced at the stables before reaching up and kissing him on the cheek, "Sorry, I seem to be making a habit of this but I've got to go. One of the elephants is due her medication. When are you leaving?"

David was still reeling from the kiss. "I'm going to head down there now, why?"

"I just wondered if you had time to have dinner before you go. I mean you've still got to eat don't you?" She shoved her hands into the lab coat's pockets. "I'll be finished in about half an hour if you're interested?"

David thought about Damo and the other rangers guarding Koinet. He should be well on his way to Mombasa by now. He convinced himself that a couple of hours wouldn't make any difference.

"I'll be waiting."

"You better be!" she smiled. He had been right about the figure, her pert bum wiggled as she walked away from him.

CHAPTER TWENTY
Hankook Garden, Nairobi
August 17th, 1996

The LandRover tilted over to almost forty-five degrees as David mounted the inclined verge. Driving a 4x4 had its advantages, even in the city. There wasn't a single space available in the packed car park.

"Chinese?" guessed Caitlyn.

"Close," David smiled. "Hankook Garden is the best Korean restaurant in the city."

As he struggled to open his door against the incline Caitlyn was almost ejected, as hers swung open.

"What, you mean there's more than one in town?" she was straightening out her dress when he joined her on the other side of the jeep. He'd waited outside her apartment so that she could change on the way. She was wearing an ankle length red and black ethnic print. The fabric clung to her body and accentuated her amazing figure. Gold sandals exposed Caitlyn's dainty painted toes and her hair was tied up in a bun. David felt somewhat unworthy dressed in his t-shirt and combats.

David smiled, "It's a big city and more cosmopolitan than you might think. There are a few that I know of."

As they entered between the bamboo pillars he noticed a few of the men look their way and give Caitlyn an appreciative look. An older gentleman with olive coloured skin and liver spots covering his baldhead let his gaze linger for too long. Or at least his companion must have thought so, a woman with big blonde hair and an even bigger voice. She turned to see what he was looking at and then gave him a mouthful in what sounded like Italian.

The four cooking stations were busy and David wanted somewhere a bit more private. They wove their way between the tables of noisy diners and found a space out on the terrace. The restaurant's clientele supported what David had said about Nairobi. He counted at least five different nationalities before they took their seats.

"What are you drinking?" David beckoned the waiter as he walked by.

"I'll have a Tusker please."

She had just gone up another notch in his estimation, "I'll have the same."

The waiter had ridiculously thin sideburns, joined together by a pencil line of stubble across his chin. After giving them two menus from another table he went off to fetch their drinks.

"I'm starving." Caitlyn decided quickly, "I'll have the sliced beef with special sauce, whatever that is, and some spicy noodles."

"Good choice, I think I'll have the same."

The waiter returned with the beers and took their order. David took a swig. The lager was cold and crisp but he'd only had a couple of hours sleep in the last forty-eight and was beginning to feel the effects of fatigue. David covered his mouth as he yawned.

Caitlyn laughed and shook her head. A lock of hair fell to her cheek and she brushed it back behind her ear. "Charming! Boring you already, am I?"

"Sorry," David smiled. "I just haven't had a good night's sleep in a while. Tell me a bit about yourself. Apart from the fact that you're a vet and work at the orphanage I know nothing about you."

"Not much to tell really. Good catholic girl, brought up in a town on the coast called Dundalk. It's near the border." A shadow crossed her eyes for a second and then the sparkle was back. "I always wanted to be a vet so I went to University in Dublin and got a degree. Worked in a country practice near Dundalk for a while looking after farmers' sheep. Giving them their yearly vaccinations that kind of thing. But it got boring and routine pretty quickly. Then the opportunity came up to work for the Sheldrick Trust. Obviously I jumped at the chance."

"How long are you planning on staying?"

She smiled, "I suppose that depends on a lot of things, but I had planned on being here for at least a year, maybe two."

"Don't you miss your friends and family?"

Caitlyn shrugged, "I suppose so. But there's really only my mum, sister and a couple of friends from university that I bother to stay in touch with. I guess I'm a bit of a loner. What about you?"

David wondered what happened to the father she didn't mention. He might have just run away with another woman but her tone and eyes said otherwise. He wanted to ask but his better judgement told him not to probe and wait until Caitlyn decided to bring up the subject.

"Well, I'm happily married with two kids, boy and a girl," David smiled.

Caitlyn's face dropped, "Oh, I see."

David laughed, "Not really, I just wanted to see how you would react."

"You bastard!" She reached across the table and slapped his shoulder. "That was unfair. Now, what's the real story?"

"Like you, I'm a bit of a loner. I've only got one friend to speak of. Then there's my mother and sister Kiira, they live with my Aunt in Kisii." David smiled thinking about her, "She's great."

"Kisii?" Caitlyn raised an eyebrow. "What a great name. I bet a lot of that went on when you were at school."

David shrugged off the backhanded compliment, "Not really. I was always too busy on the farm."

"Helping your father?"

Caitlyn was much better than him at asking difficult questions but he didn't want to go into all of that right now. Not on their first date. "Yes, we used to do a lot together."

"He's not around anymore then?"

She was persistent. But then he kind of expected that of her, "No, he died when I was sixteen."

"I'm sorry," she grabbed hold of his hand. "I shouldn't have pried so much. Being nosy is a bad habit of mine."

"Don't worry, it was a long time ago."

"But the pain never really goes away does it? You just lock it away somewhere deep inside so that you can function properly," her eyes had a faraway look in them and then she snapped out of it and smiled. "There I go getting all morbid. Shall we talk about something else? What made you decide to become a ranger?"

David was relieved that she changed the subject, "It was a natural choice really. I love wildlife and the freedom of being out in the bush, have done ever since I was a kid. It beats the hell out of being cooped up in an office or factory all day long."

The waiter arrived with their food and wished them a pleasant meal before scurrying off.

"What about the danger? Don't you worry about the fact that you could be killed?" she forked up some noodles and stuffed them into her mouth.

Caitlyn obviously had a good appetite. David liked the way she didn't pick at her food like some women he'd dated. As if they were embarrassed to be seen eating anything other than a salad.

"You just don't think about it. We take all the precautions that we can and minimise the risks. But I guess there's also a bit of the 'it will never happen to me' mentality. Otherwise we wouldn't be able to do the job."

"Do you really think it's worth risking your life?" Her eyes were hypnotising. "After all, they are only animals."

"Are you sure that you're a vet?"

Caitlyn laughed, "Don't get me wrong. I love working with animals. But would I sacrifice my life for one of theirs, or even another human being come to think about it?" She shook her head. "I don't think I've got the guts. It's very endearing though, quite a turn on."

David didn't know where to look.

"I hope that I haven't embarrassed you, Captain?" she smiled mischievously. "Surely not? A big strapping ranger like yourself."

David smiled, "Are you always this forward?"

"Only with men who've got a death wish and you never know if you're going to see them again." Caitlyn's smile faded and she took his hand in hers, "I'm sorry, that was a stupid thing to say."

"Forget it." David nodded at her plate, "Come on, we better eat up before it gets cold."

The food was fantastic as always. They ate in comfortable silence for a while before Caitlyn spoke.

"Do you really have to do this?"

"Is there something wrong with the meal?" David realised that it was a pathetic attempt at humour.

"You know what I mean!" Caitlyn scowled at him. She looked good even when she was angry. "Why does it have to be you?"

David sighed, "Somebody's got to do something before there are no elephants or rhino left. What am I supposed to do? Just walk away?"

"I don't expect you to walk away from it but you need help." She frowned, "Isn't there anyone else in the KWS that you can turn to?"

"Right now the only one I trust is Damo and he's stuck guarding the poacher that we caught. Hopefully that will all change once I've been down to Mombasa."

"Is Damo the friend that you spoke of?"

David nodded, "The one and only."

"That sounds like a bad song lyric," Caitlyn smiled, "You know, Chesney Hawkes?"

David raised an eyebrow, "Why do I get the feeling that I'm lucky not to have heard of him?"

She laughed, "I can't believe you don't know who he is, good looking fella with long blonde hair. I had quite a crush on him about five years ago."

"Sound's great." David smiled, "Are there any other pop stars that I should be worried about?"

"Only about ten or twelve off the top of my head." She grinned, "Probably more if I really try to think about it."

David held his hands up in mock surrender, "OK, I shouldn't have asked."

Caitlyn stared at the table, "David?"

"Yes?"

"You're probably going to think I'm a right tart, and believe me I've never done this before on a first date." She looked up at him, "Would you like to come back to my place?"

David knew that he should get going. But looking into her eyes he just couldn't resist. Pushing reason to one side he motioned for the waiter to bring the bill.

*****

There was a mass of people outside the American Embassy as they drove by. He guessed there were over two hundred demonstrators, men women and children. Some holding placards, most of them shouting and chanting. The repeated call and the signs above their heads bore the same message. 'MOI MUST GO' made it pretty clear what they were protesting against. Presumably this was both a public spotlight and a safe place to do it, under the watchful eye of the US marines.

A hard-core group of more radical demonstrators were at the front egging the crowd on. Two of them were holding on to the poles of a banner that read 'AMERICAN APATHY TOWARDS HUMAN RIGHTS ABUSE'. A coffee skinned man with a megaphone led the chanting. David could see the tension on the Marine Guards' faces that were manning the checkpoint in the perimeter fence. He looked up at the non-descript grey building behind them. Man's obsession with concrete during the sixties had a lot to answer for. Considering the Embassy was meant to represent American interests in Kenya it sure was ugly.

A line of light blues was preventing the crowd from spilling out onto the street. Unlike the police he'd seen in Narok earlier that day they were on their best behaviour. Then he spotted the TV cameras on the corner across the street, one of them from the American news channel CNN. That explained the lack of truncheons.

"They're out here demonstrating almost every day. How come Moi is still in power when there are so many people against him?"

David sighed, "Unfortunately it's not that simple. He's got a lot of supporters in high places, and most people are too scared of being shot or branded traitors to speak out."

"Why doesn't the West do anything? Moi's obviously a dictator."

"For the same reason they don't do anything about the Nigerian President, or Robert Mugabe. There's not enough mineral wealth to make it worthwhile and Kenya is of no strategic importance." He shook his head, "Its just Africans killing Africans. Unless the country is swimming in oil or next door to Russia they're not really interested."

"Do you really believe that's how it is?"

David nodded, "Hundreds of thousands of people have been reported murdered or missing but nothing is ever done about it. What do you think?"

"I didn't realise it was quite so bad. It puts a whole new perspective on the troubles."

"The troubles?" David raised an eyebrow. He knew a little bit about Ireland's history and the British occupation but had never heard the expression used before.

"I guess old habits die hard." She took a sip of beer, "That's what my parents' generation used to call the war in Ireland between the North and the South."

David was beginning to realise that despite being born worlds apart they actually had a lot in common. He was itching to ask about her father but didn't.

They pulled up outside her apartment building on Monrovia Street, a four-storey block facing Jevanjee Gardens. Despite the great location it was another faceless example of sixties architecture, boxlike terraces hanging beneath metal patio doors painted white.

"Are you sure that you want me to come up?"

Caitlyn rolled her eyes, "I think you'd better shut up before I change my mind." She got out and slammed the door so hard the jeep rocked.

CHAPTER TWENTY-ONE
Biashara Street, Nairobi
August 17th, 1996

The girl who called herself Katia was naked and tied to the four-poster bed, her mouth gagged in case she screamed too loudly. Maliki knew that besides wanting anonymity the leggy blonde's real name wasn't very easy on the tongue. Sviatoslava Gruzinsky was an eighteen-year-old refugee from the Ukraine. Brought to Kenya two years previously by a Russian prostitution ring to work in one of their clubs.

After seeing her gyrating at the Cocodome Palace Maliki simply had to have her. Her tight golden buttocks were pointing in the air, propped up by a couple of pillows. Maliki pulled back his cane and brought it down viciously, adding another angry red welt to the ones already criss-crossing her bum. The leather gag that she bit into muffled Katia's screams. Maliki glanced at himself in the mirror above the bed and grinned. His lean body was dripping in sweat, veins and muscles bulging, his penis standing out proudly in front of him.

He swung back to take another swipe but the shrill ringing of the telephone caused his arm to freeze in mid-air. Only one person had the number for Katia's penthouse apartment in Biashara

Street, and he knew not to call unless it was an emergency.

Maliki dropped the cane to his side and marched over to the dressing table, antique mahogany to match the bed. He picked up the receiver.

"What you have to say better be fucking important," he snarled into the phone.

"Sorry sir, I wasn't sure whether to call but then Sabore persuaded me that it was the right thing to do," he heard ruffling, as if Lembui was holding the phone to his chest, and Sabore's voice in the background. There was a delay of a few seconds before Lembui came back on the line, "What I meant to say was that we decided it was the best thing to do."

"Well spit it out you idiot." Maliki was watching Katia writhing around on the bed.

"Sorry...sir," Lembui stammered. "Captain Nbeke isn't at the Outpost sir."

Lembui suddenly had all his attention, "What do you mean he's not there? Are you sure that you've looked everywhere?"

"That's just it sir, there's nobody here at all. The place is completely deserted." He heard Lembui swallow, "What do you want us to do?"

Maliki felt the stiffness leaving his penis and his lip twitched. He was going to enjoy getting his hands on Nbeke and making him pay for the interruption.

"Get Sabore to stay there in case he comes back. You go to the other rangers' stations and see if Nbeke is at any of them. If not, find out where he was last seen and where he's going. Get the registration and description of the vehicle that he's driving and put out an all points bulletin for his arrest. I want this bastard caught! Do you understand me Lembui!"

"Yes s..." Lembui's was cut off as Maliki smashed down the receiver.

Maliki's hands were trembling as he searched through the pockets of his jacket, hanging from the chair next to the desk. Because he was flustered it got caught in the lining but eventually his address book came free. Maliki thumbed through the pages and found the number he wanted. He actually dialled the first three digits before realising what he was doing and replacing the receiver.

His face went into spasm. He had nearly called the Deputy Director at home from Katia's apartment. It would have been a stupid, amateur error. The fact that he had come close to it filled him with rage. With only Katia there to take his fury out on he turned back to the bed and raised the cane high above his head. He whipped her again and again. So hard that it broke the skin and she started to bleed. He dropped the cane and used his fists instead, the rewarding feeling of flesh meeting bone. Her dampened cries for help were far too faint for anybody to hear.

*****

"You can get some sleep now Gakere. But be ready at 6am. I might need you," Maliki dismissed the driver that regularly replaced Lembui and slammed shut the door of the Mercedes.

Gakere was another one of Maliki's handpicked bodyguards, a veteran GSU officer with over eight years in the field. Including Lembui and Sabore there were sixteen officers living in the grounds of his mansion. One of the biggest on Gigiri Road the two storey colonial palace backed onto Muthaiga forest.

Maliki lived alone and eleven of the bedrooms were rarely in use. Only occupied when he was using prostitutes to coerce VIPs into sexually explicit acts. Maliki had tapes that revealed a darker side to quite a few of Kenya's public figures, many of them high court judges. He kept them in the walk-in safe, hidden behind the false wall in his study. They were both Maliki's tools of the trade and his insurance policy. Just in case the shit ever really did hit the fan.

Six guards were on duty at any one time, two at the gate and four patrolling the perimeter with Alsatians. He could hear one of them barking at their arrival and being told to be quiet by its handler. The fence on top of the walls that enclosed the garden was electrified and the building alarmed. Maliki had taken every possible precaution to protect the property from external attacks but still he was paranoid.

He constantly scrutinised his men for any sign of disobedience or mutiny, afraid of being brought down from within his own ranks.

He ran his hand along the marble balustrade as he bounded up the stairs towards the entrance. Arched oak doors surrounded by pairs of elegantly ribbed columns that rose up to the roof. He shielded the security panel next to the door as he tapped in the six-digit number. There was a second's delay and a click before it opened inwards.

Only Maliki and Jozi knew the code for the alarm and it was changed regularly. He had rescued Jozi from the streets, taking the then sixteen year old with him from Mombasa three decades ago. Jozi was the only man that he trusted and the closest to what most people would call a friend. Maliki considered him to be more of a necessary dependant.

The Indian influence went down the east coast as far as South Africa, like a lot of Swahilis Jozi loved curries and was a great cook. He looked after the house and prepared Maliki's meals. Despite the years they had been together Jozi wasn't allowed to sleep in the house. He had his own room in the shed-like building that acted as the officer's living quarters.

Maliki flicked a switch that illuminated the atrium and twin staircases in soft yellow light. He closed the door and went over to the master panel to reset the alarm. The panelled oak doors to the lounges and two wings of the building were closed. His footsteps echoed as Maliki continued across the marble tiles to his study.

After punching a separate code that only he knew into another panel Maliki inserted the key and entered his inner sanctum. Made to look like the rest of the Georgian style doors it was really three inches thick, solid steel hidden under the wood. The door swung back easily on specially engineered hinges. The lights came on automatically and Maliki stood behind the leather topped desk. He took his diary from his pocket and dialled the Deputy Director's number. The number he was calling from didn't exist as far as the telephone company was concerned.

It took a while for Tanui to pick up and he sounded irritated, "Hello, who is this?"

"It's Commander Abasi," Maliki barked. "I thought you told me that you had Nbeke under control?"

"Do you know what time it is?"

Maliki was well aware of the time, it had been past midnight when he left Katia's apartment. She was in a right state and he'd left her a few hundred dollars to cover the extra damages. The bitch was moaning that she never wanted to see him again but Maliki knew that she would answer the next time he called. Business as usual once the bruises healed up and the swelling went down.

"If I'd wanted the speaking clock I would have dialled a different fucking number! Now where's Nbeke?"

"I told you this morning. He's up at the outpost in Purungat. Now what's all this about?"

"You fool! Nbeke's not in Purungat, nobody is," Maliki wished that the receiver was Tanui's neck. "If by some miracle you manage to find him I want Nbeke brought to me. If not you will be stripped of your command. I'm already considering it!"

Maliki slammed down the phone and started pacing behind his desk. His face began to twitch. Captain Nbeke was going to regret the day that he was born.

CHAPTER TWENTY-TWO
Caitlyn's Apartment, Nairobi
August 18th, 1996

David woke in a cold sweat and it took him a few seconds to work out where he was. There was an empty space next to him and an indented pillow but no Caitlyn. Then he heard her clattering pans in the kitchen. He swung his legs out of bed and rubbed the ridge of bone on the back of his head.

A gentle breeze blowing through the patio doors cooled his skin. The double doors were swung wide open and led onto the terrace that connected the bedroom with the lounge. Thin white drapes hung from ceiling to floor and billowed in the wind. David looked around the room as he searched for his clothes. The only decorations were a few photographs of her family and friends, most of them of what must be her mother and sister. An older picture on the nightstand beside the bed was the only one that showed both her parents. Standing with Caitlyn and her sister on a cold looking pebbled beach.

At the end of the bed a cheap flat-pack wardrobe was sagging in the middle and looked ready to burst. Next to it and supporting one side from collapsing was a bookshelf, crammed with a mixture of thrillers and medical journals.

David retrieved his pants and combats that were scattered between the bed and the door. He pulled them on and followed the delicious smell wafting down the corridor.

Although basic the apartment was large enough to be comfortable and showed signs of being recently decorated, fresh cream paint and newly laid laminate flooring. Caitlyn's room and a reasonable sized lounge overlooked the park, while the galley style kitchen, cosy bathroom and second bedroom faced the rear of the building. The smaller bedroom was tiny, big enough for a baby's cot, but it was difficult to see how a normal sized bed could fit in. Caitlyn obviously used it as a study. As David walked past the open door he could see a plastic fold up chair and a desk crammed with more medical journals and reference books. There was one on Kenyan wildlife at the top of the pile.

Caitlyn raised an eyebrow as he walked into the kitchen. She was wearing nothing but an apron with a map of Kenya on it, holding a spatula in her hand.

"Last night you were underdressed and now you're wearing too much." Her eyes twinkled with mischief.

"Sorry, I just can't seem to get it right, can I?" David smiled back at her.

"I don't know," she stepped over and looped her arms behind his neck. "You do have some talents." Then she reached up and kissed him, slow and lingering, their tongues gently probing each other's mouths.

Eventually she pulled away from him.

"What are you cooking?" asked David looking at the frying pan. "English breakfast?"

"Do I sound feckin' English to you?" said Caitlyn emphasising her accent. "This is the real thing, an Irish breakfast. You sit yourself down and get ready for a real feast."

David admired her toned body as she busied herself with the eggs and bacon, humming a tune that he didn't recognise. He started to think about the day ahead and his trip down to Mombasa. The drive to the coast would take him around eight hours, plus another hour south to Gupta's place on Diani Beach.

"Did you sleep OK?"

The question caught him by surprise, "Yes thanks."

"That's strange." Caitlyn turned her head towards him, "You were moaning and moving around quite a lot. It sounded like you were having a nightmare, you mentioned your father a couple of times."

"Oh." David looked away, "I hope I didn't disturb you too much."

"Don't be stupid David." She came over and put her hand on his shoulder, "I just wondered if you wanted to talk about it, that's all."

"No thanks, it doesn't really make for pleasant conversation."

She moved her hand to his chin and lifted his face up, "Have you ever talked to anyone about what happened to him?"

David nodded, "I spoke to Damo about it once when we were drunk."

"Great as this friend of yours sounds I don't think that really counts as a professional consultation." She smiled, "I meant a psychiatrist."

"You think that I need to see a shrink?"

"I think that it might help you come to terms with losing him," she shrugged. "It couldn't hurt and you're obviously affected by his death. I went through the same thing when my pa was murdered."

Voicing the unspoken bond between them opened some kind of mental floodgates. David stood up and held her in his arms as she started to cry.

"What happened to him?" he asked softly, stroking her hair. Feeling her silent tears run down his neck and chest.

"Bloody bomb in a coffee shop," she started sobbing uncontrollably. "Nobody even claimed responsibility, the cowardly bastards!"

He pulled her closer and felt a tear burst from his eyes and drip down his cheek, "Mine was murdered too. They shot him in front of us."

"Who are they?"

David let the tears flow for the first time since his father's death, "That's just it. I don't know either, he was wearing a mask."

"Shit!" Caitlyn pushed away from him and ran over to the cooker. David could smell it too. "I'm burning the bloody breakfast!"

She pulled the pan away and turned off the gas before putting it to one side. Then she started to laugh, "We're a right pair. You know that don't you?"

"I do," David walked over and wrapped his arms around her slender waist.

She reached up and kissed him, "Since breakfast is ruined let's go back to bed?"

"That sounds like a great idea," David picked her up in his arms and carried her through to the bedroom. Their lovemaking was more frantic than the night before. As if they were clinging on to each other for dear life.

*****

David didn't want to make any calls from Caitlin's apartment in case they were traced. He left her sleeping with a note on the pillow beside her. He closed the front door softly and took the staircase down from the fourth floor. Outside the building he found a public payphone and dialled the number for the hospital. Relief flooded him when Damo eventually came on the line.

"How's the patient?"

"He's conscious but not saying much, at least the power's back on so the equipment's working again."

"Have Chege and Makori arrived?"

"Yeah, they got here late last night," Damo sounded distracted. "Why didn't you mention that you were supposed to be confined to barracks? The Deputy Director phoned last night and I almost dropped you in it."

"Sorry, I should have said," David guessed that Tanui must be spitting nails. "What did he want?"

The bigger question was how did the Deputy Director know that he wasn't in Purungat so soon?

Days or weeks could go by without anybody visiting the remote outpost. Tanui must have sent someone there specifically to check up on him.

"He asked whether I had seen you and how the prisoner was. Wanted to make sure that he was being watched. He offered to send up a reinforcements but I told him that we had it covered."

"Thanks," David still wasn't sure whether Tanui's interest was professional or personal. "Sounds like you've got everything under control."

"It would be easier if I knew what the hell was going on. What all the cloak and dagger stuff is about." Damo sounded angry.

"I'm sorry Damo, but until I've got some proof things are going to have to stay the way they are. As soon as I've got anything positive to go on I'll let you know."

Damo seemed to calm down, his voice softened, "Is there somewhere I can reach you if I need to?"

"No." David wanted Damo to think he was staying in Nairobi, "The phones don't work at the motel. I'll call again later to see how you're doing."

David replaced the receiver. He took Bernstein's card from his wallet and dialled the hotel. The receptionist told him that Bernstein was out so he decided to leave a message.

"Are you sure that's it sir?"

"Please just make sure that he gets it!" said David before hanging up. His conscience was a little clearer but he feared that his note might arrive too late for the American. It read simply, "You're being watched."

David walked over to the LandRover and fished for the keys in the pockets of his combats. He could feel the gun digging into his spine and irrationally half expected a tap on the shoulder any second. He climbed in and put the key in the ignition. The heat plugs seemed to take longer than usual to warm up as he waited to start the engine.

When he was well out of the city and sure that he wasn't being followed David allowed himself to relax. He sat back in his seat and the tension started to go out of his arms as he loosened his grip on the steering wheel. Once again he found himself alone and with far too much time to think. David kept running events over and over in his mind on the drive south, knowing that if he had done things differently Haji would still be alive.

CHAPTER TWENTY-THREE
Kilindini Harbour, Mombasa
August 18th, 1996

David followed the road parallel to the railway line. Driving across the fifty-meter wide strip of man-made rock and earth that joined Mombasa to the mainland. There were two lanes running in both directions but very few cars using them. The town's residents resting in or out of the Sunday afternoon sun somewhere.

The calmer waters of Tudor Creek on the left of the dual carriageway branched off into lots of different sized tributaries. The various streams and rivers that fed the huge lagoon reaching out into the rich green delta of tropical forest like the fingers of a giant hand.

Kilindini Port and the choppier harbour were on the other side. David could see five huge cargo ships towering above the warehouses that lined the dockside. One of them was being loaded. Wind gently buffeted the sails of a few smaller dhows as they slowly crossed from one side of the harbour to the other.

He heard the long deep blast of a ship's horn and looked to where people were stood out on the decks of a cruise liner as it sailed out of the port. Only the top two rows of cabins and the three smoking funnels in view above the town as it headed out to where David guessed the Indian Ocean must be.

The air smelt of salt and he began to feel like a kid wanting to see the ocean for the first time. His knowledge so far was restricted to his geography textbook and the odd photograph. The island, surrounded by turquoise water, was littered with new buildings. Russet coloured roofs tucked away amongst more modern, taller, office blocks and apartment buildings. Between the town and the docks were row upon row of two-storey warehouses.

The railway veered away from the road towards the port and David continued down Mombasa Road. He followed the signs for the Likoni ferry and the south. On his left was the old part of town, where arched windows and doors showed the extent of Portuguese and Middle Eastern influence. The buildings were crammed in like sardines between narrow alleyways. A lot of signs in the shop windows were written in Arabic, most of them by hand. A few people were milling around, some wearing turbans and robes, others in western dress, colourful t-shirts and shorts. Most of the people he saw were men. The few women had veils or scarves covering their faces to retain their modesty. One or two coffee shops were open for business, but that was about it.

Some empty cricket grounds and the athletics club next door seemed to be the only bastions of greenery. The rest of the town he passed on the way to the ferry had given way to high-rise buildings and new developments. He joined the handful of vehicles rolling through the tollbooth.

David paid a small fee before parking behind a Bedford truck and killing the engine.

He got out to stretch his legs and spotted a phone booth next to the almost deserted bus station. Around eight people were sitting on a covered bench. Their slumped shoulders and bored expressions evidence that they had been waiting for a long time.

Behind the terminal was a small triangular shaped park, the curve as the road swept away to follow the coastline filled with short thick-trunked trees that had been pruned for hundreds of years. Behind the thin strip of park was a row of ugly four storey buildings that seemed out of place with their tropical surroundings. To the right of them David could see a small section of the ocean at the end of the harbour. Waves broke on an unseen sandbar with an endless swathe of blue water in the background.

David pumped some change in and dialled the number for the hospital. After a few short rings it was answered and he asked to speak to one of the guards outside Koinet's room.

"Are you the same officer who was here the other day?" it was the plump nurse on reception again. He could imagine her twiddling with her crimped hair as she spoke.

"Hi, is that Nurse Dafina?" David smiled to himself.

"Oh...you remembered," she actually giggled like a fifty-something schoolgirl. "I'll go and fetch one of the officer's myself. Just hold the line."

A few minutes later she returned, puffing and panting, "I've got one of the rangers here for you Captain. I'll hand you over."

"Thanks Dafina you're a star."

"No trouble at all," he heard her giggle again as she passed the phone over.

"I think you've got some explaining to do," Damo sounded annoyed but he was talking quietly into the phone, almost whispering. "Not long after I spoke to you this morning a couple of gorillas from the GSU turned up. Guess who they were looking for? They practically interrogated us. Even threatened to arrest us for aiding and abetting a fugitive if they found out later that we had seen you or knew your whereabouts. It's a good job Rashid didn't see you at the hospital or I think the boy would have cracked."

"Shit!" David thought for a moment, "Are you sure they were from the GSU?"

"How the hell do I know? They had ID badges and looked the part," hissed Damo. "Sort of guys you wouldn't want to meet in a dark alley, if you know what I mean."

If they were for real then it meant that the scar-faced man he had seen leaving Tanui's office might be involved in all this. The man Ngozi had said was Commander Peter Abasi. If he was then David was in a lot deeper than his previous estimations, which were already bad enough. Then again it could all be a bizarre coincidence.

"Was one of them a stocky guy with a flattened nose? Looks like he might have been a heavy-weight boxer."

"That sounds like the short one with bad breath." There was a pause, "How did you know?"

"Just a wild guess."

"Who is he?"

David avoided the question. "Believe me Damo until I'm sure of the facts the less you know the better."

There was another awkward pause before Damo replied, "OK. I guess I'm going to have to trust you. But whatever you're doing you'd better do it fast. These guys didn't seem to be messing around."

"I'll bear that in mind." David had almost forgotten the reason for his call, "How's Koinet?"

"He's been awake for a couple of hours now and has got movement in his leg. The surgeon seems to think that he's out of any real danger and won't need further surgery."

By further surgery Damo meant amputation.

"That's good news. As soon as he's fit enough I want him moved somewhere safe."

"The doctor said that he won't be able to walk on the leg for weeks," replied Damo dismissively.

"I don't care if you have to drag him," snapped David. "We need to get him out of there as soon as possible." Then he remembered who he was talking to, "I'm sorry, it's just I get the feeling that we haven't got much time. Do you think that you could grab whatever medication he needs and stretcher him out of there?"

There was a long pause before Damo answered, "I suppose so, where am I taking him?"

The only suitable place to hold Koinet for a while that immediately sprang to mind belonged to

Spencer Scott. David didn't really want to involve Caitlyn's ex-boyfriend any more than he had already but there seemed to be no other alternative.

"This is what I want you to do..." He gave Damo directions to the lodge belonging to the Friends of the Masai Mara and instructions on what should be said to Scott and the other rangers.

"And Damo..." a blast from the ferry's horn as it approached caused him to pause mid-sentence. "Be careful. Make sure that you aren't followed."

Unfortunately Damo heard the sound too, "Is that a boat?"

"Look Damo I've got to go, I'll call again tomorrow."

David hung up and sprinted back to the LandRover. By the time he got inside the ramp was being lowered down to meet the concrete causeway. About thirty pedestrians and a few cyclists were waiting to get off the open topped ferry. Behind them were a truck and a couple of cars. He waited for the inbound passengers to disembark and file past before following the Bedford truck onto the ferry.

*****

The crossing took around thirty minutes. David enjoyed the time, feeling the refreshing spray on his face as he hung onto the rail at the edge of the deck. He got a better view of the Indian Ocean when they were half way across. The mouth of the estuary opened up to turquoise waters, a huge sandbar to the right that curved like a scimitar.

The cruise liner David had seen earlier was gradually getting smaller as it sailed towards the horizon.

All too soon he was back in the LandRover and driving along the coast road, heading south towards Diani Beach. The difference between Likoni and the main island of Mombasa was dramatic. There were few buildings to speak of, just an endless shantytown that stretched for miles. Eventually he came across a petrol station with a large kiosk that looked open. The windows and door protected by metal mesh.

He pulled over and made sure that the LandRover was locked, it was getting a lot of interest from a group of kids in their early teens on the other side of the street.

David went in and bought a map of the city to make his life easier. Armed with one that showed a good section of the coast including Diani Beach, a sandwich and a bottle of water, he left the shop just in time.

"Hey, beat it!" David shouted as he ran towards the jeep. The taller boy holding the coat hanger left it dangling from the window and sprinted off with his accomplice. They vanished from sight through a gap between two of the rusty tin shacks and David knew better than to chase them. Once inside the shantytown you were on their turf. Worse things could happen to a person than getting lost in the maze of interconnecting alleyways.

David got back in the jeep and carried on down the A14 towards Ukunda. Traffic was almost non-existent, only a few cars passing in the other direction. About fifteen minutes later David saw the sign he was looking for and turned off towards the coast.

When he hit Beach Road David realised that the place was bigger than he had expected. On instinct he went north and few minutes later pulled up in the car lot of one of the larger hotels.

The Diani Beach Resort and Spa was a small piece of man-made heaven. Date and palm trees next to thatched roof buildings. As he headed towards the entrance David caught a glimpse of people sunbathing on loungers at the edge of a bleached white beach. David shrugged. He had to start somewhere.

CHAPTER TWENTY-FOUR
Ngara West, Nairobi
August 18th, 1996

Maliki had decided to pick up Professor Onesimus personally. He needed a distraction, an outlet for the rage he felt eating him up.

"I'm sick of your lies!" spit flew from Maliki's mouth. "We know that it's you who has been leaking information to the Americans and the press."

He whipped back his arm and put all his weight into the punch, the professor's bottom lip burst open, ballooning up instantly and dripping blood.

"Monster!" spat Onesimus. "You and Moi's reign of terror will be over soon. I'm not the only one who knows what you've been up to."

Maliki punched him again. His knuckles were bruised but he ignored the pain and kept reigning down blows to the back of the professor's head. Long after he slumped forward.

"I think he's unconscious sir."

Gakere was one of the guards struggling to hold the professor in an upright position. The other was a Kalenjin called Kamau.

Maliki lifted up Onesimus's head and slapped his face. The professor flinched but didn't wake up.

Maliki let go and his head flopped back onto his chest.

Maliki sighed to himself and walked over to the window. He pulled back the curtain and peered out into the street.

The professor lived on the top floor in an old block of flats on Ngara Road, not far from the university. The four-storey building was falling apart. Crumbling concrete and broken windows, the stairwell stank of urine. Taking the moral high ground obviously wasn't working out that well financially for Onesimus.

"Take him down to the car and wait for me there."

"Yes, sir," replied Gakere.

Maliki watched them drag Onesimus out of the room, his floppy arms looped over their shoulders, feet dragging along the floor.

Once they were gone he started to search the apartment. It didn't take long, apart from a writing desk in the lounge and three kitchen drawers there was no other storage space. Maliki leafed through the papers lying on the flip-down desk, mostly lecture notes and household bills, the odd bit of correspondence from students or the faculty. He closed the bureau and noticed a thin drawer concealed beneath it. He pulled on the handle but nothing happened, he increased the pressure and it slid open reluctantly, squeaking in protest.

Inside he found one of Konde's anti-Moi pamphlets and a thin file containing copies of half a dozen police reports. He put the pamphlet inside and tucked the file under his arm before going through the other drawers. Emptying the contents onto the floor as he went. Satisfied that there was nowhere else to search Maliki left the apartment and closed the door quietly behind him.

As he walked down the corridor he heard the rattle of a safety chain being taken off and one of the doors in front of him opened.

An almost skeletal woman stepped out wearing a dress made from what appeared to be paisley curtains. Doubled over with the weight of the bag she carried. She glanced at Maliki through hazy white eyes and scowled before scurrying back inside her apartment and slamming the door shut. He walked past the crazy old woman's room and down the stairs.

Outside Gakere was facing away from the armoured Mercedes, watching the street. Kamau was keeping the professor company. Maliki got in the front passenger seat. There was no way he was being sandwiched in the back next to the fat academic. He glanced over his shoulder but the professor was still out cold. Gakere got in without a word, gunned the V8 engine into life and slammed on the accelerator pedal. Tyres screeched and the faint smell of burning rubber came through the air conditioner as they sped away.

*****

They slipped through the narrow archway and the Mercedes pulled to a stop in the courtyard between the main building and the cells.

Maliki turned towards Gakere, "Take him to the basement and soften him up. Let me know when he's ready to talk."

Gakere nodded, Maliki got out and strode over to the entrance. He looked up at the CCTV camera and pressed the button on the intercom. The offices were always manned, even on a Sunday night, the men taking turns to do the late shift from the barracks next door. The desk sergeant on duty must have been warned of his arrival by the guards at the gate. He answered immediately.

"Good evening Commander, what brings you in to headquarters so late?"

"Just open the door," snapped Maliki. "Or I'll have you thrown in the sand box."

Situated next to the parade square the sandbox was a three-foot square hole covered with a sheet of corrugated iron. Recruits were put inside for days on end for offences such as insubordination or not maintaining their kit. Known to the men as the 'hothouse', during the summer it was over fifty degrees in the hole. Occasionally one of the men died from dehydration. As far as Maliki was concerned it was all part of the process of weeding out the weakest.

"Sorry sir..." the rest of what the mumbling desk sergeant said was drowned out by the loud buzzing of the electronic lock as it opened.

Maliki glared at the sergeant and noticed the young man's hand trembling as he tried to hold the salute. On another day it might have pleased Maliki, but not today. He was far too preoccupied with events that seemed to be spiralling out of his control. Maliki bounded up the stairs to his office. The light was flashing on the answer machine and Maliki felt his pulse quicken. He sat down in his leather recliner and played the tape.

There were hushed voices in the background and then Lembui started speaking, "Just checking in sir. We've been outside the hospital all night and Nbeke hasn't shown up. One of the nurses on reception claims that he called this morning and the display showed the Nairobi area code. He's driving an old LandRover. We've put out an all points bulletin with a description of the vehicle as well as one of Nbeke. We're going to head back to Nairobi in the next hour. Time now is 11.40am. Our first point of call will be KWS headquarters." There was a pause and more muffled discussion before Lembui came back on, "That's all sir."

The line went dead and the machine beeped to signify that there were no more messages. Maliki's face started to twitch. He pressed the button to get a new line and dialled Gupta's number in Mombasa. He let it ring about twenty times before hanging up and trying the lodge in Tanzania but got the same result. Maliki roared as he slammed down the phone. He should have trusted his gut instinct and had this Koinet picked up from the hospital straight away, something that would be rectified in the morning. The more time that passed the surer he was that the man caught by Nbeke worked for Gupta.

There was a tap on the door, so light that Maliki wasn't sure that he had heard it. Then there was another slightly louder one.

"Come in!" he barked.

Gakere poked his head through the door, "He's awake sir and asking for a lawyer."

"Is he now?" Maliki sneered, "Tell him that I'll be over in a minute to explain his human rights."

Gakere looked confused, "Sir?"

"Just do it!"

"Right away, sir," Gakere backed out of the room and the door closed softly.

Maliki rubbed at the scars to ease the discomfort. He hated not being in control of his own face. Once Nbeke and Gupta were taken care of maybe he would take that trip to Switzerland. A plastic surgeon there claimed that he could use skin grafts from Maliki's buttocks to cover the welts. Maliki nodded to himself. Once Gupta's mess was cleared up he would get rid of the annoying tic.

CHAPTER TWENTY-FIVE
Diani Beach, Mombasa
August 18th, 1996

David walked past the busy reception desk, heading for the steps that led down to the lounge and bar area. An overweight man wearing floral swimming shorts, his bald scalp and shoulders burnt red, was holding up the queue of guests waiting to check in. His accent was thick and guttural. The pot-bellied tourist spoke using slang that David didn't recognise.

"Give away man! Are you telling me there's not one spare room in this whole bleeding hotel? A posh place like this, it's a disgrace." The man turned to look at the couple behind him and shook his head before continuing, "If that really is the case then you better get wore air conditioner fixed and pronto or there'll be hell to pay. Come on henny we're gan doon the beach."

There was something unnatural about the colour of the woman's skin that David assumed to be his wife. It was an almost luminous orange. She followed him with her head down as he stormed off. Her straw sunhat almost touching his hairy back, flesh overflowing from a polka-dot bikini.

There were a few wry smiles from the other guests. An olive skinned lady in her fifties, wearing a white see-through dress over her gold bikini, raised a manicured eyebrow. A man carrying a sleeping girl, her head drooped over his shoulder, moved aside to let them pass.

David noticed that there were quite a few children waiting with their parents, a mixture of tiredness and excitement evident on their young faces. With most of Europe on holiday he guessed that this would be the hotel's busiest time of the year.

The lounge was sleek and stylish. Square-cut sofas and chairs that were low to the floor, made from teak and covered with yellow leather cushions. Some of the sculpted armchairs were clad in zebra print to make them stand out from the others. A single barman was serving drinks to a handful of people.

David glanced out through the patio doors. The guests not enjoying the beach were bathing in the kidney shaped swimming pool or one of its smaller satellites. A man made river ran out from one end of the main pool, it looped lazily around a pumice stone island covered in flowers and small palms before returning to rejoin the other side.

David couldn't help noticing that nearly all of the people using the hotel's facilities were white. He perched on one of the cubist bar stools and caught the barman's attention.

"What can I get you sir?" the welcoming barman had an instant smile that reminded him of Haji.

"I'll have a Tusker please."

The barman nodded as if it was a fine choice and returned a few seconds later with a cold bottle and a chilled glass from the freezer. He placed them on a couple of paper drinks mats, taken with a flourish from a silver dispenser.

"Will there be anything else, sir?"

David glanced at the bronze nametag on the breast of his jacket. He nodded and lowered his voice, "Information, if you have it Samuel. I'm looking for a man called Deepak Gupta."

Samuel's smile vanished for a split-second. He shook his head, "I'm afraid I've never heard of him." This time the smile didn't reach his eyes, "Is he a friend of yours?"

"Not exactly." David poured some beer into his glass, "More a friend of a friend." He took a swig, his lips almost sticking to the frosted glass, "I was told he might have some work for me."

"What kind of work?" Samuel picked up a cloth and started to polish the bar-top. Something in the way he did it told David that he wasn't just making polite conversation.

"Taking tourists hunting that kind of thing," he watched Samuel's face for a reaction over the rim of his glass. "My friend told me that Gupta runs safaris."

The barman stopped polishing and glanced up and down the counter before answering, "If I was you I would look for work somewhere else. From what I've heard around town he's not someone you want to get involved with."

David's pulse quickened, "Do you know where I can find him?"

Samuel shook his head, "Weren't you listening to me?"

"Look, thanks for your concern but I can look after myself." David took a 200-shilling note from his pocket and placed it on the counter, "Now, where does he live?"

*****

Gupta's house was the last one on Diani Beach Road. Overlooking the sandy delta where a small river met the Indian Ocean. The other side of the creek was thick jungle, the odd coconut tree rising above the canopy.

A group of six men wearing shorts were using a square shaped net to catch the fish trapped against the sandbar by the low tide. Their skin the deepest black David had ever seen. Another fisherman was stationed in a canoe shaped boat with a cross-frame connected to wooden floats for stability. From time to time he slapped the surface with his paddle to drive the tiny silver-blue fish skipping across the water into the net.

David turned left up a sandy track heading away from the ocean. He drove past the chain-link fence with grey-rattan matting attached that belonged to Gupta's property. Gated driveways lead off to four other thatched villas down the track, none of them quite as grand as Gupta's. After a few hundred yards the track came to an end amongst some palms. David threaded the LandRover between the trees until he was sure that he was out of sight and killed the engine.

He took his pistol from the glove box. David checked that the safety was on and stuffed it into the waistband of his combats. Then he made sure that the gaffa tape, torch and tape recorder where in his rucksack before zipping it shut. David hesitated before opening the door. Although he had stretched the boundaries a little everything he had done so far was strictly speaking legal.

He took a deep breath and turned the handle. Taking care to make as little noise as possible, David locked the dust covered LandRover and made his way over the matt of fallen palm fronds. He stopped behind some bushes at the end of the track and a quick glance confirmed that it was still empty. David slipped out from cover and sauntered down the road.

A couple of the villas were obviously in use, cars in the driveway, towels hanging from the verandas. Voices and splashing coming from what must be the pool of another. Although the rattan was supposed to act as a screen it was old and weathered. As he walked along the track David caught glimpses of Gupta's place, enough to see that the shutters were closed. He reached the main road and turned left towards the creek. As he walked by the entrance his suspicions were confirmed.

The drive was empty and the house locked up, all the shutters battened and padlocked security gates covered the front door.

David felt his hopes start to fade, Gupta was the only real lead he had. What if the poacher decided to go on the run and not come home? No, David shook his head. Even if Gupta did intend to disappear he would need money and want some of his clothes and possessions. It was only a matter of time before he came back.

There was a rumble from his stomach and David realised that he hadn't eaten all day. An open stretch of scrubland separated him from the strip of resorts and the beach. Nearest to him was an older cafe set apart from the newer developments. The thatched roof and bamboo walls were more faded than its neighbours. David hooked his thumbs into the straps of his rucksack and walked towards it.

*****

David felt much better after wolfing a steak baguette and washing it down with bottle of water. What he really wanted was another beer but didn't want to slow down his reactions. While he ate David kept one eye on the entrance to Gupta's but nobody showed up. After hanging around for a little over an hour, he paid up and thanked the bikini-clad girl behind the counter.

David left the few patrons eating ice creams and drinking sundowners behind him and found a tree near to the creek to sit down. He leant against it facing the river, keeping up the appearance of a holidaymaker enjoying the scenery. As the light faded the fishermen packed away their nets and went home for the night. The beach stretching up the coast in front of him soon became deserted.

He nodded off a few hours later and woke with a start, unsure of how long he had been out. Worried that Gupta might have been and gone whilst he was asleep. The house was still shrouded in darkness and eventually David convinced himself that he was being paranoid. The minutes and hours passed by slowly and David struggled to stay awake. He got to his feet and stretched his legs a few times, wandering over to the creek to splash water on his face. Light gusts of wind brought the sound of faded music from further down the beach in waves, garbled by the noise of the surf. A full moon reflected off the ocean, bathing the surf in an ethereal white light.

As midnight came and went David started to think about what he would do if Gupta didn't come back. There was still Koinet, but without his boss that was where the trail ended. Against his better judgement David suspected that Tanui was involved, and by the sounds of it so was the head of the GSU. The two goons turning up at the hospital in Narok could be standard procedure but it was too much of a coincidence that they were the same ones he had seen outside KWS headquarters. The more he thought about it the more it made sense that Tanui and Commander Abasi were working together. The GSU officers who had been snooping around must have tipped off the Deputy Director that he wasn't in Purungat.

A pair of headlights appeared and bobbed their way down the bumpy road towards him. David was instantly on full alert but avoided any movement as the lights drew closer. By the deep-throated sound that the engine made it was something larger than a car, maybe a 4x4.

Eventually the vehicle slowed down and pulled to a stop in front of Gupta's gates. A tall thin man in flowing robes and turban got out from the driver's side of what appeared to be some sort of small truck. Possibly a Nissan Atlas guessed David looking at the shape. He went over to the gates and a few seconds later David heard the sound of a chain rattling before they were swung open. As the man turned back towards the truck he was caught in the headlights. David glimpsed a bony face, thin nose and long grey beard before the Indian shielded his face against the glare and got back in the cab.

David bolted across the few hundred yards to the gate. He reached for the handle of the pistol in his waistband and pulled it out before following the truck trundle down the drive. It came to a stop in front of the garage. David crouched behind it and waited for the door to open. His signal was the sound of crunching gravel as the driver's feet made contact. He rounded the vehicle and shoved the pistol into the man's back before he could close the door.

"Don't make a sound. If you do I'll put a bullet right through your spine." David pushed the muzzle of his pistol into the man's back for emphasis. "As long as you do exactly as I say then you won't be hurt. Nod if you understand me, Mr Gupta."

The man jerked his head repeatedly, "Yes, yes. Now what is all this about? Who sent you?"

At least he had the right man. David lifted his arm and brought the butt of the pistol down.

Gupta fell to the floor like a sack of lead. David leant over and felt his neck for a pulse but couldn't find one.

CHAPTER TWENTY-SIX
Gupta's Residence, Mombasa
August 19th, 1996

David started to panic thinking that he must have hit Gupta too hard. Then he felt it, the faintest flicker beneath his fingertips. He sighed with relief and stuffed the gun back into his pants before shrugging out of the straps of his rucksack. He fumbled around, wondering why it was so hard to find the gaffa tape when there were so few items in the bag. Eventually he did and taped the unconscious Gupta's arms behind his back. He pulled off another strip of tape and covered the poacher's mouth for good measure.

David searched Gupta's robes and the ground around him for what seemed like ages but couldn't find the keys. The process of elimination led him back to the truck, where they were dangling from the ignition. It took him a few minutes to locate the right keys for the metal recas and open the door. He carried Gupta inside and dumped him unceremoniously in the hallway. David closed the front door behind him and turned on his pocket torch. Hooding the beam with his hand he made sure that all the other doors and shutters were firmly shut before finally hitting the light switch.

Gupta started to writhe on the floor and then his eyes opened. At first dull and distant, then realisation must have hit home and they opened wide with terror. He was struggling to say something beneath the gaffa tape.

David ignored him and took in his surroundings. There were a number of doors leading off the tiled hallway. A double set straight ahead that must lead to the back garden and two single doors to his left. Between them a leopard skin hung from the wall, its glassy eyes stared back at him and appeared to come to life for a second in the torchlight.

To the right was a boxed archway with squat granite pillars on either side that led to the lounge. He had a brief look inside but there was nothing suitable, it was all soft-backed sofas and upholstered chairs. Amongst the various hunting trophies a huge buffalo's head dominated one of the walls, but the centrepiece of the room was above the stone fireplace. Two crossed tusks over six feet in length, held in place with wrought iron brackets. Gupta must be doing well if he could afford to leave them hanging up as decoration. They must be worth at least $15,000 each. David gritted his teeth, and getting more valuable with every elephant that Gupta and his men slaughtered.

David resisted the urge to kick Gupta where he lay and tried the doors on the other side. The first belonged to a long hallway with a series of doors that he guessed were bedrooms. He opened the second one and found what he was looking for.

A few minutes later he had Gupta strapped to one of the kitchen chairs with gaffa tape, arms pinned behind his back. David put his rucksack on the worktop behind Gupta and took out the tape recorder. Coughing to mask the sound he pressed record and set it down quietly. He went around to the other side of the table and pulled the pistol from behind his back, took the safety off and pointed it at Gupta's chest to get his attention. David took a seat and placed the gun on the surface between them. The evidence might not stand up in court but David didn't care. He smiled at Gupta, trying to act as if he did this sort of thing all the time.

"I'm only going to give you one shot at this," David nodded at the gun. "In a moment I'm going to take the tape off your mouth and ask a few questions. If I don't like the answers that I hear, or you try to shout for help, then this discussion will be terminated. Nod if you agree Mr Gupta."

Gupta's eyes bulged like an animal caught in a trap. He twisted his head around as much as he could, as if expecting salvation to be found in the kitchen units. Fortunately he couldn't turn his head far enough to see the dim red light flashing on the tape recorder. Finally his shoulders slumped, he looked at David and nodded once.

"Good," maintaining the smile he reached across and ripped the tape from Gupta's mouth. A significant amount of Gupta's beard came with it.

"Shit!" Gupta's face was red raw around his mouth. In almost any other given situation David would have found it amusing. "You bastard, you'll pay for this!"

David put his hand on the gun, "Now, now, Mr Gupta, I'm trying to be patient but one more little outburst and I really will have to end this interview."

"You're either stupid or have no idea who I am! Now untie me and maybe you will be allowed to live!"

"Right now I seem to be the one holding all the aces Mr Gupta." David twisted his hand so that the butt of the gun was resting on the table and pointing at Gupta's chest before continuing.

"Maybe I should introduce myself before we go any further. My name is Captain David Nbeke. I'm a ranger in the Kenyan Wildlife Service. A couple of nights ago one of my men was shot dead whilst out on patrol in the Masai Mara."

"I don't know what you're talking about! I've been in Mombasa for the last..."

"Please," David held up his hand. "Let me finish before you say anything else. It will save us both a lot of time and you a lot of pain." David kept his tone neutral, trying to maintain the impression that this was all business as usual. He found himself beginning to get into the role of bad cop as he glared at Gupta.

"On the same night that my officer was murdered we encountered one of your employees in the south the reserve, attempting to poach the horns of two black rhino. He was shot in the leg during the resulting firefight and taken into custody. When questioned the man identified himself as Koinet and you as his employer. He's willing to testify and based on what he's told us I could have you arrested and held without bail until it goes to court."

The last part was stretching the truth a little but Gupta obviously believed it. He closed his eyes and let out a deep breath before opening them and speaking, "You can't arrest me. When he finds out that I'm in custody he'll have me killed. Nobody can touch him."

The way he said it was matter of fact, a statement.

"Try and concentrate on the present," David cocked the hammer of his Browning. Untouchable didn't fit the Deputy Director's status. He took a gamble, "I'm assuming you mean Commander Abasi?"

Gupta's nod was barely perceptible and David needed him to respond for the tape recorder, "Sorry, I didn't quite catch that?"

"Yes, of course I mean Commander Abasi. Who else would I mean?" Gupta shook his head, "You didn't know, did you?"

"To tell you the truth I wasn't a hundred percent sure but I am now, thanks." David smiled, "What about Deputy Director Tanui?"

"Who's Tanui? I've never heard of him."

Gupta was either a very good actor or he was telling the truth. David decided it was the latter, he had already given up the Commander of the GSU, in comparison the Deputy Director was small fry. If there was a connection between them then it was obvious that Gupta didn't know anything about it.

"You said earlier that Commander Abasi would have you killed if you were put in jail," David changed tact, half out of curiosity, half for the benefit of the recorder. "What makes you think that."

Gupta started to tremble, "Because that's where he found me in the first place."

"What do you mean?"

Gupta looked up at the ceiling for a few seconds before answering, "I'll talk if you can guarantee my protection. I want immunity and safe passage out of the country, with a British or Canadian passport and a new identity."

David noticed that Gupta wasn't asking for money. Then he remembered the tusks hanging up in the lounge.

"I can't offer you a new identity. But we'll make sure that no harm comes to you until this is all over and Abasi is safely locked away behind bars."

"That's not good enough. Haven't you been listening to me? As long as he's alive and I'm still in Kenya I won't be safe." Gupta's eyes misted over.

David nodded, "From what you've told me Commander Abasi isn't going to be happy when he finds out that you've been talking to me. As far as I'm concerned you deserve to die for what you've done but right now you're more useful to me alive."

Gupta's head drooped forward and his eyes seemed to be fixed on the table. Then he began mumbling to himself in what David guessed must be an Indian dialect.

"Let's start at the beginning," David leant back in his chair but kept the gun trained on Gupta.

"You said that you met Commander Abasi in prison. Is that when you started working for him?"

Gupta didn't answer.

"I asked you a question!" David slapped the table to get his attention, "When did you start working for Abasi?"

Gupta looked up, his eyes puffy and bloodshot, "I was arrested for poaching and put in Kamiti Maximum Security Prison..."

He paused, as if considering his next statement. "There was a shootout in Tsavo when we were ambushed crossing the border with a shipment of ivory." He shrugged dismissively, "One of the rangers died."

So this wasn't the first time Gupta had killed one of his colleagues. David put the gun down on the desk and rested his hands in his lap. He didn't trust himself not to pull the trigger and blow the snivelling turd away.

Gupta continued, "Abasi came to prison and said that he could arrange for my release if I agreed to work for him." He shook his head, "Of course I agreed. You can't imagine what it was like in there...the stabbings...the rape...I would have sold my own mother to get out." His head dropped back down, "Now I know that I would have been better off taking my chances and serving the time. Abasi is like the devil, once he gets his claws into you he never lets go."

"When did this happen?"

"More than a decade ago." Gupta sighed, "It was 1982."

"And you never tried to leave?"

"Others did and they ended up at the bottom of the harbour." Gupta shook his head, "You can't run away from him, he has spies everywhere. Like I said, he's the devil."

"So you've been poaching elephant and rhino for Abasi for around fourteen years?"

Gupta either didn't notice that David was structuring the questions or didn't care, "Something like that, does it really matter how long it's been?"

David leant forward and put his hand back on the Browning, "I'll decide what's important and what's not. So how does it work?"

"What do you mean?"

"Don't play dumb Mr Gupta. I'm beginning to lose my patience," he put his finger on the trigger. "How do you get the tusks to Mombasa and where are they shipped to?"

Gupta mumbled something under his breath and then shrugged as if it didn't matter, "Abasi owns a timber export company. We hide the goods inside pallets of wood and bring them by truck to Kilindini Harbour. From there they are shipped out to Hong Kong."

David digested what he had just said, "How do you get across the border into Kenya?"

"We come through Holili. The guards there are on Abasi's payroll. He's got connections everywhere."

A few trucks carrying timber from the rich forests in the north of Tanzania to Mombasa probably wouldn't arouse much suspicion. Abasi was obviously taking extra precautions in paying off the border guards.

"What's the name of Abasi's company?"

"The 'EAST AFRICA TIMBER COMPANY', there's a warehouse on the waterfront near the docks."

"Have you ever met any of the buyers?"

"No," Gupta swayed his head like a snake. "Abasi would never allow that. But there is only one buyer as far as I know, he's Chinese."

"How do you know if you've never met him?"

Gupta laughed for the first time and David was hit by a foul mixture of tobacco and what smelt like decaying meat, "I heard Abasi calling him a yellow belly bastard once when he was on the phone to him." His brow furrowed in concentration, "They were talking about a meeting the next day in Nairobi."

"How did Abasi get the scars on his face?" he wanted Gupta to confirm Abasi's description for the record.

"I don't know," Gupta shrugged. "He's always had them."

David had heard enough, he pointed the gun away from Gupta and gently lowered the hammer before putting on the safety. Getting up from the chair he tucked the weapon back into his trousers and walked behind Gupta. Turning the recorder off first he stuffed it back into the rucksack and slipped his arms through the straps. David picked up what was left of the roll of gaffa tape and walked back around to where Gupta could see him.

"You stay there a minute while I fetch the car."
He tore off another strip, "I promise that I'll be
right back."

The life force seemed to have gone out of Gupta
and he hung limply from the chair. He made no
attempt to resist as David put the tape over his
mouth.

He left Gupta in the kitchen and went outside.
As he walked past the Nissan he noticed the half
hidden logo on the side of the cab for first time. The
top of what resembled a Christmas tree with
writing shaped in an arch above it was poking out
of the mud covering the door.

David scraped off the dirt with his hand, 'EAST
AFRICA TIMBER COMPANY'. Instinctively he
went around to the back of the truck and lifted the
tarpaulin. David expected to see a pallet of wood or
the creamy tip of an ivory tusk, there was nothing
but a dark void.

CHAPTER TWENTY-SEVEN
Maliki's Residence, Nairobi
August 19ᵗʰ, 1996

Maliki had become increasingly agitated over the last twenty-four hours. There had still been no sign of Captain Nbeke, or any word from Gupta. On top of that Professor Mutungi was proving to be a stubborn old fool. They had to resuscitate him twice after overdoing the electric shock treatment but the fat bastard still wouldn't talk. He allowed himself the briefest of smiles, which only served to set his lip off and annoy him further. He had left the badly beaten and dazed Professor in one of the cells in the early hours of the morning, instructing the guards that he should receive no food or water. The arrogant academic would be singing like a canary by sundown.

As a result of the late night activities Maliki woke up later than usual and it was nearly 10am by the time he sat down for breakfast in his study. Jozi served him scrambled eggs, toast and orange juice on a silver tray at his desk.

"Will that be all?" asked the benevolent Swahili.

"For now," grunted Maliki.

The years of service had taken their toll. Jozi looked twenty years older than Maliki even though he was a few years younger. His skin was weathered and wrinkled like that of a rhinoceros hide. He moved slowly and deliberately with a bent back and stooped posture, as if in constant pain. Jozi's subservient demeanour was that of an old dog that had endured years of physical and mental abuse from its master but remains faithful. Cowering, keeping his eyes on Maliki as he retreated from the room.

Jozi had always been afraid of him, ever since they had met on the streets of Mombasa. They once shared a blanket to keep warm in the dilapidated warehouse. After being disgraced and expelled from the tribe Maliki needed someone to take his anger out on. Jozi had been the unfortunate recipient on many occasions.

Maliki felt no gratitude. Even though it was Jozi who had set him on the course to wealth and power. He had got the information by threatening to kill Jozi one cold and windy night under the blanket. The Masons were supposed to be on holiday in England and the house empty, ripe for the picking. But they weren't. Maliki was shot while trying to break in. Luckily the Masons took pity on him. Rather than hand him over to the mercy of the police they decided to take him in and educate him in the Christian way.

Maliki was given his own room and went to school with the Masons' children, Douglas and Katie. On the surface he responded well and did as he was told, all the time resenting their stupid beliefs. Jozi was the only person alive who knew that he had slit the Masons' throats as they slept and emptied the safe. Maliki smiled to himself as he absentmindedly forked scrambled eggs into his mouth. Ironically it was Jozi's fear that kept him alive.

The telephone on the corner of his desk started to ring. The long shrill tone signifying that the call was being patched through from his office at GSU headquarters. Maliki put down his fork and picked up the receiver.

"Yes?"

"It's Sabore, sir."

At least it was the more intelligent of the two. He was well aware that Lembui was being talked into making all the calls bearing bad tidings. Maybe it was good news.

"Have you found Nbeke?"

"Err...no sir." Maliki's question put Sabore off his stride but he recovered quickly, "We have found out that someone at the Elephant Orphanage has been spending a lot of time with him recently. The new vet there, an Irish woman called Dr Caitlyn Brennan. According to one of the keepers Captain Nbeke was seen leaving with her on Saturday afternoon."

Maliki digested the information quickly, "Have you questioned her yet?"

"No sir, I wanted to speak to you first. She's out in the Park with the elephants and Lembui's keeping an eye on her car to make sure that she doesn't leave."

Maliki rubbed at the scars on his face with his free hand and took a moment to think, "You've done the right thing Sabore. Don't talk to anyone else there. I want you to follow her and see where she goes. Find out where she lives. Call me when you have something. Don't go anywhere near this Dr Brennan or Captain Nbeke without informing me first. Is that understood?"

"Yes sir. I'll let you know immediately..." Sabore's reply was cut short as Maliki pressed the button in the cradle of the rotary phone.

He dialled '0' and was put through to headquarters on the line reserved for his use only.

"Good morning Commander," the sergeant on duty who answered after a couple of rings tried to sound friendly but Maliki could hear the resentment in his voice. "What can I do for you, sir?"

"I want somebody picked up and brought to the cells for questioning, have you got something to write with?"

"Yes sir, go ahead."

"His name's Koinet," Maliki allowed himself the briefest of smiles. Deputy Director Tanui would probably blow a blood vessel when he found out, "A poacher that was caught in the Maasai Mara by the KWS. He's currently under guard at Narok hospital."

He instructed the sergeant to inform him when it was done and then hung up. Maliki grinned and stood up from behind his desk, pleased that at least something was happening. There was work to do, first the obstinate Professor and then the Irish woman. Instinct told Maliki that she would lead him to the interfering Captain.

CHAPTER TWENTY-EIGHT
Voi, Northwest of Mombasa
August 19th, 1996

David checked the clock on the dashboard, nearly 10am. For over three hours they had been driving through the monotonous and unforgiving landscape. The lush green tropical forests that hugged the coastline and the hills around Mombasa left far behind them. It had been a stressful wait for the ferry in Likoni and they had to fight their way through the rush hour traffic. But since then the rest of the journey had passed uneventfully.

The railway running beside the road drew a red line through the grey desert tundra. Richer earth concealed below the surface had been turned over to lay the tracks. Elsewhere patches of rusty red stood out from the chalky whites and sandstones of the veldt around them. An endless savannah of dry grassland only interrupted by the odd stunted tree.

Surprisingly the barren wasteland still supported some life. A herd of impala skipped and jumped gracefully as they ran away from the sound of the approaching LandRover. They were dainty looking antelope with short curved antlers that pointed forwards above hare like ears. Black teardrop markings around their eyes and white bellies. The adults had matching dark lines down their sides and the backs of their hind legs.

Later he saw a flock of five ostrich digging in the dirt for grubs. Three drab brown females and two dark black males with white tail feathers. They popped their heads up from the sand and pointed duck-like beaks towards the jeep as they drove past.

The going was tortuously slow. The road surface riddled with potholes, some of them over half a meter in depth. Navigating the craters made it almost impossible to overtake without risking losing a wheel or breaking an axle. David had been stuck behind a crawling refrigerated meat truck for over half an hour. The company's address in Nairobi and telephone number written on the doors at the back imprinted on his mind. To make matters worse there was little airflow inside the jeep and it was baking hot.

Looking at the state of the road David wondered how many people were actually employed by the highways agency. He sighed to himself, AWA, Africa Wins Again. To most Africans the phrase was a proud statement of achievement but to David it represented the corruption that riddled the continent.

David glanced over at Gupta in the passenger seat. He was snoring and appeared to be sleeping soundly. His arms were still bound behind his back and David had taken the added precaution of taping his feet together once he was inside the LandRover. He had removed the strip from his mouth to stop Gupta looking like a kidnap victim.

He spotted the spattering of ragged hills around Voi in the distance and could see the tops of low buildings poking above the trees. The savannah gave way abruptly to a stark line marking the edge of an aloe vera plantation. The farm stretched for almost a mile along either side of the road. David marvelled at so many cacti growing in one place. With funding and medicines in short supply his Aunty Farisi often used the healing qualities of the sap to treat bruises and small lacerations. He resisted the urge to stop and pick her some of the huge spiny leaves. David felt guilt a pang of guilt. He hadn't spoken to them since leaving Kisii to meet Spencer Scott.

He pulled into the Shell petrol station on the outskirts of Voi and parked the LandRover at the far end of the lot. Facing away from the kiosk so that Gupta couldn't draw attention to himself. He tuned the radio into 98.4 Capital FM and turned up the volume to some soulless pop music. David locked the doors and walked over to the kiosk.

The payphone was out of order. After some haggling with the Kikuyu attendant he paid fifty shillings to use the staff telephone behind the counter. David took Bernstein's card from his wallet and dialled the number for the hotel on the back. This time he was put through to the room and Bernstein answered.

"David!" exclaimed the American. "Good to hear your voice. I've been worried since I got your cryptic message. What's been happening?"

David brought him up to speed on events, including his chat with Gupta and suspicions regarding Commander Abasi. He failed to mention that he was holding Gupta prisoner, or that he had taped his interrogation.

"Shit! You have been busy." Bernstein put his excitement on hold for a moment, "Sorry to hear about your friend, but what exactly do you need me for?"

"I want you to use your contacts and do some digging, find out everything you can about Commander Abasi and this 'EAST AFRICA TIMBER COMPANY'." David frowned to himself, "And while you're at it the Deputy Director as well. I've got a feeling that he's involved in all this."

"Am I going to get exclusivity?"

"You're the only person I've spoken to about this," grunted David. "And remember not a word to anyone until we've got more proof. Lives are at stake, yours and mine included. I'll call again this evening when I get to Nairobi."

"OK, but you won't find me at the hotel. I'm moving somewhere a little safer." David dug for the pen in his combat pockets and scribbled down the number.

"Ask for Seymour Dewitt, he'll know where I am." Bernstein paused, "What do you plan to do next?"

"I'm not sure yet but I'll be in touch."

He hung up before Bernstein could ask any more questions and dialled Caitlyn's number. As expected there was no answer, she would probably be at work by now. He considered calling the orphanage but decided against it. As part of the KWS facility all calls would go through the switchboard and be easy to monitor. Not for the first time he regretted involving her, albeit indirectly. If Abasi's goons started asking questions at the orphanage then she could be in real danger. The less contact he had with her until this was all over the better. But he needed to warn her somehow that the GSU were involved.

He made one more call to the hospital in Narok. An indignant receptionist, whose name David didn't recognise, informed him that Koinet and the rangers had disappeared in the middle of the night.

"This is most unorthodox and a complaint will be made by our Chief Surgeon. There are procedures to be followed you know..."

David cut her off and replaced the receiver, hoping that Damo had followed his orders and moved the prisoner. With no way of contacting Spencer Scott he would just have to wait until he got there to find out.

A 'POSTA KENYA' sign hung above the counter and there was a stationary stand next to it. Before returning to the jeep David picked up a pack of envelopes and a book of stamps, along with some stale looking chicken sandwiches and a bottle of water.

Gupta was awake and watched him lean on the bonnet and scribble a note to his Aunty. David wrote that he was fine and asked her to put the tape in a safe place until his return. He shielded the letter from Gupta with his free hand and wrote the address on the envelope. As he walked back to the post box he took the miniature tape from his pocket and slipped it inside the envelope.

Once again he hated having to involve someone close to him but travelling with Gupta and the evidence was too much like carrying all his eggs in one basket. As he dropped the incriminating package through the slot David consoled himself with the fact that nobody else knew about the tape and his Aunty Farisi was not connected to the investigation in any way.

*****

"I really need to piss," grunted Gupta.

He had been moaning for over an hour and David could do without the stench of urine being added to Gupta's body odour. They were about ten miles from Nairobi, close to a settlement called Athi River. There would be little other opportunity to stop before they hit the town centre. David reluctantly turned onto a small track. Half a mile found later he found a dry riverbed out of site from the main road. He followed it for a few hundred yards, pulled to a stop and left the engine running.

He took the gun from his waistband and pointed it at Gupta's lap, "Alright let's make this quick and no funny business, or I'll blow that thing off."

David got out and had a look around before opening the door and helping Gupta out, "Here will do, squat down there next to the jeep."

"What?" Gupta looked put out.

"I thought you needed a piss?" David smiled, "You didn't really expect me to untie you? If you're wearing underpants then I'll pull them down for you but that's as far as it goes."

As it turned out Gupta wasn't wearing any so David was spared the experience. He watched from a distance as Gupta squatted next to the door of the LandRover. Leaning his back against the side for support. Some of the urine splashed off the sun baked ground and stained the hem of his robes.

"You bastard!" exclaimed Gupta. "You'll pay for treating me like a dog!"

"That's all you are Gupta, a rabid dog." David grinned, "Now get back inside before I decide to put you down."

Gupta looked like he might say something else but the pain stopped him. David pulled him to his feet by his ear and bundled him into the passenger seat. He slammed the door shut before Gupta had a chance to react.

By the time they rejoined the highway the traffic had built up going into Athi River. Vehicles were nose to tail and crawling forward at a snail's pace. Eventually a bus driver allowed David to enter the stream of motorists.

He wondered whether it was an accident or road works causing the hold-up. As they approached the bridge into town the reason for the delay became apparent. GSU officers armed with machine guns were manning a temporary roadblock. A series of oil barrels forced the vehicles to slow down between them. Adrenalin pumped through his veins and a voice inside his head screamed at him to floor the accelerator.

David calmly pulled off into a side street and passed a weathered looking sign that read 'GREENPARK ESTATE'.

"Please Captain, I'm begging you! Turn around and take me back to Mombasa and I will pay you handsomely. I can get a boat from there to Karachi or Mumbai. Shall we say $50,000?"

When David didn't answer he kept talking, the panic evident in his rapidly spoken words, "I told you that as long as I am in Kenya then I am not safe...let's call it $100,000. Think about what you could do with all that money. You would be set up for life."

David ignored Gupta's blabbering and continued to where the street and rows of unfinished bungalows ended in an unnatural sand dune. David guessed that bulldozers had created the ridge when they flattened the land to make way for the new development. He gunned the engine and the LandRover careered up the slope, wheels tearing into the sand as they bit for purchase. The jeep flew off the top of the mound and the engine revved wildly as the wheels came free of the ground. They landed with a crash and the chassis groaned in protest. Gupta cried out in pain as he was thrown forward and his head struck the dashboard. The front wheels were jolted off course on impact and the jeep threatened to topple over. David wrenched the wheel back in the opposite direction and accelerated gently to correct the skid.

Then they were tearing across the tundra, heading north away from the town. He checked the mirrors and looked back over his shoulder towards the abandoned development but there was nobody following them. His extravagant manoeuvre seemed to have gone unnoticed. David lifted his foot off the accelerator and slowed to a less reckless pace.

"You're fucking crazy!" exclaimed Gupta. There was blood running down his face from a cut on his forehead.

All things considered David was beginning to think that Gupta might be right. But his gut told him that the roadblock was no coincidence. Commander Abasi was stepping up the search for him.

After a few miles they hit a dirt road and David turned west towards Nairobi, heading for the maze of villages and townships that surrounded the city.

CHAPTER TWENTY-NINE
Outside Caitlyn's Apartment, Nairobi
August 19th, 1996

Maliki peered up through the bulletproof glass at Caitlyn's apartment. It was the only one on the top floor with the lights on.

His car was parked on the opposite side of the street, next to the park. Beside the sedan that Lembui and Sabore were using. The two GSU officers had joined him in the Mercedes ten minutes earlier and briefed him on Dr Brennan's movements. Maliki tried not to breath through his nose. Gakere was at the wheel and it was beginning to stink of sweat and testosterone.

"Turn the AC up!" snorted Maliki. He didn't want to take the risk of opening the window and lowering the defences of his armour plated sanctuary. He turned and looked at Sabore, "You're sure that's her apartment?"

"Yes, we followed her here after work," Sabore nodded. "After Dr Brennan went inside we spoke to the caretaker. He confirmed that she lives in apartment 4C on the fourth floor facing the park."

Lembui was checking the action on his Glock. There was a loud click from the front seat as the mechanism slid back into place.

"And nobody fitting Nbeke's description has been in or out since you arrived?"

"No sir."

Maliki had another thought, "Were the lights on when you got here?"

Sabore frowned, "No, they came on about twenty minutes after Dr Brennan got home."

"Good, Gakere you stay here and keep an eye out for Captain Nbeke. If he shows up let him get inside the building, but don't let him out. The rest of you are coming with me." Maliki smiled wickedly, "Let's go and pay this Dr Brennan a visit."

Despite the bravado Maliki was as on edge and the smile turned into a grimace as his face started to twitch. He had been interrupted interrogating the Professor that afternoon by a call from one of the officers sent up to Narok. According to hospital staff the KWS had removed Koinet from his room sometime during the night. There was no trace of the officers or the patient when the nurse went to do her rounds at 6am. Maliki warned the lieutenant who was leading the four-man team not to bother coming back to headquarters unless they found Koinet.

The Deputy Director had sounded surprised when Maliki called him afterwards. Tanui vehemently denied any knowledge of Koinet or the rangers' whereabouts. There was of course the possibility that the arrogant bastard was lying to him, but he sounded genuine. By all accounts the Captain had gone off the reservation and taken some of his braves with him.

At first he had thought that Nbeke was a thorn in his side that could easily be pulled out and forgotten. Now he was beginning to think there was more to it than that. Nbeke and Koinet's disappearances were somehow connected to Gupta's. The Captain had also been seen with Bernstein in the Maasai Mara. What was he doing with the meddlesome reporter? He needed to know what was going on. Maybe this Irish woman could give him some of the answers.

Lembui got out of the front and checked the street before opening Maliki's door. Staying close to his flanks they waited for a gap in the traffic and then shepherded him across the street. Sabore glanced into the lobby and rang the caretaker's buzzer.

"Yes, who is it?" the voice was male and elderly.

"It's Lieutenant Kibet, we talked earlier Mr Chigwe," said Sabore leaning close to the intercom. "Can you open the door please? We need to come inside."

Maliki's men carried fake badges identifying them as regular Kenyan Police. People were generally less scared of the local officers and it helped to cover their tracks when the circumstance required it.

There was a brief delay before Mr Chigwe replied, "Do you have a warrant?"

Maliki's lip started to twitch and he pushed Sabore out of the way, "Listen Mr Chigwe we only want to talk to Dr Brennan. If you don't open this door right now we'll arrest you for obstructing police business."

"Oh." There was another pause before the caretaker continued, "I suppose you'd better come in then."

The intercom went dead and the door clicked open. Lembui lead the way and they rode the elevator to the fourth floor in silence. The two bodyguards drew their weapons and released the safety catches before they got to Caitlyn's apartment.

Sabore and Maliki stood on either side of the door and Maliki nodded. Lembui kicked at the lock with his boot. There was a loud cracking noise as the wood splintered and the door was flung inwards.

Lembui charged into the apartment headfirst like a wounded bull, with Sabore and Maliki close behind. The light was on in the lounge ahead and Lembui ran towards it. Over his shoulder Maliki saw a woman appear in the corridor on the other side. She was dressed in a white towelling robe. Her deep red hair pulled back from her oval shaped face in a ponytail. Her skin was flushed and radiant like she had just come out of the shower.

"What the hell?" her jaw dropped when she saw Lembui running at her. The flannel she was holding fell to from her hand.

"Police!" shouted Lembui. He stopped a few meters away and aimed the Glock at her, "Get to the floor and put your hands over your head!"

"You've got no right to be here!" she shouted, real anger in her voice.

Lembui stepped forward and hit Dr Brennan with a punch to the stomach that doubled her over.

Then he struck her on the back of the head with his pistol. She fell to the floor with a thump, moaning and clutching her wound. Lembui hardly broke stride and continued on into the room that she had come out of.

He and Sabore searched the rest of the apartment whilst Maliki stood watching over Dr Brennan, blocking the corridor in case she tried to escape. He needn't have worried. She took her time to struggle into a sitting position and then touched the back of her head. There was a puzzled look on Dr Brennan's face as she examined the blood on her hand and realised it was her own.

"He's not in the bedroom," said Sabore returning from the room at the end of the corridor.

Maliki turned on his heel and walked into the lounge, "Bring Dr Brennan in here, I want to have a little chat with her." He tried to make himself comfortable in one of the wicker armchairs and crossed his legs. He picked a piece of flint from his trouser leg as Dr Brennan was dragged into the room and shoved into an identical chair on the other side of the glass coffee table.

"You bastards!" she tried to get up. Lembui pushed her back down with one hand.

Maliki turned to Sabore, "Go and guard the front door." Sabore smiled nervously and hurried off towards the hallway. Maliki knew that he didn't have the stomach for what was coming next.

"What do you want?" Dr Brennan was holding the back of her head with one hand.

"Go and check the place for any sign of him," he dismissed Lembui and waited for him to go off down the corridor. Maliki decided to play it softly for now.

"I'm sorry about the rough treatment Dr Brennan," he held his hands out, palms facing up in a gesture of apology. "My associates can be a little over zealous at times."

"You're pigs! Bullies! That's what you are! There's plenty of your sort where I come from," her eyes flickered and there was a lyrical edge to her voice. "Who the hell are you?"

Maliki ignored the question, "Why don't we make this intrusion as brief as possible, Dr Brennan. We're looking for a deserter from the Kenyan Wildlife Service, a man called David Nbeke."

"I've never heard of him." Her gaze wavered for a split-second, "You've got no right to come barging in here like this. I demand to speak to a solicitor."

"Things don't quite work that way here in Kenya, Dr Brennan. And I assure you that I am well within my rights. Now let's cut the crap shall we? You were noticed leaving the orphanage with Captain Nbeke on Saturday and you've been seen together a number of times."

Her head dropped.

"So what if I know him?" She looked up at him and thrust her chin out defiantly, "David's no criminal."

"Where is he now?"

"I don't know."

"When did you last see him?"

"At the orphanage on Saturday," she glared back at him with glowing eyes but a single blink gave her away.

Maliki let it go for the time being, "Where was Captain Nbeke going when you parted company?"

"He didn't say."

"Come now," he tutted. "Do you really expect me to believe that? Aiding and abetting a fugitive is a criminal offence, Dr Brennan. You really don't want to end up in one of our prisons. Let's just say that they are not a suitable place for a woman such as you."

"I told you, I don't know where he is."

Maliki smiled thinly and shook his head.

"Are you fucking Captain Nbeke, Dr Brennan?"

She jumped to her feet, hands clenched into fists by her sides, "What business is that of yours?"

Maliki grinned back at her. She had real spirit this one and was quite stunning. The robe had opened slightly during the struggle with Lembui to reveal the pale skin between her breasts. There was a rush of blood and stirring in his pants. He would enjoy breaking her. He stood up and slapped her so hard across the face that the force jerked her head and torso to one side. The stinging sensation in his palm only aroused him further and Maliki swung his arm back to do it again.

Dr Brennan's reaction almost caught him off guard. Instead of backing away or collapsing into the chair she picked it up and used it as a weapon. As she swivelled back towards him with it in her hands he raised his right arm to block the attack. The leg of the chair hit his arm and broke. Maliki ignored the pain and lashed out with his other fist, catching her on the cheek. Before she had the chance to recover he pulled the knife from the

270

sheath strapped under his armpit in a back handed stabbing move.

The blade sank deep into the Irish woman's hip. She squealed out in agony and dropped the chair. It shattered the coffee table and sent shards of glass across the floor.

Maliki yanked the knife out and thick arterial blood spurted from the wound. He was overcome with rage and stabbed again but somehow she got an arm in the way. The knife jarred in his hand as it glanced off bone and she let out another howl before collapsing to the floor. She curled into a foetal position and tried to cover her head with one hand whilst feebly attempting to stem the flow of blood from her side with the other.

That was when Sabore and Lembui came running into the room from opposite directions.

"I told you to guard the door!" he snapped at Sabore. The veteran was staring down at Dr Brennan's crumpled form. Sabore turned towards him with his mouth open as if about to reply but closed it again when he saw the look on Maliki's face. He shrugged and went back to his post.

"Get this bitch into the bedroom!" Maliki returned his attention to Dr Brennan.

Lembui leant over and grabbed a handful of hair to pull Dr Brennan to her feet. Her attempts to resist useless as she was dragged kicking and screaming down the corridor. Maliki stayed near the edge to avoid the trail of blood as he walked behind them.

Lembui stopped underneath the light in the middle of the room and pulled Dr Brennan upright, pinning her arms behind her back. Maliki held the knife to her throat and stared into her eyes. The blade was razor sharp, he applied some pressure, just enough to break the skin and leave a shallow cut.

"Put her on the bed and then find something to tie her other hand with," he undid the bow and yanked the chord from around her waist but kept the knife against her neck. "We're going to have some fun making this bitch talk."

She spat in his face and Maliki's lip started to spasm as the phlegm dripped down his cheek. He wiped it away and then cleaned his hand on her robe.

"You really shouldn't have done that, Dr Brennan," he said quietly and then punched her hard in the temple. She slumped forward in Lembui's arms, her head hung limply to one side and her eyes shut.

Biceps bulging under his suit jacket Lembui bundled the unconscious Dr Brennan onto the bed. Maliki sheathed his knife and tied one of her arms to the wooden bedstead using the belt. Lembui found a scarf to tie the other.

Maliki slapped her face but she barely stirred. He struck her again, harder. Dr Brennan groaned but her eyes stayed closed. She was semi-conscious, muttering the odd incoherent word.

"Go and get some water to wake her up with," snapped Maliki, standing up beside the bed.

Lembui's wide face remained impassive as he walked off towards the kitchen. Maliki stripped out of his clothes as he waited for him to return. He took the knife back out from its sheath and went over to the bed. Using the tip he prised open Dr Brennan's robe carefully so that her breasts were exposed and played the knife over them. She stirred but didn't wake. He grabbed her face and squeezed his thumbs into her cheeks so that her mouth opened. Dr Brennan's eyelids flicked open for a second but her eyeballs were rolled back in their sockets. They closed again as Lembui returned with a pan full of water.

"Throw it over her," Maliki grinned at Lembui and took a step back from the bed. "Let's find out what she knows and then you can have a turn."

His bodyguard's usually stoic face cracked into a grin as he doused Dr Brennan's head and torso with the water. She woke up spluttering and coughing. Lembui carried on emptying the pan into her open mouth as she gasped and choked for breath until she threw up some of the water.

After a few deep intakes of breath she turned her head towards them. Her dazed eyes focussed on Maliki, widening in fear as they dropped down his naked torso to the knife. Then she screamed and started writhing wildly on the bed, trying to pull her hands free from their constraints. He covered Dr Brennan's mouth with his free hand to silence her. She tried to knee him in the balls but Maliki deflected the move easily with his hip.

"Hold her legs down!" he barked at Lembui.

Maliki waited for her legs to be pinned down and then straddled her, one of his knees sitting in the blood seeping from her hip. Keeping one hand over her mouth he dragged the knife across her chest.

Tracing a line from above her right nipple between her cleavage and ending below the other breast. The blade left a gash in its trail.

Maliki kept his hand over Dr Brennan's mouth to muffle her screams and leant forward so that their faces were inches apart. He held the tip of the knife near to the corner of her eye and pricked the skin. A single red bead emerged like a clown's macabre teardrop. His penis was now rock hard and pressed against her navel. He could feel her coarse pubic hairs rubbing the tip.

"You've got spirit Dr Brennan and I like that, makes all of this a bit more interesting. But believe me you will talk. Everybody does." He watched her pupils dilate, "It's simply a question of how much you can take."

CHAPTER THIRTY
Jomo Kenyatta International Airport, Nairobi
August 19th, 1996

Avoiding the major routes took much longer than David expected. It was dark by the time he pulled into the deserted supermarket car park a few blocks from the airport. Guessing that Commander Abasi must have an APB out on the LandRover he had smothered the licence plates with a mixture of oil and dirt to conceal them. The vehicle was caked in dust and mud so to the casual observer the registration wouldn't appear out of the ordinary. But still he knew that if they stayed in the jeep it was only a matter of time before they were caught.

After using the last strip of gaffa tape to silence Gupta he shouldered his rucksack and locked the jeep. Ten minutes later he was walking along Airport North Road with his head down, avoiding looking into the headlights of the vehicles as they left the terminal.

David doubted that the airport was being watched. Abasi wouldn't be expecting him to try and leave the country. But he could still feel his heart beating rapidly in his chest as he walked into the brightly lit foyer. He spotted the Avis sign and walked over to the desk.

"I'm afraid that all we've got available at such short notice is a Mitsubishi Colt," the immaculately groomed representative straightened the bit of tie showing above his red waistcoat and smiled sympathetically. His long jet-black hair was pulled back and tied in a tight bun on the top of his head.

"That will do fine," David smiled back. "How much is the deposit?" He winced at the amount.

After withdrawing the last of his savings from the Barclays ATM machine across the foyer he completed the paperwork. Reluctantly handing over the 30,000-shilling deposit plus a week in advance.

"You can't miss it sir, its white," the Asian desk clerk handed him a worn set of keys. "If you have any problems with the vehicle please call the number at the bottom of your hire agreement."

Something told David that the agent was expecting the call but he thanked him politely and left the terminal. As promised the two-door Colt was easy to find. It was the oldest most battered looking vehicle in the lot. A common model and colour in Kenya it would help them blend in with the crowd.

The engine coughed a bit when he turned the key but surprisingly started first time. A few minutes later he was back outside the supermarket, parked next to the LandRover.

Apart from Gupta there was little else to transfer and they were soon driving towards the city centre. David shrugged off the momentary feeling of guilt in abandoning the KWS vehicle that had served him so well. In less than a few hours at most local thieves and hooligans would strip the jeep bare. Within a couple of days even the engine parts and seat covers would be sold on the local black market.

Feeling a lot less conspicuous in their new mode of transport his confidence grew the closer they got to Caitlyn's apartment. He found a space facing the park and turned off the ticking engine. David wasn't sure whether the noise was normal or it was low on oil. He decided it would be prudent to check the levels before continuing north to the Maasai Mara and made a mental note to stop at a garage. David was taking Gupta up to Scott's lodge. It was the best place to hold him for now, assuming that Damo and the other rangers had made it there safely.

"Now stay here and be a good boy," David turned towards Gupta and smiled before ripping the tape off his mouth. A few more long grey hairs came with it. "And don't go shouting for help."

"Bastard!" muttered Gupta but they both knew that he would obey. If he was found with his hands and legs taped together the first thing his rescuer would do is call the police. And then Commander Abasi would find out.

David took the precaution of checking the area for Abasi's men. He walked past the apartment building on the opposite side of the street and surveyed the cars and people for anybody out of the ordinary. There was the odd shopper taking advantage of the fashion boutiques' later opening times and a few office workers returning home but that was about it.

He stopped and pretended to examine the goods in a closed sports shop, using the window to check whether he was being followed out of the corner of his eye. He couldn't see anybody acting suspiciously.

When David reached the intersection he crossed onto Caitlyn's side of the street and doubled back towards her apartment. He went into an open grocery store and paused in the doorway as if looking for change in his pockets. David used the opportunity to steal a look back towards the traffic lights but there was nobody there.

He went in and bought a packet of biltong and a bunch of bananas that the grocer stuffed into a brown paper bag. David thanked him and paid the extortionate price, living in the city obviously didn't come cheap. He could have bought a carrier bag full for the same amount in Kisii.

Holding the bananas under his arm he ripped open the plastic packet and took out a strip of biltong. The dried beef, cured with salt and vinegar, softened as he chewed and released the intense meaty flavour. David glanced into the deserted foyer of Caitlyn's building and walked on to the end of the block. He stopped around the corner and pretended to tie his shoelace. Satisfied that nobody was following him David went back down the street and pressed the buzzer.

There was no answer so he pressed it again. He was about to give up and try the public phone box outside when a smartly dressed couple arrived. They were both in their mid-twenties and seemed to be a little wasted but they politely held the door open for him. David guessed that they had stopped off for dinner on the way home from the office and drank too much wine. The red stain on the white shirt the man was wearing looked like it might have come from something full bodied like a Rioja. His hands were all over her short grey skirt as they went up, she kept giggling and telling him to wait. David couldn't help noticing she had long toned legs below the thigh-length skirt.

They got out of the elevator on the third floor but the smell of alcohol remained in the air. That's when it started to bother him that Caitlyn hadn't answered the buzzer.

As he walked down the corridor towards the door of her apartment the hairs on the back of his neck stood on end. Maybe he was being paranoid but David couldn't shake it. After placing the groceries gently on the floor he put one hand behind his back onto the butt of his pistol and rapped on the door. It swung open a few inches and he could see broken bits of wood around the lock.

His stomach knotted up instantly. David took a step back, pulled out his gun and thumbed off the safety. Holding the Browning close to his chest in a two handed grip David kicked open the door and rushed in at a crouch. Trying to avoid being silhouetted by the lights in the hallway. Apart from the dim glow of the streetlights coming through the drapes the lounge was swathed in darkness.

He was like a duck in a shooting gallery and didn't wait for his eyes to adjust. Staying low he stopped at the end of the short entrance corridor and felt around on the wall for the switch. When he finally flicked on the light his heart skipped a beat as he surveyed the damage.

One of the wicker armchairs had been smashed through the middle of the coffee table and was resting there with a broken leg. Shards of glass scattered around it. Another chair was toppled on its side and David noticed a dark circle on the floor next to it. The air was expelled from his lungs as if he had been hit in the chest with a sledgehammer. He bent down for a closer look and was overcome by another more powerful wave of nausea. David forced himself to dip his finger into the small puddle and hold it up to his face for inspection.

It was wet and fresh between his thumb and forefinger. The blood was still bright red, not yet brown from oxidisation. Where was she? Forcing himself to stay calm he took a few deep breaths before standing up. He wiped his hand on the leg of his combats and turned towards the corridor leading to the kitchen and bedrooms.

Gun stretched out in front of him he took the first step and felt the anger rise within him. It started in the pit of his stomach and climbed up through his chest to engulf him. Turning on the corridor light revealed a sinister trail of large splatters leading across the fake parquet flooring to her door. There was a streak on the white gloss paint near the middle where she must have brushed against it. David had no doubt that it was Caitlyn's blood and that she was bleeding badly.

He ignored the other rooms and rushed forward, heart pumping and grabbed the handle. David swung the door open. The light cast from the corridor illuminated the fixed mask of terror on Caitlyn's face. Her eyes and mouth were open wide, tongue hanging to one side, bruises on her face and neck.

She was laying spread eagle on the bed with her arms tied to the headrest. Someone had used a knife on her repeatedly. There were gaping slashes across Caitlyn's abdomen and breasts. Another deeper stab wound just above her hip. The white towelling robe was soaked in Caitlyn's blood, open and pulled up to her waist. Her legs were straight and stretched apart. There were tell tale rings of purple bruises around her ankles where she had been held whilst she was tortured. Caitlyn's genitalia were a bloody mess and a large pool of blood had flowed onto the sheets to form a puddle between her thighs.

David walked over to the bed as if in a trance and let the gun drop to his side. He fell to his knees beside her and touched her cheek. It was still warm. If he had got there just half an hour earlier he probably could have saved her. It was then that he started to sob, short silent intakes of breath that racked his chest as he struggled to breath. The pain she must have suffered was almost unimaginable. Surely only an animal could do this kind of thing to another human being?

Whoever was responsible for this was going to pay, and pay dearly! An 'eye for an eye' seemed more than a fitting punishment in the circumstances. David was reasonably sure that it was Commander Abasi's eye that needed taking out. Maybe Tanui's as well.

He wiped away the tears with the back of his free hand and used the bed to push himself to his feet. David put the gun down and reached up to untie the hand nearest to him. She deserved to have some dignity. He wanted to cover her up at least before he called the local police and the circus arrived.

She had pulled hard on her restraints in an attempt to escape. The knots were tight solid lumps of rope. David pulled at the first one for almost a minute before it came free. As he lent over her to reach her other hand a single tear rolled off his cheek and landed on her forehead. Finally the second knot came undone and he closed the soiled dressing gown over her mutilated chest. Then David folded Caitlyn's arms loosely on top so that her hands rested over her lap.

"I'm so sorry Caitlyn." He leant over and kissed her on the lips before closing her eyelids, "I promise that I'll get whoever did this to you."

He heard the footsteps coming up behind him and started to turn around but it was too late. David was struck on the back of the head by something hard and everything went black.

CHAPTER THIRTY-ONE
GSU Headquarters, Nairobi
August 19th, 1996

David's mind flitted between the dream world and reality as he came out of the nightmare. It was the usual one about his father and the masked murderer wearing the medallion. But for some reason that David didn't fully understand Caitlyn was there, trapped inside the burning house instead of his mother. He could still hear the echoes of her screams for help as he regained consciousness.

His head was throbbing worse than it did after a night out on the town with Damo, and David's eyelids felt like they were made of lead. He attempted to open them but nothing happened. Screwing up his eye sockets first he tried again, pulling down with his cheek muscles and raising both eyebrows to give them assistance. This time they opened but he still couldn't see anything. There was some kind of hood over his head. When he tried to investigate David found that his hands were handcuffed behind his back. He pulled at the restraints, heaving around face first on what felt like concrete and reeked of urine and human defecation.

The handcuffs were clasped so tightly around his wrists that he could barely move them, let alone slip them over his hands. But he carried on trying anyway. After a few more minutes of pointless thrashing around that left his skin raw he began to feel light-headed. Realising that he was close to passing out David stopped for a moment to catch his breath.

"Arrrggghhhh!"

The howl that broke the silence came from somewhere beneath him. Although high-pitched it was too deep to be a woman's, more like the sound of a man in some serious pain. Then the louder voice of someone else, his angry shouting overlapped another cry of agony.

As if struck by a bolt of lightning it all came flooding back to him. The screams that he had heard in his dream weren't Caitlyn's at all. How could they be? Caitlyn was dead, her face twisted in agony. Murdered because he hadn't protected her. David had failed to save her, just like his father. He rolled onto his side and started to weep silently, tears flowing over the bridge of his nose. Caitlyn's face kept changing between one of beauty to the grotesque death mask that he had found in her apartment.

David wasn't sure how long he lay there lost in his own thoughts but it felt like an eternity. Slowly his self-pity and self-loathing was replaced with anger. It started like a hot ember in his belly and grew until it consumed him.

There was no doubt that Commander Abasi was the sick bastard responsible. Just before being knocked out David recognised the thug he had seen opening the car door for Abasi at KWS headquarters. Maybe he was the one who held Caitlyn down? Judging by the marks on her legs more than one person had been involved. He fought the urge to vomit. One way or another he was going to find out who they all were and make them pay. But first he had to get free somehow.

He rolled onto his back, his hands trapped uselessly beneath him. Then he performed an awkward sit-up, thrusting his head and shoulders forward to compensate for the ungainly position. The effort seemed super-human and made him gasp for breath under the hood. Star-like pinpricks of light started to spin in the darkness and he came close to passing out again.

The hood was so tightly tied around his neck that it was making him hyperventilate. David forced himself to calm down and took shallow breaths until the spinning stopped and the feeling of nausea faded.

Maybe it was the lack of oxygen or a protection mechanism but he found himself imagining a bizarre news story. In the article David was discovered naked in a ditch. He could see the headline.

'UNKNOWN MAN CHOKES TO DEATH ON OWN VOMIT'

He straightened his back and shook his head. Besides not being ready to die, Abasi needed to suffer for what had been done to Caitlyn. The promise of retribution stiffened his resolve and David began to assess where he was.

His feet were bare. They must have taken his boots and socks, so he used his toes to explore the space around him. The walls on either side were less than a few feet away. Shuffling around on his bum it took David less than a minute to work out that he was in a small rectangular room less than eight feet long.

The door set in one of the smaller walls felt cold to the touch but he kicked it with his heel to make sure. A dull clang confirmed that it was metal.

Combined with the smell it didn't take a genius to work out that he was being kept in a cell. KWS holding facilities were much the same and he had smelt the mixture of sweat and piss before. It was a distinct odour that David had come to associate with human fear.

"Hey!" he shouted to anybody that might be listening. "Let me out of here!"

The screams and shouting stopped and it went quiet. He waited for over a minute but nothing happened. David kicked at the door, "Bastards! Where are you?"

Then the man's pitiful screams started up again. David kept kicking at the steel and shouting until his voice was hoarse and his heel felt bruised. But still nobody came. Wherever he was being kept they obviously weren't worried about the noise. He was somewhere that they felt secure, probably at a GSU facility. Realising eventually that it was hopeless he shuffled away from the door, turning ninety degrees so that he could lean against the wall.

Knees bent and feet touching the wall opposite David arched his spine to accommodate the handcuffs. He tried to rest his head but a sharp shooting pain told him that it was a bad idea.

Examining his situation objectively David came to the conclusion that the Commander must think he knew something. Otherwise he would be dead already. It had to be Koinet, or more precisely his whereabouts. He hadn't told Caitlyn about his decision to move the prisoner to Spencer Scott's lodge. A wave of guilt hit him, imagining Caitlyn being tortured for information she didn't even have. He should have tried to warn her sooner, before he left Mombasa with Gupta.

"Shit!"

David had forgotten all about Gupta, he'd left him tied up in the rental outside Caitlyn's apartment. Maybe they hadn't found him and he was still sitting there. He shuddered, or maybe the screams coming from the depths of the building belonged to Gupta. Thinking about it everything had been quiet for a while, how long was impossible to tell. Seconds seemed like minutes, minutes like hours.

Straining his ears he heard footsteps first, then the jangling of keys and the scraping noise of a lock being opened. The keys clanged against a metal door somewhere outside his cell. Judging by the squeal they made the hinges needed oiling. As the laboured wheezing got closer he painted a mental picture of the heavyset bodyguard. His jail cell suddenly felt positively luxurious. A regular sanctuary compared to what might be waiting for him. David backed himself into the corner and held his breath.

Although he was expecting it the noise of the key entering the lock made him jump. He pulled his knees up to his chest and hung his head forward as if asleep. Thighs tensed, his whole body sprung like a snake ready to strike. The door to the cell was swung open and some light came through the hessian sack. Then it dimmed as the man stepped inside the cell. Although David couldn't see properly through the thick material the changing shadows allowed him to make out a shape. His brain put the pieces together and the shadows came together to form the vague outline of a man.

"Are you still asleep?" the man's laugh was deep and booming. He took a step closer, "Come on wake up, there's somebody who wants to see you."

David didn't move and continued to exaggerate his breathing.

"You better not be faking it!" The dark shape got bigger as he leant over, "I'll..."

His threat was cut short as David unleashed the pent up energy in his coiled legs and kicked out. He was hoping to connect with something hard like the man's head but his feet drove into something soft and squishy.

The man grunted, his voice sounded strained and had gone up a few octaves, "You little bastard!"

Thrashing out again David found nothing but air, before he could withdraw his legs steely hands locked around his ankles. Although he tried to resist and pull away there was nothing he could do to stop himself being dragged across the floor feet first. Skin was scraped from his forearms and his head bounced off something solid. Suddenly the hold was released and his heels hit the ground with a thud before he could get his leg muscles to respond.

His jailor was taking sharp short breaths. David guessed that he must have caught him in the balls and that it would take him a few minutes to recover. David wasn't doing so well himself. He had used up the oxygen under the hood during the brief tussle and his head was spinning again.

Maybe he sensed the attack coming, or heard the rustle of clothing, David rolled away enough to prevent the kick bursting his kidney. A steel toecap drove into his ribs and knocked the wind out of him. At the same time there was an intense stabbing pain and David thought he felt something break. It was swiftly followed by another kick that caught him above his handcuffed wrists in the small of his back. David curled into a ball to protect himself against the series of blows to his arms and back that followed. The man changed angle and aimed a kick at his head, it struck the wound he had received in Caitlyn's apartment. David cried out as a shard of pain stabbed into his brain.

"Shut up!"

He cringed expecting the next blow but thankfully the beating was over. An arm slipped through his and he was lifted off the floor to his feet, a little too easily for David's liking. The man was even stronger than he looked, if it was the bodyguard. David's legs were jelly and he would have collapsed.

Supported by his assailant David was led through a door and then down a flight of stone stairs. The musty damp smell got worse as they went deeper. So did the stench of death. The escaping gasses and release of bodily fluids smelt the same whether emitted by an animal or human. David didn't have to guess which these belonged to.

There was a sudden gust of air up the stairwell and his nose picked up something else. A second later he worked out what it was and recoiled from the acrid odour of burnt hair and human flesh. He dug in his heels and tried to back up the stairs but the man behind him prodded David in the back and propelled him forward.

The change as the floor levelled out caught him by surprise and he tripped, scuffing his knee on the concrete. David was yanked roughly to his feet and marched blindly forward. He was guided along a long corridor and then they turned right. The acoustics changed to signify that David was in a different room and after a few paces they stopped and the grip on his arm released.

The handcuffs were removed and he was shoved into a wooden chair. He started to nurse his aching wrists but his arms were pulled behind his back gain and the handcuffs replaced. David tried to move his hands but the chain of the handcuffs was looped around one of the struts.

His ankles were bound tightly to the legs of the chair with what was probably gaffa tape. He felt tugging as the chord holding the hood over his head was untied and then the blindfold was whipped off. The noose caught his nose on the way up and smarted. David dipped his head and closed his eyes to the glare of strobe lighting.

"Ah, Captain Nbeke," the man standing in the shadows spoke calmly, his tone soft like velvet. "So good of you to join us."

David looked up towards the voice, squinting against the light. The man stepped forward from the darkness, he blinked and the blurry image came into focus. Commander Abasi's scarred face was staring back at him smiling.

CHAPTER THIRTY-TWO
GSU Headquarters, Nairobi
August 20th, 1996

"You bastard!" David's voice sounded croaky. "I'll kill you for what you did to Caitlyn!"

"What?" his grin exposed teeth that were filed to a point. Abasi looked more shark-like than human as he tilted his head back and laughed.

When he looked back down at David the smile was gone and there was a fanatical zeal to his eyes, "Do you really think that you are in a position to threaten me, Captain Nbeke?"

Commander Abasi turned and gave his minder an almost imperceptible nod. David had identified the big man correctly when he was in darkness under the hood. It was the suit-wearing gorilla from the KWS car lot.

The burly bodyguard was quicker on his feet than he looked. Crouched in a boxer's stance he stepped forward and delivered a swift right hook. He led with his left foot and put all his weight into it. Hard calloused knuckles smashed into David's cheek, dislodging one of his teeth and whipping his head to the side.

He turned back to face him and spat out the tooth with a mixture of saliva and blood. David smiled, "Is that the best you've got?"

Enraged he swung his arm back and punched again. David was expecting it this time and ducked his head a split-second before impact. The fist connected with his forehead and he was rewarded by the sound of at least two knuckles cracking against his skull. The GSU goon yelped out in shock and took a step backwards.

"Now look what you've done, Captain," Commander Abasi's voice was smooth as chocolate. He shook his head and tutted, "You've hurt Lembui's pride."

As if to confirm what he was saying the disgruntled thug's expression changed from one of shock to anger. Teeth bared, he rushed forward and extended his left fist like a pile driver. He hit David squarely on the nose, flattening it against his face and splitting the bridge. His eyes watered instantly and the force sent him and the chair toppling backwards. David's head hit the deck as he went over and his hands were crushed beneath him.

"I think that the Captain has had enough for now," barked the Commander. "Pick him up!"

David felt rough hands under his shoulders and then he was propelled upwards. The chair pivoted on two legs and met the floor with a jarring impact that reverberated through his teeth. He stared at Abasi. The hatred inside him felt like something physical that he could somehow project across the space between them.

The Commander was wearing a tailor made suit that accentuated the slope of his athletic shoulders. White shirt, black tie and a pair of gold Armani sunglasses perched on the top of his closely cropped head. Abasi looked over-dressed for the occasion. Although he was too tall to be well built there was muscle on him. David decided that he would make a good middle-distance runner. If it wasn't for the scars that twisted his mouth up into a sneer on one side and the pointed teeth the Commander might have been good looking. But he wasn't. Gupta was right when he called him the Devil.

Then he noticed the bloodstain on the white shirt poking out from underneath the sleeve of his charcoal jacket. A dark heart shaped splatter that touched one of the gold cufflinks. He felt a cold chill pass over him.

"Did you kill her?" he could picture the slash wounds on her chest, the look of terror on her face, "Did you do those things to Caitlyn?"

Commander Abasi raised an eyebrow, "If you mean Dr Brennan, then yes." He smiled like a shark about to eat its prey, "What a woman! But I guess you know all about that, eh Captain? She put up quite a fight that one. Until I was inside her, then she seemed to enjoy it a lot. If you know what I mean?"

David felt the blood drain from his face and his stomach churned. So she had been raped. David had pushed the idea from his mind.

"I think you do, Captain." David wanted to wipe the sick smile of his face. "There were screams of pleasure from the good doctor before she died."

"You filthy bastard!"

David tried to shuffle towards him but the best he could hope to achieve was toppling face forward in the chair. He glared at the Commander.

"You're sick Abasi, there's a disease inside you. When I get out of here I'm going to hunt you down and cut it out. You won't be safe anywhere." David nodded, more to himself than the Commander, "I won't rest until it's done."

"Brave words indeed, Captain." Abasi clapped his hands together, "Unfortunately for you they won't come to pass." He nodded towards something hanging from the wall on David's left, "I'm afraid that, like the late Mr Gupta here, you have gravely underestimated me."

The smell was stronger in this part of the room and he could see something out the corner of his eye. Until now David had been too preoccupied with the Commander and his henchman to look. Now that he did David actually found himself feeling sorry for the despicable poacher.

By the looks of it Gupta had suffered terribly before he died. He was chained to an iron bed frame that was fixed to the wall. His arms spread wide like a crucifix, legs dangling a foot from the floor, head hung to one side. An electric jump lead was attached to the frame on one side, the other still connected to Gupta's exposed scrotum. The skin was burnt black around the crocodile clip and there was a crop circle of singed pubic hairs. David traced the cables back to a control panel plugged into the mains. He couldn't help looking at Gupta again. He must have bit his tongue badly during one of the convulsions, there was a thick trail of blood coming from his blue lips and down over his beard. The hair turned red and matted with blood.

David remembered reading somewhere about a man in the States who was struck by lightning whilst wearing rubber boots. Without any earth to conduct the electric charge it concentrated in his chest and cooked his internal organs. The same thing had happened to Gupta. His robes were burnt off to reveal a blackened pit of charcoaled flesh.

Gupta's bowels had emptied before he died. The robes tied up around his waist were wet and stained yellow. They must have doused his genitals to aid the flow of electricity. There was a puddle of water on the floor by his feet and a metal bucket nearby. Maybe they used it to put out the flames when his chest caught fire?

The worst thing was that Gupta wore a look of sheer terror that was similar to the one that David had found on Caitlyn. He looked away from the charred corpse that was once Gupta, back towards the Commander.

"You're insane. You won't get away with this."

"That's where you're wrong Nbeke." Abasi shook his head, "This business will soon be over and my life can get back to normal. What happens to yours depends on whether you cooperate. Now, where's Koinet?"

"Who the hell is Koinet?" David kept a straight face. Abasi was only confirming what he had already guessed. The fact that he was still alive meant that Damo must have got Koinet safely to Spencer Scott's lodge.

"Come now, Captain." The Commander's face twitched with another spasm that pronounced his sneer, "There's no point making this any more painful than it needs to be."

On cue, Lembui came in from the side and gave David a quick rabbit punch to the temple that sent him spinning. Straightening up again in the chair he shook his head to get rid of the grogginess.

"You punch like a girl," he stared at Lembui.

The giant's eyes widened and his nostrils flared in anger. This time he hit David so hard that it stunned him and his vision blurred.

"That was better!" David grinned, he could feel the air coming through the gap where his tooth used to be. "But you're still not getting all your weight behind it."

The infuriated bully raised his arm again.

Commander Abasi coughed once. It was obviously a signal and Lembui froze, fist in the air. He looked over at his master, wearing a despondent frown. His expression reminded David of a child whose favourite toy had just been taken away.

The Commander dismissed Lembui with a gentle wave of the hand, "He's no good to me unconscious."

Abasi's enforcer sighed loudly but obediently dropped the clenched fist to his side and took a step back. He might be built like a brick but Lembui was out of shape. His breathing was ragged and sweat poured from his thickset brow. He kept his eyes fixed firmly on David, like a vulture waiting for the next opportunity to feast.

"Why don't we stop playing games, Captain," Abasi's right hand snaked inside his jacket and came out holding a four-inch blade. He held the knife in the palm of his hand as if testing the weight. "Koinet led you to Gupta and he told you all about me and my involvement. The stupid old fool just couldn't keep his mouth shut."

Commander Abasi took a step towards him and closed his fingers around the knife. He held it close to his chest in a backhanded grip so that the tip pointed at the floor. His lip twitched again as he leered down at David.

"The idiot gave you details about my buyer and the EAST AFRICAN TIMBER COMPANY. The question is who did you tell?"

"I still don't know what you're talking about," David couldn't be sure that Gupta had said anything.

"This is getting boring, Captain. I'm going to give you one last chance before this starts to get really unpleasant," Abasi paused and rubbed at the scars on his face as if waiting for his words to sink in. "Gupta said that you stopped in a petrol station near Voi and posted a letter. He saw you writing it. What was in it?"

So he must have blabbed everything. Considering the screams of anguish he had heard and the state of Gupta's fried testicles it wasn't much of a surprise.

"It was my resignation," David smiled. "I sent it to your friend...Deputy Director Tanui."

Commander Abasi's face twisted into a snarl and he lunged forward, thrusting with the knife. Half of the razor sharp blade sank into the hollow of David's shoulder, slicing through muscle and tendon.

"Ahhhh...shit!"

David looked down at the knife in disbelief. Then Abasi slowly and deliberately twisted his hand ninety degrees and the pain intensified to a level that David had previously thought impossible.

"What did you put in the letter?" screamed the irate Commander. "How much does Tanui know?"

He was so close that some of his spittle hit David on the cheek. Despite the fact that he had the upper hand Abasi looked scared. David felt a split second of relief that Tanui wasn't involved. A feeling that was immediately replaced by guilt for doubting the Deputy Director.

"Nothing," muttered David, worried that he might have already inadvertently dropped Tanui in it. "Why would I when I thought that he was working with you?"

Abasi's laugh was like a hyena's bark, "With me?"

"It seemed to make sense at the time," David gritted his teeth and tried to ignore the flaming agony spreading through his chest and arm. He needed to think of a way out fast. Otherwise he was going to die down here with Gupta. Then it came to him. The idea was so simple it might actually work, or at least buy him some time. Another wave of agony went through his shoulder as Abasi adjusted his stance and the knife moved around inside him.

He looked Abasi in the eye, "If you promise to let me go then I'll take you to Koinet."

The Commander's face slowly relaxed until finally he smiled, "That's more like it, Captain. But if for one second I think that you're pulling the wool over my eyes. Well, let's just say I won't be too happy."

David eyelids closed and he nearly passed out as the knife was twisted another quarter turn.

"Do you understand, Captain?"

He opened his eyes and managed to nod.

"Good," the Commander withdrew the knife and wiped it on David's sleeve before slipping it back inside his jacket. Blood started pumping out of the wound. David could feel it running down his chest and soaking his shirt.

"Get rid of Gupta and patch him up."

"Then what shall I do with him?"

Lembui's question stopped Abasi half way to the door. He turned and smiled at David, "Put him upstairs in the cell for now and wait for me to get back. Then we'll go and pay Koinet a visit."

CHAPTER THIRTY-THREE
GSU Headquarters, Nairobi
August 20th, 1996

Maliki wanted to check something and make a few arrangements before departing from headquarters with Nbeke. He strode across the courtyard feeling pleased with himself for leaving Lembui to watch over Dr Brennan's apartment. He stopped outside the main building and rang the buzzer. The officer on the nightshift must have been sleeping and took an age to answer the intercom.

"Open the damned door!" ordered Maliki, glaring up at the camera. It was the second time he had been made to wait outside in one day.

His mood shifted like the tide, switching from one of annoyance to euphoria as he thought about what happened inside her apartment. Reliving the moment that Dr Brennan died aroused him, thinking about the sheer terror in her eyes. Maliki chuckled, Lembui was more than a bit pissed off that he didn't get a turn but he would get over it. Lost in these thoughts he forgot all about the lazy desk clerk and found himself sitting in his office.

Maliki leaned back in the leather recliner and thumbed through the back few pages of his diary until he found the Lieutenant's home number. He glanced at the display of the digital clock on his desk as he dialled. The time was 2:07am.

"Yes, who is it?" there was a hint of irritation in the sleepy voice that answered after several rings.

"It's me," barked Maliki.

"Oh...sorry, I didn't realise it was you," Idi Tikolo was stuttering. "What can I do for you, sir?"

"What's the latest?" He could picture the weasel reaching for the inhaler he always kept close by for his asthma. Sure enough there was a long pause and a sharp intake of breath before Tikolo replied.

"Nothing new, the Deputy Director was going crazy this afternoon. He's got pretty much the whole of the KWS searching for Captain Nbeke and the missing poacher. When I clocked off at midnight there was still no news of either of them."

"You're sure of that?"

"Of...course sir," stammered Tikolo. "I would have called you straight away."

"Let me know the minute anything changes."

Maliki smiled as he hung up the phone, the greasy Lieutenant was probably wetting the bed.

Unlike most of the people that Maliki recruited, Idi Tikolo had actually come to him. Over eighteen months ago the pompous little Kalenjin approached him after one of his regular meetings with Tanui at KWS Headquarters. Tikolo claimed to be a fan of President Moi and asked if there was a job for someone like him in the GSU.

Both ambitious and an ass licker Maliki had disliked the snivelling little Lieutenant almost immediately. He dismissed him at the time with a shake of the head but thought about it afterwards and relented. Having someone inside the KWS was just too valuable a prospect.

A few months later, after pumping Tanui for information on the rangers' movements, he made a point of stopping in reception and getting Tikolo's number. Since then the eager Lieutenant had proven to be a veritable goldmine. Keeping Maliki so well informed that he rarely bothered visiting the Deputy Director anymore. That was until recent events, starting with Nbeke saving that stupid elephant.

Once the misguided Captain had taken him to Koinet he could dispose of him and forget about the whole sorry affair. Then he could get back to more important matters that needed his attention, like the Professor and the Committee on Human Rights. Maliki smiled at the irony. When he had last seen him Onesimus Mutungi was lying in a pool of his own blood and vomit.

More importantly, Maliki needed someone to replace Gupta and quickly. The next shipment of rhino horn was due in less than six weeks. Wei might try to find another supplier if he didn't deliver. Maliki smiled, if the Counsellor showed any sign of reneging on their arrangement he would have his balls cut off and sent back to China.

But it would have to wait for now. When Koinet was in the hospital he was being guarded by at least two of Captain Nbeke's Rangers. They were probably still with him and Maliki wanted to make sure that he had more firepower. He picked up the phone and entered another number from memory, one that only his select guard knew. This time it was answered almost immediately.

"Yes Commander?" the man sounded alert despite the lateness of the hour. "Sergeant Wangari here."

At forty-six years of age Wangari was the oldest of the sixteen GSU officers living in the barracks outside Abasi's mansion. A veteran who had proved himself many times over, his main role now was administrative, organising the other officers' rota and manning the phone. But he remained fit as a fiddle and loved a good skirmish.

Maliki thought about Wangari's experience and made the decision, "Sergeant, get a troop of six officers together, including yourself, I want you fully kitted out and over at headquarters within the next twenty minutes. Bring night scopes and torches."

"Is there anything else sir?"

"No, that's it," Maliki imagined him pen poised above a notepad taking notes. He thought of something else as he was about to hang up, "Just make sure that the vehicles have a full tank of gas. I don't know how far we'll be going."

Guessing that Koinet was being held in the Maasai Mara, or somewhere nearby, he expected it to be a long drive. Feeling even more pleased with himself he settled back into the chair for the wait. The tide had turned and things were starting to go his way. Maliki massaged his cheek and smiled. The journey north would end with the tragic death of Captain Nbeke, Koinet and any other witnesses that were unlucky enough to be around.

CHAPTER THIRTY-FOUR
GSU Headquarters, Nairobi
August 20th, 1996

The rational part of his brain told him that this couldn't be happening. The scene before him was so surreal it was difficult to comprehend.

Lembui detached the copper clip from Gupta's genitals and threw it to one side. Then a rattling noise filled the room as he unchained his legs and arms. As the final restraint from the makeshift torture device was removed Gupta's burnt corpse collapsed to the floor.

His eyes closed and the sound started to fade. David forced them open and shook his aching head, the worst thing he could do now was pass out. He wasn't sure whether the numbness or the fact that the blood had stopped flowing from his shoulder was a good sign or not. One of his ribs had been busted by Lembui's boot and was cutting into his lung. It hurt every time he drew breath. By comparison his missing tooth and his broken nose seemed cosmetic. Although thinking about it the gum would probably need a couple of stitches, he could already feel swelling around the broken root. David spat to get rid of the metallic taste in his mouth.

Lembui hoisted Gupta over his shoulder in a ghoulish fireman's lift and turned to David. His face cracked into a wide grin, "Don't go anywhere, I'll be right back."

Echoes of his laughter still booming off the walls the smile vanished and the one hundred yard stare returned. After glaring at him for a few seconds Lembui nodded to himself and then headed out of the door. His footsteps gradually got fainter and then disappeared off into the distance.

Blocking out the pain he concentrated on taking deep breaths and regaining his strength. With each piercing intake he felt a little better and flexed his arms and legs to improve the circulation. His shoulder was numb and cold but there was nothing he could do about it for now. The punch that broke his nose and sent him over backwards had weakened the wooden joints. When David wriggled the chair wobbled.

He rocked the chair back and forth, praying that it didn't fall forward. David experienced a moment of weightlessness before he tipped backwards. Gravity took over and he accelerated towards the floor, David tilted his head forward to protect it, chin on his chest.

His bound arms took most of the impact, which in turn was transferred to the slats on the back of the chair. There was a satisfying crack as one of them snapped. David threw himself onto his side and pulled with his arms. A dagger of pain went through his shoulder and nothing much seemed to happen but then the wood creaked. He tugged again, this time kicking out with his legs and pressing hard against the chair with his back.

The wood groaned, trying to resist the pressure that he was exerting on it. David's whole body trembled with effort. Finally there was a cracking sound as the frame gave way and the back of the seat tore from its base. His handcuffed arms came free of the chair. He kept kicking until there was nothing left but the two wooden legs taped to his calves.

David rolled away from the debris onto his back and sat up. Pulling one leg under him David threw his good shoulder forward and transferred his weight so that he was on his knees. After taking a few deep breaths he got to his feet. Feeling unsteady and more than a little ridiculous with the bits of wood stuck to his legs he walked over to the bucket. Thankfully he could see his battered reflection in the water.

The pail was more than half full. With or without his hands handcuffed behind him David didn't rate his chances taking on Lembui in a fight. The man was nearly twice his size and way out of his weight class. Squatting over the bucket he felt around for the handle and picked it up. Holding it a few inches off the floor between his legs he edged slowly towards the door in a crab-like shuffle. Careful as he was the precious liquid sloshed about and David swore as some of it spilled over his combats.

Lembui could return at any moment so he hurriedly tipped the water over the floor, making sure that it reached the door. After taking a quick look down the corridor David took the empty pail back to where he had found it. The jump leads were lying on the floor next to the wire bedframe. David dragged the first one over towards the puddle near the door but it wouldn't reach. He noticed there was some slack on the cable between the trolley housing the control panel and the wall. Facing away from it he grabbed the handle and wheeled the metal gurney towards the door. The damn thing nearly toppled over when the cable reached its limit and snapped tight.

Thankfully the distance travelled by the trolley was enough and with the help of his toes David soon had the jump leads in position. He turned his attention to the control panel, which seemed simple enough. There was a dial to adjust the voltage and a switch to turn on the power. Already at the top end of the red line with the output set at 300 milliamps all he had to do was flip the little chrome lever. He walked over to the door and used his forehead to turn off the light. Treading carefully through the semi-darkness David stepped over the cables and slowly edged his way around to the back of the device.

He didn't have to wait long. A couple of minutes later he heard Lembui coming down the corridor, whistling out of tune. Hoping that he was deep enough inside the room to be hidden David's fingers trembled on the switch.

"What the hell?"

For one dreadful moment David thought that he might not come in. Lembui hesitated in the doorway his shoulders practically touching the frame. Then he stepped inside and reached for the light switch.

David threw the lever and the room lit up in a blaze of blue arcs. Fingers of electricity reached up from the puddle and enveloped Lembui. The huge bodyguard was frozen to the spot. Juddering and vibrating as the sparks flew off him. Lembui fell forward onto the floor like a felled tree and started to convulse. David kept his hand on the switch. He waited a full thirty seconds after Abasi's henchman stopped moving before cutting the power. A blue-white imprint of Lembui's death throws on his retina was all that remained as the room descended into darkness.

Lembui was motionless for another minute before David deemed it safe enough to leave cover and walk towards the door. As he got closer the smell of burnt hair and flesh got a hundred times worse. Fighting the urge to retch he knelt down next to the Mike Tyson lookalike. Suddenly there was movement and David's heart skipped a beat as Lembui's hand brushed up against his leg. He started breathing again when he realised that it was just a death spasm.

The bunch of keys was attached to Lembui's trousers. He tried to prise the ring open and thread it through the loop but the blunt end of the metal kept catching. David spent nearly a minute fumbling behind his back before the key ring came free. Choosing the smallest he managed to get the key into the lock of the handcuffs but couldn't turn his hand far enough to unlock it. When he attempted to adjust his grip the bunch fell noisily to the floor.

David scrabbled around on his haunches. Worrying more with every resounding heartbeat that he would be discovered.

"Got you!" muttered David triumphantly when his trembling fingers bumped into them. The keys were lodged next to Lembui's thigh.

Another nerve-racking minute later and one of the cuffs finally came open. David briefly massaged his wrist to help return the circulation and then opened the other lock. He shoved the keys and the handcuffs into the thigh pocket of his combats thinking that they might come in handy. The bleeding red raw skin around his wrists the least of his worries. Tentatively he touched his nose and winced, it was swollen to double its normal size.

The pain in his chest seemed to get worse with every breath he took. David turned on the light so that he could see properly and opened the buttons on his bloodied shirt. Peeling it back carefully to reveal the stab wound. There was a small amount of seepage, a mixture of blood and puss, but it didn't look that bad. A quick scan of the room revealed there was nothing to bandage it with. Slipping the shirt over his bad shoulder hurt like hell, blood started to flow from the puncture mark as he tore it into strips. He pulled the material as tightly as he could, using his teeth to hold onto one end and tie it. David eyed his handiwork. Messy, but it would have to do until he could get some proper medical attention.

His first priority was to put some distance between himself and the Commander's chamber of horrors. David estimated that around ten minutes must have passed since Abasi left the basement and he needed to get moving. But there was something that he wanted.

Bending over he took hold of Lembui's shoulder with one hand and his hip with the other. Heaving and leaning back it took David's combined weight and strength to roll him over. Lembui's teeth were bared and clamped shut in a strange grimace, blood dripping from the gaps between them. Then he noticed the small lump of pink muscle laying next the dead bodyguard's football size head. It took his brain a couple of seconds to register that it was Lembui's tongue.

David felt the bile rise in his throat, he looked away and forced himself to concentrate. Reaching into Lembui's jacket he unclipped the holster und pulled out the pistol. He checked the action and made sure that the magazine was full.

Glocks were standard issue in the KWS and David's training had involved spending hours on the firing range practicing with his. A year after being in the bush he changed to the heavier 9mm Browning as ammunition was easier to come by. The older British model was more prone to jamming if it wasn't kept clean but David preferred the increased weight. Nevertheless the Glock was more than capable of doing the job and held 17 rounds, four more than the Browning. Safety off David held the dead man's weapon out in front of him and stepped over Lembui's body.

Pulse racing and his injuries forgotten, he paused for a second in the doorway. Adrenalin heightened his senses. He checked to make sure that the coast was clear before slipping out into the corridor. David broke into a trot and padded towards the foot of the stairs. There were another three rooms leading off the wide passageway but only one of the doors was open. The set-up looked identical to the room he had just come from. David guessed that the other two were no different.

He took the steps at a crouch, arms extended, gun pointing at the crack of light coming through the open door. As he reached for the handle David froze, stopped in his tracks by a clanging noise from the other side. Then there was another, softer, duller this time.

"Please!" he heard a faint voice. "I don't want to die in here."

The man drifted off into incoherent mumbling and then stopped. Realising that it must be someone trapped in one of the other cells David pushed the door open slowly and winced. Reaching out caused the cracked bone to jab into the wall of his lung. Holding back the urge to shout out he retracted his arm and took a few painful breaths to recover. It sounded like he was sucking on a straw as the air whistled through the gap between his teeth.

He surveyed the twelve-foot wide anti-chamber and guessed this was where Lembui had dealt him the kick that broke his rib. There were six single steel doors on each side of the room and a double set made of solid oak dead ahead. Reinforced with three horizontal steel braces painted black. Standing next to them was a flimsy looking wooden desk boasting a telephone, two drawers and a chair. Camouflage raincoats hung from a row of pegs beneath the only window, it was barely two feet square and iron bars ensured that nobody could escape.

Viewing hatches at the top and longer thinner slots at the bottom for passing food identified the metal doors for what they were. What must have been David's was the only cell open, the rest looked securely shut.

David wondered what the hell he was doing as he dug into his pocket for Lembui's keys. His legs wanted him to run, get out of there as quickly as possible. He fished them out and shook his head. This was going to take forever. There were twelve identical keys on the ring. Luckily the first six doors weren't locked and swung open easily. Then he found one that wasn't.

"Hello," whispered David as he tried different keys in the lock. "Can you hear me?"

There was no response.

With each key David's efforts got more frantic until he wasn't sure whether he had mixed up the order and should start again. Picking a key at random from the loop he shoved it into the lock and twisted his hand. There was a rewarding click as it opened.

He pulled on the handle and light filled the darkened cell to reveal a naked man lying on the floor. His flabby back facing the door.

"Come on, let's move!"

David glanced towards the entrance before looking back in the cell but there was still no movement. Holding his breath against the stench of urine and vomit he stepped inside the cell and bent over the crumpled form. There didn't seem to be a part of the man's body that wasn't covered in cuts and bruises. David prodded his shoulder gently, fearing the worst.

"No," the man cried out weakly, covered his head with battered hands. "Leave me alone."

"It's OK. I'm not going to hurt you." David tried to make his voice sound soothing, "We've got to hurry!"

The man lowered his arms and twisted his neck towards him, disbelief on his face. By the way he squinted David guessed that the man must normally wear glasses.

"Who are you?" His voice was hoarse, barely more than a whisper, "Did Dewitt send you?"

"Trust me, there's no time for that," David thought for a second that the name sounded familiar. He held out his hand, "Commander Abasi could be back at any moment."

Mention of the Commander's name got a reaction. The prisoner rolled onto his back and reached out with a chubby hand. David took hold and pulled, the strain tearing at his shoulder. A few seconds later they were stood panting and wheezing face to face. The man's legs buckled suddenly and David almost lost his grip. To his surprise the stranger grunted and pushed himself back up.

He nodded, "I'll be OK."

"Follow me," David led him over to the door and took one of the raincoats down from its peg.

Handing it to him he noticed the scorch marks around the man's genitals for the first time. The same burnt pattern he had seen on Gupta. David looked up at the man's moon shaped face with new respect.

He draped the coat gently over the quivering man's shoulders, "Here put this on."

"Thanks, whoever you are," his teeth chattered.

Putting the gun down on the desk David grabbed the other jacket and shrugged it on. Pulling the belt tight to compensate for it being a few sizes too big he picked up the Glock and looked towards the cell doors.

"Shit!" He hadn't checked all of them.

Thirty seconds later he tried the last one and was grateful to find it empty. Getting out of the facility was going to be difficult enough without bringing along any more baggage. David glanced at the overweight inmate leaning against the desk for support. What was he doing? Neither of them was in any fit state to make a run for it.

"We'll stick to the shadows." David tried to sound confident as he made his way back over to the entrance, "Whatever happens, stay close to me and don't panic. Only run if I tell you to." The man looked at him but his eyes were glazed over. "Did you hear me?"

"I heard you," the man shook himself like a wet dog. David was surprised by the strength in the deep voice that answered, "I'm ready, let's go."

CHAPTER THIRTY-FIVE
GSU Headquarters, Nairobi
August 20th, 1996

David flicked the switch and the chamber was plunged into darkness. He found the fist sized loop and twisted the wrought iron handle, the clunk as the latch released sounded way too loud. Heart beating noisily David waited a few seconds for any kind of reaction before opening the door a fraction and peeking out.

There were signs of activity in the two-storey building on the other side of the gravel courtyard. Someone inside the frosted glass entrance was moving around, casting shadows. Lights were showing on the first floor and what looked like Abasi's car was parked out front. Hard for him to be certain with the tinted glass but it appeared empty. On his right a deserted looking single floor block joined the jailhouse with the larger building to form a quadrangle. There was no doorway or entrance, just a row of identical barred windows. David glanced at the other low level building to his left and began to wonder how the Mercedes had got there. He pushed the door open a bit wider, craning his neck around so that he could see the rest of the square. There was a gap between the buildings wide enough to fit a small truck through.

David nodded to the nameless man beside him. He took a deep painful breath and went outside. The drop in temperature was noticeable as the chill night air enveloped him. Hugging the wall and keeping low he headed for the opening, stones crunched underfoot.

The prisoner's laboured breathing and dragged footsteps seemed amplified. He worried that the combined noise they were making would attract attention. David crouched in the shadows between the two buildings and waited for him to catch up. His injuries and Caitlyn's death were forgotten as he scanned ahead, looking for a way out

Directly in front of them the driveway ended at a gatehouse about three hundred meters away. Under the oasis of light created by the arcs of two streetlamps David could see an armed guard, machine gun slung over his shoulder. He was standing behind the red and white striped barrier facing in the opposite direction. The occasional glow of a cigarette in the hut beside the gates gave away the position of another guard.

Over to the right of the road was a large level expanse of ground that could have been a football pitch except that there weren't any posts. David knew that it was a parade square, having finally worked out where he was. GSU Headquarters on Thika Road. No wonder Abasi and his bodyguards were so confident. Around two hundred troops lived in the rows of Nissan huts that made up the barracks on the other side of the square. If the alarm was raised the place would be swarming in minutes.

"Sorry," he apologised for bumping into David's back.

David held up his hand for him to be quiet. He could hear something, footsteps getting louder. Leaning around the corner at knee height, he honed in on the sound and picked up the silhouette. A figure emerged from between the last two huts and headed towards them. Ducking back behind the safety of the wall he swivelled on his haunches to face the other man. He jabbed him in the chest and then pointed at the ground, signalling him to stay put. The man nodded to say that he understood.

Whoever was coming had traversed the parade ground and was getting close when he took another look. David withdrew into the shadows and switched his grip on the Glock so that he was holding it by the barrel. Firing it would be like committing suicide.

David rose slowly to his feet and pressed his back up against the wall. He lifted the gun above his head ready to strike. Fighting back the pain as his broken rib dug into his lung.

As the man drew level with him he brought the butt of the gun down hard on the back his head. There was a loud exhalation of air and corresponding thump as he hit the ground. David leant over the prostrate figure. He aimed for the same spot and hit him again for good measure. The man sighed strangely and his whole body seemed to sag deeper into the gravel. David rolled him over. The staring eyes belonged to the other GSU officer he had seen outside Tanui's office.

David straightened up and turned the gun around so that he was holding it the right way. At least two of the men responsible for Caitlyn's death had been made to pay the price. He would have to come back for their boss. His fellow prisoner was squatting next to the wall, clearly in shock, eyes fixed on the dead man's body.

Tapping the trembling man's shoulder gently to get his attention David gestured towards some narrow brick buildings with tin roofs. The man stared at him blankly.

"Snap out of it!" hissed David.

He blinked and his eyes lost their glazed look. Then he nodded and with David's help the man pushed himself to his feet. Gritting his teeth against the resulting pain that shot through his shoulder they made their way towards the firing range.

During basic training David and the other rangers had been given the opportunity to try their skills out on the course. Part of the selection process in deciding whether you ended up out in the field or behind a desk somewhere pushing paper. Designed to test reaction speeds as well as marksmanship it was the only facility of its type in the country. There were both indoor and outdoor arenas where live rounds and smoke grenades were used to keep the candidates on their toes.

They walked slowly down the length of the building and passed the briefing room where he had received his induction. Treading carefully in the dark David searched for obstacles in the overgrown grass with his bare feet. His accomplice wasn't far behind.

Pausing first to make sure that there was nobody around he went out into what was the main section of the course. They crossed through the large wasteland of burnt out cars and trailers that resembled a disorganised scrap yard. As they entered the copse of trees on the other side he realised that Thika Road was closer than he remembered. The sound of a vehicle drifted through the trees and he caught a glimpse of some headlights.

Dry leaves crunched and branches snapped underfoot as they threaded their way blindly through the patch of woodland. David's arm bashed against a tree trunk and it took all of his will power to stifle the scream that built in his throat. He saw a single headlight coming down the road a few hundred yards away, bobbing up and down. Then the beam swung in an arc towards them and he realised it was a torch. One of the perimeter guards doing his rounds.

"Get down!" David quietly dropped to the floor. Lying as flat as possible he took some of the weight with his elbows to reduce the pressure on the broken rib. Pointing the pistol at the spotlight he prayed that the sentry would walk by without noticing them. The stomping of the man's boots got closer and then he heard the dog growl.

The sentry stopped in his tracks a few yards away and spoke softly in Swahili, "What is it? Did you hear something?" A deep bark answered him, then another.

Making the split decision to shoot the animal first and then its handler David prepared to squeeze the trigger. But then common sense told him to do neither. He lowered the weapon and pressed his face into the dirt. Resisting the temptation to look up, he could sense rather than see the light probing the darkness above his head. There was rustling nearby and he almost jumped out of his skin when the dog barked a feet away from him.

"There's nothing there," snapped the sentry.

There was a thumping noise followed by the dog's whimpering.

Gradually his footsteps and cursing faded and David got to his feet. He set off without looking back. The woods ended at a footpath and six-foot high fence, some bushes on the other side between them and the road. David grabbed the bottom of the chain link and pulled, stretching the metal and bending it up to create a gap underneath.

"Hold this for me," he instructed the man breathing heavily next to him. Chubby hands took hold of the fence and David crawled underneath.

Returning the favour from the outside David couldn't make the opening big enough and the man's jacket snagged on the fence as he tried to get through.

"Shit!" David put the pistol in his pocket and used both hands but no matter how hard he pulled the man wouldn't budge. His jacket was snagged on the fence, "Try going back a little bit."

As he wriggled around somebody started shouting in the distance, only to be drowned out by the shrill ringing of an alarm bell. David yanked harder and almost lost his balance as the man shot out from under the fence like a cork from a bottle. The jolt produced another wave of agony.

David turned and started to run as the other man scrambled to his feet. They burst through the bushes onto the old Thika Road that ran parallel to the new highway feeding the city. Luckily they were hidden from view of the main gates by a curve in the road. David turned away from the entrance and started running north.

A handful of matatus and a few trucks were taking advantage of a lay-by a few hundred meters up the road. David banged on the back of the nearest minibus and skidded to a halt beside the driver's door. The scared occupant woke with a start and jumped again when he rapped on the glass.

David made a revolving motion with his hand to indicate that he should wind down the window. The driver shook his head and shrank away from him. At a guess he was in his late twenties, possibly early thirties, from one of the desert countries bordering Kenya. Either Ethiopia or Somalia. His mixed Arabic and African heritage betrayed by his thin nose and purple lips. Closely cropped hair and a cleanly shaven face above a striped tunic.

David rubbed his forefinger and thumb together to indicate that he wanted to pay. The frown changed into a smile and the window was wound down.

"Where do you want to go, boss?"

That was when the big man arrived wheezing like he was about to die. He spoke between gasps for breath, "Take us...to the...American...Embassy."

"Get in!" replied the driver excitedly. He reached over his shoulder and unlocked the side door.

Sliding it open David bundled his unlikely partner into the vehicle and closed the door behind them. The starter motor clicked and whirred and for an awful moment sounded like it wasn't going to work.

Blabbering something in a foreign dialect the driver struck the steering wheel and fiddled with the key again. This time the starter turned over and gathered momentum until the engine reluctantly kicked in. Coughing and spluttering the minibus careered out onto the road and began to pick up speed slowly. Eventually the shaking matatu levelled out at a steady pace, one that David was sure he could outrun. He leant forward between the front seats and looked at the speedometer. The erratic needle was hovering below the 50km per hour mark.

"Doesn't this thing go any faster?"

The driver smiled at him in the rear-view mirror, "Not anymore." He veered off the road onto a slipway.

They went over the bridge and rejoined Thika Road, this time heading south towards the city on the highway. David sank back into his seat as they passed the lay-by and got close to the GSU gatehouse. Around a dozen officers were lined up inside the gate. Some of them standing, others crouched down on one knee. All of them were facing away from the road with their weapons trained towards the base. A thick concrete wall in the middle of the highway separated them from him. But David still didn't feel safe.

He could see a hive of activity over near the main building. Commander Abasi towered over the men around him. He was waving his arms and gesturing towards the gate. Then the scene was gone, blocked by hedges and Nissan huts. He turned to face the man next to him in the back of the minibus.

They stared at each other seriously for a second and then the big man grinned. His nerves got the better of him and David joined in.

"I'm Professor Onesimus Mutungi," he held out his hand. "A man forever in your debt."

"David Nbeke." He took the outstretched hand and shook his head, "and you don't owe me anything."

David closed his eyes for a few seconds and let his head fall back against the seat. Now that the adrenalin was wearing off he was feeling a bit faint.

Then vivid pictures of Caitlyn lying mutilated on the bed popped into his head. Thinking about the chain of events that had led to her death he felt the hatred growing inside him.

Trying to get near Abasi at GSU headquarters would require a small army. David wanted to speak to the Deputy Director and piece together some sort of plan but first he needed to get his wounds seen to. Infection would set in soon if he didn't get antibiotics, and some painkillers wouldn't go amiss. He spoke to the driver.

"Once we've dropped him off you can take me to the hospital." He turned to the Professor, "Do you think that you can get hold of some money at the Embassy?"

All of his worldly possessions were in the rucksack that he had left with Gupta outside Caitlyn's apartment. David wondered if Abasi had found the recorder and realised that the tape was missing. Not that it mattered, only David knew where it had been sent.

"Of course, if that's what you want," replied the Professor, thoughtfully stroking his chin. "But I'm sure that we'll be able to get medical attention at the Embassy, and it will be much safer. Seymour will take care of us."

David shrugged. As long as he got patched up it didn't really matter where. Driving over the Globe Flyover he could see the taller trees of Jevanjee Gardens, the park in front of Caitlyn's apartment. The road started to descend and the painful reminder disappeared as they dropped down into the city centre.

Something clicked. Bernstein had used the same name. "Do you mean Seymour Dewitt?"

The Professor raised one of his bushy eyebrows, "Why, do you know him?"

"Not personally," David shook his head. "But it's a small world."

CHAPTER THIRTY-SIX
GSU Headquarters, Nairobi
August 20th, 1996

Maliki was daydreaming when he heard the shrill noise. At first he thought it must be the phone ringing. Then he realised it was the alarm and jumped to his feet. Running from his office he practically bounced down the central staircase to the foyer.

"What's the alarm for?" He had to shout at the duty officer behind the desk to be heard above the racket.

"Your driver told me to sound it," the veins on his neck swelled up as the lieutenant was forced to shout back. "He found a dead officer. Looks like one of the prisoners might have escaped."

"Turn that bloody thing off!" barked Maliki. The noise was disorientating and would have alerted all the men in the barracks by now. His face twitched.

Thankfully the ringing stopped as he stepped outside. Ahead of him one of the double doors to the jail was swung open on its hinges. Maliki turned right, attracted by the sound of raised voices coming from beyond the courtyard. Following them he found the group of officers he had been expecting to arrive from his mansion. Huddled together near the gap between the buildings. They were animated and seemed distracted by something near their feet. As he drew closer Maliki realised that it must be the dead officer.

"Who is it?"

Some of the men with their backs to him were so on edge they actually jumped at his question. A hush fell over them and they parted so that he could see into the centre. Gakere was bent over the body.

"Its Sabore sir." He looked up, disbelief in his eyes, "Somebody crushed his skull."

"Don't be stupid, man," Maliki stepped into the throng to get a closer look, but sure enough the back of Sabore's head was a mess. Caved in like the crater of a volcano.

"Gakere, you come with me." Maliki waved towards the front gate that was already swarming with troops, "The rest of you go and find him, he can't have got far."

A rusty brown matatu caught his eye beyond the throng at the gates, trundling along slowly on the other side of the highway. But there was no one on board except the driver in the front. His men fanned out and started to search the grounds as Maliki turned away from the gates. With Gakere beside him he walked briskly back into the courtyard, over to the detention block.

"Be careful," he instructed standing to one side. "He could still be in there."

Gakere took out his Glock and led the way. Maliki waited until the light was on and he shouted that the room was clear before following.

All of the cells were open, including the Professor's, so was the door at the top of the staircase. Maliki nodded towards it and Gakere disappeared down into the basement.

A few minutes later he returned gasping for breath, a look of disbelief on his face, "There's nobody down there except Lembui, sir...and he's dead."

Maliki had to see for himself, he pushed past Gakere and descended the stairs. Lembui's frazzled corpse face first on the floor near the doorway sent a shiver down his spine. It was a sensation that Maliki hadn't felt in a long time. Not since being mauled by the lion all those years ago. Captain Nbeke had been badly wounded and strapped to a chair the last time he saw him. Yet somehow he had escaped with the Professor and killed Maliki's two best men with his bare hands. It wasn't until he was back outside in the courtyard that Maliki recognised the strange feeling. It was fear. His cheek went into spasm.

CHAPTER THIRTY-SEVEN
American Embassy, Nairobi
August 20th, 1996

"If your name's not on the register then you don't get in." The guard from the local security company manning the checkpoint tapped his clipboard, "And you're not on it."

"Just call Seymour Dewitt and tell him I'm here," the Professor shouted, exasperation evident in his tone. "Or Ambassador Bushnell. For Christ's sake man can't you see it's an emergency? This man is bleeding to death!"

The podgy security guard peered in the window through bloodshot eyes. He frowned at David's messed up face and roughly bandaged shoulder. Obviously this was a dilemma for him. Waking up Embassy staff in the middle of the night was not a step to be taken lightly. Get it wrong and you could find yourself out of a job. The stoned guard scratched behind one of his ears with a pen and nudged his navy blue beret. A few sizes too big it threatened to topple off but somehow stayed perched on his head at a jaunty angle.

"OK." He stopped itching his ear, "Stay here, I'll be right back."

David noticed the creased white shirttails hanging over his bubble shaped butt as he walked back into the booth. Through the glass he saw him put a telephone receiver to his ear and wondered why the guard didn't have a radio. Now that David thought about it he hadn't seen a weapon either. Maybe he was expecting too much but David thought that there would be Marine Guards everywhere, armed to the teeth.

Security in the Embassy basement was worse than lax, it was practically non-existent. Even the barrier itself was temporary, the freestanding metal type that police use for crowd control. David was tempted to tell the driver to hit the gas and run through it but that might stir the Marines into actually making an appearance. Presumably there must be some of them in the building on nightshift? Inside the booth the guard was now talking into the telephone, he nodded and replaced the receiver.

"Maybe we should just go to the hospital?" the driver of the matatu sounded nervous. He started to fiddle with the gearstick.

"Just wait," snapped the Professor, speaking with an air of confidence that David hadn't heard before.

The hired security guard ambled back over to the minibus. He pointed to a spot against the wall behind them, "You can park over there for now and someone will be down to see you in a minute."

"They'd better be quick!" snapped the Professor.

Now that he was on familiar turf the Professor was a different man, far from the cowering wreck that David had found back in the cell. There was a loud bang and David was thrown back against the seat as the driver of the matatu reversed into the wall.

"Now look what you made me do!" He covered his face with both hands, "Allah, what have I done to deserve this?"

"Relax." Mutungi leant forward and patted him on the shoulder, "I'll make sure that the repairs are paid for."

"Really?" the driver dropped his hands and turned to look at the Professor.

"You have my word...sorry, what is your name?"

"Jamal," replied the driver. His face lit up and he smiled, "Like the basketball player."

Despite the pain he was in David smiled at the irony. Jamal Jones was almost seven feet tall whereas the driver could barely see over the dashboard. Somebody had a sense of humour but he wasn't sure whether it was Jamal or his parents. Professor Mutungi turned and squinted at him.

"Please excuse me, Captain Nbeke. I can't see a damn thing without my glasses." The Professor shook his head, "So how did you end up in Abasi's dungeon?"

"I could ask you the same thing," he sighed, causing a pang of pain in his chest. So much had happened in such a short space of time. How could he summarise the whirlwind of events that had led to their chance meeting in just a few words? David looked up. The Professor was peering at him expectantly.

"It's all to do with poaching. I've got proof that the Commander is involved in smuggling rhino and elephant horn out of the country. He's also responsible for the death of one of my colleagues and somebody very close to me."

"I'm sorry to hear that," the Professor sounded sincere but there was a hint of excitement in his voice. "Did you say that you have proof?"

David nodded, "I've got a witness in custody and the statement of a poacher who worked for him...Abasi killed him too, tortured him to death." Thinking about Gupta's burnt genitals almost made him retch.

"With your testimony it just might be enough." The Professor stroked his chin, "Let's see what Seymour has to say."

"What about you?"

"Sorry?" the Professor frowned.

"Why were you in there?"

He actually smiled, "All in good time Captain, let's get you patched up first." He pointed out the window, "Looks like our escort has arrived."

A detachment of six marines had materialised beyond the checkpoint. Their leader, a squat sergeant with three stripes on the shoulders of his khaki shirt, was talking to the hired help.

After a brief conversation the sergeant nodded and walked over to the minibus. Two of the other Marines followed a few paces behind him. Fingers on the triggers of the Heckler & Koch machine guns they were carrying. If he was surprised by their appearance or the lateness of the hour the sergeant didn't show it. Ignoring the driver he addressed them through the side door.

"Sergeant Krasinski," his eyes darted around the back of the minibus, examining the seats behind them. "Which one of you guys is Professor Mutungi?"

*****

The sergeant led them into the building through a fire escape in the basement. A brightly lit stairwell replaced the gloom and damp. Now that he was safe, the massive amounts of adrenalin his body had been producing were no longer needed. As the flow ceased and it broke down in his blood stream David started to tremble. He shivered as if cold, even though it must have been over thirty degrees Celsius in the subterranean level of the Embassy.

As they walked up to the first floor David suddenly felt queasy and his legs buckled underneath him. One of the marine guards grabbed hold of his arm to steady him. The procession halted in the middle of the stairs as he gathered enough strength to continue. Aware that all eyes were on him David took a few deep breaths and nodded that he was ready to go.

"Not too quickly, just take it one step at a time, sir," barely twenty with blonde fluff rather than stubble, the fresh-faced marine's words of encouragement only made it worse. "Not much further now."

David was relieved when they reached the foyer on street level and walked towards the elevator. He couldn't contemplate attempting another flight of stairs. After not sleeping for days and losing so much blood all he wanted was to find somewhere to

333

lie down and close his eyes for a while. The sofa opposite reception looked inviting, but they weren't stopping.

"We're taking these gentlemen up to the conference room on the fourth floor. Call the hospital and have them send over a doctor ASAP," Krasinski barked at the local security guard manning the desk. "And make sure that they come prepared, two trauma patients, one with a stab wound."

Not waiting for a reply he pressed the button and the elevator doors opened. Sergeant Krasinski turned to the Marine helping David, "Pierce, come with us. The rest of you stay here. Make sure that only the doctor and the RSO make it anywhere near the fourth floor until you hear otherwise from me personally."

Professor Mutungi's laboured breathing filled the silence as the tiny elevator trundled slowly upwards. The steel box was cramped with only four of them inside and didn't seem large enough for the building, either an oversight or the result of underfunding. Their ascent ended jerkily as the elevator settled itself on the fourth floor.

Krasinski took them down a long glass panelled corridor with offices on either side and opened a set of double doors at the end.

"Make yourselves comfortable," he said, switching on the light. "We'll get you some water and clothes to put on. I can't guarantee they'll fit but we'll find you something."

David was helped into one of the twenty or so leather chairs around the oval shaped conference table. Mutungi sat opposite him, his face reflected in the highly polished walnut.

"Thanks," his voice sounded weak and distant. David felt the room start to spin and closed his eyes.

*****

By the time Dewitt got there the doctor sent from the hospital had already sewn up the stab wound and taped his ribs. David winced as antiseptic was applied to his nose but he was feeling a lot better. Probably had something to do with all the morphine.

After everything he had been through in the last few days it didn't surprise him when Aaron Bernstein turned up with the Embassy's Regional Safety Officer. Bernstein looked scruffy as usual, wearing torn jeans and a collarless shirt. The reporter walked into the room ahead of Dewitt, acting as if he belonged there. In contrast, the RSO was immaculately dressed. Despite the fact that he must have been dragged out of bed he wore a crisply ironed shirt that hugged his square cut shoulders

"What the hell happened?" exclaimed Bernstein seeing his face and fresh bandages. "You look like shit!"

"Thanks," replied David. "It's good to see you too."

What did seem strange to David was that once the introductions were over Dewitt took a back seat. It was Bernstein who asked all the questions.

He was obviously a skilled interviewer and only interrupted David a couple of times to ask for Gupta and Caitlyn's addresses. Dewitt took notes, scribbling away noisily with his pencil.

"It's a miracle that the two of you managed to escape," said the reporter, shaking his head when David finally finished recounting events.

"I owe my life to Captain Nbeke here," announced the Professor glancing over at him. "If it wasn't for him I'm certain Abasi would have killed me."

Bernstein addressed David, "How much do you know about Commander Abasi?"

"Only what I've told you," replied David. "Until a couple of weeks ago I'd never even heard of him."

"Makes sense, Abasi likes to keep below the radar," Bernstein nodded. "If that's even his real name."

"What do you mean?"

Dewitt coughed, "Unfortunately poaching is not the only crime that Abasi is guilty of, in fact it's just the tip of the iceberg. He first appeared on our radar in 1978 not long after Kenyatta died and Moi came to power. A group of MPs were falsely accused of plotting against the President after a failed assassination attempt. The Ministers declared their innocence and claimed that the trumped up charges were being used as an excuse to get rid of them.

Commander Abasi led the enquiry against them as the head of Moi's secret service. By all accounts it was a brutal investigation that ended in the disappearance of two Kikuyu MPs."

Professor Mutungi's powerful voice took over, "Since then he has been President Moi's enforcer and implicated in numerous crimes. Including the ethnic cleansing of the Kikuyu people in the run up to the election. His job was to keep them away from the ballot polls. Which he did to great effect, killing and detaining tens of thousands."

David felt disbelief turning into raw hatred. Abasi was connected to his father's death as well as being directly responsible for Caitlyn's. As head of the Secret service Abasi would have ordered the death squads to do his dirty work. He slammed his fist on the table and sent a shockwave through his shoulder that managed to override the painkillers.

He gritted his teeth, "If you know all this, why hasn't anything been done? Why isn't Abasi behind bars?"

"We are talking about the President's right hand man." The Professor sighed deeply, "Every time a witness comes forward they mysteriously disappear along with any police reports. People who know are too afraid to speak out, even members of the Human Rights Committee."

"Where does he come from?" David couldn't shake the feeling that his and Abasi's fates had been intertwined for some time.

"Before 1978 there doesn't appear to be any official record of Peter Abasi, at least not one that we can find," it was Bernstein who replied.

"What, nothing at all?"

"We believe that the name Peter Abasi is invented." Bernstein turned to Dewitt, "What do you think. Have we got enough to go on?"

"I'm not sure that there is enough evidence to convict Abasi." Dewitt furrowed his brow, "But with Captain Nbeke and the Professor's testimony it's probably enough to have him brought in for questioning. And to obtain search warrants. I'll call Minister Kamotho and ask him to speak to the Police Commissioner. Maybe we'll get lucky and find something at Abasi's house or his office."

"Hold on a minute," said David, as the RSO got up from his chair. "This is a KWS investigation and it stays that way."

"I don't understand?" Dewitt clenched his jaw and examined him through steely grey eyes.

"From what you've been telling me we can't be sure that Abasi hasn't got the Minister and the Commissioner in his pocket," David wasn't ready to take the risk. "If not them, one of their members of staff. Start asking for his arrest or search warrants and he's bound to find out."

"I suppose you're probably right." Bernstein gave him a sideways look, "Just what are you proposing?"

"A set up. Abasi wants Koinet and we've got him," replied David simply. "Is there a CB radio in the Embassy?"

Dewitt nodded, "There are two down in the coms room on the ground floor."

David held onto the edge of the table for support and got up from his chair, "Would you mind taking me there? I need to make a couple of calls."

CHAPTER THIRTY-EIGHT
Waiyaki Way, Nairobi
August 20th, 1996

Bernstein drove them northwest out of the city. Dawn was breaking and the streets were already bustling with people on their way to work. The American drove confidently and weaved the Datsun hatchback expertly through the traffic.

"So, who do you really work for?" David already knew the answer but he wanted to hear it from Bernstein.

The American glanced over at him and then turned his attention back to the chaos in the street ahead. Five lanes of traffic were sandwiched into what had been built for three. Bernstein gave a long blast on the horn and forced his way into a lane that was moving.

"You've probably figured it out already anyway." He shrugged, more to himself than David, "I work for the CIA. I'm what they call a Collection Management Officer, CMO for short. It's my job to collect information in the field and relay it back to Langley for analysis. Find out who the bad guys are and suggest affirmative action."

"You make it all sound very corporate."

Bernstein smiled, "I guess it is, in a way. That's why we call it 'the company'."

Bernstein had the perfect cover. Nobody would suspect a reporter asking questions or poking his nose in, it was part of the job description.

"How long have you been investigating Abasi?" David grimaced as they went over a pothole in the road and it jarred his shoulder.

"Like the RSO said, we've known about him for years. But things escalated when the Professor contacted the Embassy a few months ago. I was called in to do some digging around. Once I found out that Abasi was familiar with Counsellor Wei it didn't take long to figure out what was going on. Wei's family own a string of carving factories back in China, we figure that he's been shifting the ivory for Abasi. We also believe that Deputy Director Tanui's involved, passing on operational information so that the poachers can avoid your patrols. But that part's conjecture, we've got no proof."

David shook his head, "I thought so too but Tanui's not the leak. Abasi must have someone else inside the KWS."

"How can you be so sure?"

"Abasi let slip that there's no love lost between them when he was interrogating me." David shivered when he thought of the basement, Gupta and Lembui.

"Well someone's been giving Abasi the heads up," Bernstein accelerated into another gap. "Until you came along he's been getting away with it for years. We've traced regular transfers from an account in Zurich to Abasi's local bank. Going back over a decade. As usual the bloody Swiss crooks won't break client confidentiality so that's where the money trail ends."

Once they got past the Kabete Telephone Exchange the traffic began to thin out and Bernstein picked up speed. They soon left the city behind them and the land beside the road fell away as they reached the edge of the rift valley. They dropped down from the escarpment and turned onto the B3, heading through the dry grasslands towards Narok.

David ran things over in his mind. Spencer Scott had taken the news of Caitlyn's death badly. David just hoped that he kept it together and didn't become a hindrance. The likelihood was that they were going to be outnumbered and they would be relying on the element of surprise. If Scott acted recklessly it might endanger them all.

Back in the Embassy he thought about calling KWS Headquarters but decided against it. Not knowing the mole's identity he didn't want to risk the possibility of tipping off Abasi. David would have to come clean with Deputy Director Tanui when this was all over, a conversation that he wasn't looking forward to.

He checked the display on the dashboard, nearly eight o'clock. Damo would probably be back at base camp in the Mara by now.

"You should try to catch some shut-eye," Bernstein interrupted his thoughts. "You look like you need it."

David leant his head back against the seat and winced, he'd forgotten all about the bump on the back of his head. It seemed superfluous compared to his other injuries, yet he had to turn sideways in the seat to get comfortable. He closed his eyes. The vibration and rocking motion of the car soon put David to sleep.

"We're here," announced Bernstein, the hatchback skidded to a halt in a cloud of dust. "Which way now?"

David opened his eyes and shook his head to get rid of the drowsiness. He must have been asleep for over an hour, his troubled mind torturing him with new nightmares, Caitlyn being raped by Abasi as he was forced to watch.

They were outside the KWS camp behind Serena Lodge. He pointed to a track leading to the left of one of the barracks, "Damo should be down there."

Bernstein ground the gearstick into first and the Datsun lurched forward. Damo and the six additional men he had requested were sitting under the shade of an acacia tree. Next to them was a Bedford truck with green canvas covering the back. Damo stood up as they approached and patted down his jacket to get rid of the dust. Bernstein pulled up behind the truck and killed the engine. Damo was opening the door for him before David could reach for the handle.

"Jambo sana, I was beginning to think that you weren't coming back," his friend's smile vanished when he noticed the extent of David's injuries. "Man, you look like shit. What happened?"

"I'll tell you later. Is everything ready?"

"Yes." Damo nodded towards the truck, "We've got enough in there to take down a small army."

"Good, I've got a feeling that we're going to need it." David turned to the American, "Damo, this is Aaron Bernstein. He's here to help us. Make sure that he's fully kitted out. I'm assuming he knows how to use it."

Damo raised an eyebrow, "Are you sure?"

Bernstein smiled, "Don't worry. I'll try not to get in the way."

"OK," David nodded. "Get everybody loaded up, we leave in five minutes. Did you bring the other things that I asked for?"

Damo handed him the rucksack he was holding, "All in there."

"Thanks, I won't be long."

Turning his back on them he headed back up the track towards the hotel. It was time to put the call into Commander Abasi and stir the hornets' nest. David just hoped that he could make it sound convincing.

CHAPTER THIRTY-NINE
GSU Headquarters, Nairobi
August 20th, 1996

Maliki rubbed at the scars on his face. The twitching was worse than it had ever been. A thorough search of the grounds failed to reveal anything. Captain Nbeke and the Professor must have escaped. The question now was where would they go?

Hoping that the pair would head straight for KWS headquarters he had dispatched men to watch the various entrances to the Park. He decided to call Idi Tikolo and see if the plump little weasel knew anything.

The lieutenant sounded surprised, "No there's been no sign of him here."

"There's nothing on the phones or radio relating to his whereabouts?" As the Chief Communications Officer Tikolo would know if there was anything on the wires.

"Like I said, sir." Tikolo lowered his voice, "There's been no unusual activity."

"Has anybody else been to see Tanui?

"No, the DD's not here." Tikolo's voice was muffled as he covered the phone, "And he's not expected back for a couple of days. He's on a scheduled visit to the training camp in Tsavo to brief a new batch of recruits."

"Let me know the moment there's any change," his cheek twitched as he hung up the phone.

Everything Maliki had was at stake. If the President got wind of this he would be disgraced and used as a scapegoat. There was no doubt about that. His years of loyal service would mean nothing if Moi's reputation was compromised. The President had made a lot of political mileage on the international stage by preaching Kenya's no tolerance policy on ivory trade. He was under no illusion. The President would drop him like a tonne of bricks if the press got hold of the story.

Maliki reached for the chain around his neck and pulled the amulet out from underneath the polo shirt he was wearing. The texture of the soft metal as he rubbed the gold between his thumb and forefinger didn't provide him with the usual comfort. The family heirloom was the only physical link to his former life with the tribe. Unless he was bathing or having sex it remained securely around his neck. His mother once told him that the talisman was forged by a powerful witch doctor. Instilled with supernatural powers that would protect him. Maliki believed her then as he did now. He gazed reverently at the two-headed figure of Engai Narok as it glowed in the palm of his hand.

The phone on his desk started to ring and Maliki shoved the amulet back inside his shirt. He grabbed the receiver off the hook and pressed it to his ear.

"Yes?"

"Sorry to disturb you, Commander," it was the annoying desk clerk again. "I've got a Captain Nbeke on the line for you, says that you'll want to speak to him."

Maliki's chest froze up and he stopped breathing for a second. Then anger replaced his disbelief. Who the fuck did this Captain Nbeke think he was?

"Put him through!"

"Yes sir."

There was a series of clicks and then Nbeke spoke, "Is that Commander Abasi?"

"What do you want?" barked Maliki.

"Now, now, Commander, is that anyway to talk to someone who is trying to help you?"

"And why would you want to help me, Captain?" sneered Maliki.

"I just want to be left alone. I'll give you Koinet and resign from the Service if you agree to let me live in peace."

"Is that all?"

There was a brief pause, "And $250,000. Let's call it my retirement fund."

"That's a lot of money, Captain," Maliki smiled to himself. So that's what all this was about. Everybody had a price, even the good Captain. "What do you intend to do with it?"

"I don't think that's any of your business," replied Nbeke. "Now do we have a deal or shall I turn Koinet over to the Deputy Director?"

"Calm down, Captain." Maliki decided to go along with the charade, "I think that I can accommodate you but it will take a few hours to

346

raise the money. Bring Koinet to me at lunchtime and I'll have it ready."

"Don't try and play me for a fool, Commander." Nbeke paused, "Do you really think for one second that I would go back there? If you want Koinet then you'll have to come to me."

"And where might that be, Captain?"

"A lodge near to the Maasai Mara," Nbeke gave him directions. "I'll wait there until nightfall. If you don't show by then I'll assume that the deal is off and turn Koinet in to the Deputy Director. Tell him all about you and Wei's little business venture."

Maliki was surprised that Nbeke knew about Wei. He was sure that Gupta hadn't known the Councillor's identity, someone else must have told Nbeke. But now wasn't the time to ask. He would enjoy finding out later, when he got his hands on the annoyingly resilient ranger.

"There's no need for that, Captain," Maliki's lip pulled up as his cheek contracted. "I'll meet you. But how do I know that it isn't a trap?"

"You don't!" replied Nbeke. "Just make sure that you bring the money. This is the only chance you'll get. If I smell a rat I'll be off into the bush before you know it and you'll never find me."

The phone went dead in his ear before Maliki could reply. He smashed the receiver repeatedly on the edge of his desk. The plastic cracked and sent grey shards flying over the Persian rug. Eventually it broke in half, as it did a piece of plastic dug into his hand. Maliki dropped the broken earpiece so that it hung over the desk and clashed against the wooden drawers, the two ends held together by a couple of wires.

Ignoring the gouge he'd made in his finger, Maliki pushed back his chair and stood up. This time there would be no mistakes and he would take care of Captain Nbeke personally. The meddlesome ranger would be begging for his own life to be ended by the time Maliki finished working on him with the knife.

CHAPTER FORTY
Spencer Scott's Lodge, Maasai Mara
August 20th, 1996

"We're nearly there," said David as they passed the Kawai Damn. This time there were no cattle or herdsmen to be seen, the midday heat probably too much for them. Damo was already reducing speed and guided the old Bedford gently onto the dirt track.

"Bit on the remote side, isn't it?" Bernstein was sat between them in the cab of the truck. The rest of the men were in the back.

"Exactly."

David didn't bother to expand any further. He gritted his teeth as the Bedford bumped over a rock. The painkillers were beginning to wear off. He would take some more when they stopped.

Damo squeezed the Bedford through the open gates and down the drive to the cluster of huts by the waterhole. Scott appeared on the porch of the main lodge with something dangling from his hand. As they drew closer David realised that it was a bottle. The brakes made a high-pitched squeal as Damo pulled up in front.

Scott looked more dishevelled than the last time he'd seen him and was obviously drunk. The big man would have fallen head first down the flight of steps if he hadn't somehow grabbed hold of the wooden handrail.

"Shit," David pulled on the handle and pushed the door open. He looked across at Damo before getting out, "Whatever happens don't do anything."

"I told you to look after her. You bastard!" shouted Scott as he staggered towards him waving the half full bottle around for effect. He stopped a couple of feet away and prodded David in the chest, swaying on his feet. His eyes were all puffy and red and there was a strong smell of whisky on his breath, "Now she's dead!"

David knew what was coming but let Scott hit him anyway, turning his head to reduce the impact as a huge fist caught him on the jaw. Luckily it was wild and had none of the big man's weight behind it, or he would have been on the deck. David straightened up and rubbed his chin, the movement sent a stabbing pain through his chest. Scott swung back his arm to take another shot but a loud click stopped him as Damo released the safety on his rifle.

"That's enough."

"Put it away Damo, I deserved that."

His friend looked confused but lowered the rifle so that it pointed at the ground.

Scott started to sob, "You deserve more than that, you bastard. You're the one who should be dead, not Caitlyn."

David nodded. It was something he would have to live with for the rest of his life. He could feel the tears welling in his own eyes, "I know. It's my fault for involving her."

"Actually, that's not strictly true." Bernstein coughed nervously, "Caitlyn was supplying me with information long before you came along."

"What?" David turned around to face him, "Are you telling me that Caitlyn was spying for the CIA."

"No, nothing quite that dramatic. She told me when orphans were brought in or heard reports about poaching for my newspaper articles." Bernstein must have read the look on his face, "She did it willingly, David. Nobody forced Caitlyn to do anything. She was far too strong a woman for that. Caitlyn cared about the animals and wanted to make a difference."

"Why didn't she tell me?"

"I don't know," Bernstein shrugged. "Maybe she was going to. You guys had just met. I thought that you knew, after our conversation in the Hankook Garden"

David had forgotten about the hint Bernstein dropped that first night in the restaurant, alluding to the fact that he had been talking to Caitlyn. He'd never really had the chance to ask either of them about it. How much more was there that he didn't know?

"So it's your fault then," roared Scott as he blundered past him. David stuck out his foot and ankle tapped him before he could reach Bernstein. To his credit the American didn't budge as Scott collapsed in front of him.

"Didn't you hear any of that?" David knelt beside him, "The man who's really responsible for Caitlyn's death is on his way here. Now, if you want to be part of what I've got in mind for him then you need to sober up. Or you'll be no good to me. Do you understand?"

Scott nodded.

"Good." He looked over at Damo, "Take him inside and get some coffee on the go. Lots of it."

Damo shouldered his rifle and Bernstein helped him get Scott to his feet. The rest of the rangers had filed out of the truck and were watching as they supported him up the short flight of steps to the lodge. Some of them were laughing, obviously amused by Scott's antics.

"Wipe those smiles off your faces," shouted David. "We've got work to do. Everybody on me."

Many of the men were familiar to him and he had worked with them before on patrol. A hush came over the group of rangers as they gathered around him.

"Good to see you two," said David as Chege and Rashid emerged from one of the adjacent huts and joined them. "Where's Makori?"

"He's inside sir." Chege grinned at him and saluted theatrically, "Guarding the prisoner, as instructed."

"You can drop the act, Chege, save it for later," David needed everybody to focus. He raised his voice and addressed the eight rangers listening, "I want you guys to unload the truck and put everything on the porch. Then get fully kitted out and check your weapons. Make sure that you are carrying extra ammunition. Then get something to eat and fill your canteens, we might have a bit of a wait on our hands. Back here in half an hour."

Comfortable in the knowledge that they must be at least a couple of hours ahead of the Commander, David went inside.

*****

After throwing up and drinking another pot of foul looking coffee Scott started to sober up. Bernstein raided the fridge and found some cheese to make sandwiches with. David wolfed one down as he examined the local map above Scott's desk. There were a number of tracks leading north, if they needed to make a run for it. With his finger he traced the line of trees along the dry riverbed to the west of the waterhole. It was pretty much how he remembered it. The end of the smaller waterhole to the east was open where it faced the lodge. The rest was surrounded by a U-shaped copse of trees.

"You said that the man responsible for Caitlyn's death was on his way here," Scott sounded much more coherent. "I think I have a right to know who he is."

David turned to face him. Scott was sitting in his armchair by the fireplace. "His name is Peter Abasi. He's the head of the GSU."

"I'm guessing by all the men you've brought that he isn't coming alone?"

"That would be a fair assumption."

David was under no illusions but he had a few surprises that would help level the playing field.

"Do you mind if I borrow this?" the map was stuck to the wall with sellotape and the corners tore off as he ripped it down from the wall.

353

"Do I have a choice," grumbled Scott.

"Not if you want to live."

He took one of the marker pens from the pot on the desk and added the four huts to the map. He put a big circle around an area of open land to the northwest. Then he put two small crosses on the copses of trees that overlooked it from each side.

Damo came over and stood beside him, Bernstein and Scott were talking by the fireplace. Damo spoke quietly so that they couldn't hear, "You can't seriously be thinking about taking on the head of the GSU?"

"What would you like me to do?" replied David. "Walk away as if nothing has happened? Let the man responsible for the deaths of Haji, Caitlyn and countless others get away with it Scott free." David realised that he had raised his voice. The others stopped talking and were no doubt listening. He glanced over his shoulder. Sure enough they were looking his way. "Sorry Spencer, no pun intended."

"None taken." Scott hesitated for a second before asking, "Did you say *countless* others?"

Bernstein answered on his behalf, "That's right, our best estimate is that he's ordered the deaths of somewhere between fifty and a hundred thousand people. The majority of them Kikuyu killed in the run up and aftermath of the last general election."

David's father was one of them, but he didn't say anything.

"That's one hell of statistic." Scott frowned, "If the CIA knows all this then why haven't they done something about it? Taken this guy out? I thought that you assassinated people all the time?"

"In the real world it's not that easy," Bernstein shook his head. "Abasi is too well protected and has Moi's support. If the President knew that we were involved at all it would jeopardise American interests in Kenya."

David was hit with a sudden realisation that was so obvious he couldn't believe it hadn't come to him before. Bernstein had been playing him all along. "So you rely on local people to do your dirty work for you?"

"I'm sorry David. But like I said our hands are tied," Bernstein shook his head in apology. "All we can do is point people in the right direction."

David started to wonder what might have happened if the CIA hadn't got involved. Would Caitlyn still be alive? That question would have to wait for another day. It was nearly time to brief the troops and he wanted to speak to Makori alone first.

"We'll talk about this another time." David headed for the door, "Be outside in five minutes."

*****

Makori didn't take the news very well.

"Why do I have to go," he kicked the wall with his steel toecap. "Can't one of the others take him?"

"It has to be someone that I can trust," David appealed to Makori's ego. "And our lives may depend on it." Koinet was the only bargaining chip he had and David wanted him as far away from the action as possible.

"If you think that it's important then I'll do it," grunted Makori. "But don't expect me to be happy. I would rather stay here than babysit this scum."

Koinet was handcuffed by one of his arms to the metal bunk bed, his mouth covered by a strip of gaffa tape. The wounded leg was so heavily bandaged that he couldn't bend it at the knee. His heel rested on the wooden floorboards.

"Let's take him outside to the truck." He patted Makori on the shoulder, "The sooner you get going the better."

David was killing two birds with one stone, the truck needed to be out of sight before Abasi got there. Makori was to wait near the police station in Migori. The nearest town of any size about twenty-five miles to the west. In the opposite direction to where Commander Abasi would be coming from.

The rest of the men, including Bernstein and Scott, were waiting near the front of the truck when they got outside. David opened the passenger door and Makori bundled Koinet into the cab.

"Where's he taking him?" Bernstein asked as the disgruntled ranger jumped into the truck and slammed the door shut.

"He's taking him somewhere safe," David shouted to be heard over the noise of the Bedford's engine but avoided answering the question.

Once the truck went out through the gates and turned onto the track he faced the others, "Against his will, Makori has agreed to take on a special mission. It is imperative that the prisoner doesn't fall into the hands of our enemy. His job is to keep him safe until this is all over."

A couple of the men shook their heads as if they were disappointed not to be chosen but nobody said anything.

"Most of you will be wondering what the hell you are doing here. All I can tell you is that we will probably be up against a superior force of equally armed GSU combat veterans." Murmuring broke out amongst the men but David continued, "They are being misled by one of their superior officers. A man connected with the death of one of our colleagues, Ranger Haji, amongst many others."

The talking ceased.

"He is also behind one of the largest poaching rings this country has ever known and is responsible for shipping tonnes of ivory to China every year."

He waited a few seconds for it to sink in, "Although as Rangers we are sworn to protect Kenya's wildlife and bring this man to justice, the mission hasn't been sanctioned. Anybody who doesn't want to be involved should leave now, whilst they've still got the chance."

"We're wasting time," said Chege. "How are we going to catch this bastard?"

David smiled briefly as he unfolded Scott's map and laid it on the ground, the men huddled around him to get a better view. The decisions to have Koinet brought there and use it for the showdown with Commander Abasi hadn't been made randomly. Nor was the list of confiscated items he had asked Damo to bring

"I'm expecting them to arrive in two, possibly three, helicopters. As you can see the four huts back onto the waterhole making them easily defendable from the rear," not many men would be willing to cross the crocodile infested waters. "The only real place to land is here." David pointed to the circle he'd drawn.

"Chege, I want you to take one of the rocket launchers and hide in these trees here," he pointed to the one just north of their position. "Rashid, you hide to the east of the clearing with the other RPG. Wait for the shooting to start and then take out the helicopters. Then I want you to come at them from the rear."

Both men nodded but bore opposing expressions, a look of disbelief on Rashid's face, a smile on Chege's.

"Before they get here we're going to put down some perimeter defences to make sure that they can't outflank us. I want you to space the snares out in two rows either side of the clearing. Between the trees and our position." He pointed to the lines he'd drawn between the corners of the furthermost huts and the trees.

"Then the land mines need to be divided up and placed in these two areas outside the snares. We're going to funnel them down to our position."

By doing so, David hoped that he would reduce the effectiveness of their superior numbers. His men would be able to concentrate all their firepower on the neck of the funnel. With Chege and Rashid surprising them from the rear it might just tip the balance. David rehearsed the plan with them a couple of times until he was sure that every man knew the details off by heart.

"Right, their ETA is about an hour from now so we'd better get the snares and mines in place and take up our positions. Remember, nobody is to fire a shot until I do. The key to this succeeding is drawing them onto us before they know that we're here. Good luck gentlemen."

Even Chege was strangely silent as the men dispersed and went off in pairs.

The butterflies started to flutter in his stomach, as they always did when a mission got going. David walked with Damo up the stairs between the piles of munitions into Scott's lodge.

CHAPTER FORTY-ONE
Spencer Scott's Lodge, Maasai Mara
August 20th, 1996

The seconds ticked by agonisingly slowly. Minutes became an hour, then two, eventually dragging into three. Inside the lodge the tension mounted between them as the waiting took its toll. Outside the light started to fade.

"This is crazy," muttered Damo. He was staring out of the window towards the gates. "It will be dark soon."

"Why don't you relax and sit down, you're starting to get on my nerves." David instantly regretted snapping at his friend, "I told you before, this might be the only chance we'll get to stop him."

"And that's so important that you're willing to risk all of our lives, including your own?" Damo shook his head, "You don't even know who he really is."

Bernstein must have told him that part of the story. David was about to ask when he heard the drum of rotors in the distance. Seconds later a pair of Bell helicopters appeared over the brow of the hill in the distance.

"They're here." David took charge, "You'd better get in position."

Damo mumbled something under his breath but made his way over to the window.

As the ungainly glass-fronted beasts got closer the noise of the double-rotors became deafening. They hovered over the clearing. So close that David could see the manifold of the exposed Pratt & Whitney engines housed in their tails. Ponderously they descended into the clearing, creating a huge cloud of dust.

David rested his rifle on the edge of one of the armchairs that they had dragged near the window and adjusted the scope. The hatch located behind the cockpit of the nearest helicopter opened and a figure in combat fatigues appeared. His finger tightened on the trigger but it wasn't Abasi. He released the pressure and let the GSU officer disembark, followed by nine others, also armed with machine guns and wearing bulletproof vests. They fanned out from the Bell and dropped to their knees in the grass, forming a semi-circle facing the lodge.

Another squad emerged from the second helicopter in tight formation, protecting someone in their midst, using their bodies as a human shield. David guessed that it must be the Commander but there was no way of telling through the mass of camouflage uniforms. The second troop stopped behind first and crouched facing the lodge.

In unison the first squad of officers rose to their feet and started to advance towards the huts. They held formation well, about five meters apart.

He centred the cross- hairs on one of the faces in the middle of the line and waited. When the man was about a hundred meters away he took a deep breath and pulled the trigger. His head snapped back and the GSU officer was thrown backwards. The air was instantly filled with the sound of gunfire as David's men started shooting from the other buildings. Three more GSU officers were riddled with bullets and collapsed.

A couple of Abasi's troops started to return fire. Aiming at the hut that Bernstein and Scott were in. There was a whooshing sound followed by an enormous explosion that shook the posts supporting the lodge.

The helicopter furthest from them burst into flames and sent a huge mushrooming fireball up into the sky. Black smoke started to pour from the back of the Bell as what was left of the fuel continued to burn. The force of the blast had broken the beast's back, the hull torn open below the main rotors. The flaming metal carcass groaned and rolled over onto its side with a crash. Still spinning one of the huge rotors buckled as it dug into the ground. For some reason Rashid didn't fire at the second helicopter. David could only assume that there was something wrong with the rocket launcher.

Not that it mattered. The group that had previously been guarding Abasi picked themselves up and started running away from the Bell. Dry grass around the downed helicopter had caught fire and a wall of flames was spreading rapidly towards the second. Unfortunately the group were heading straight for the snares and landmines to the west of the clearing. There was a dull pop as one of the anti-personnel mines went off and the man at the front disintegrated in a spray of blood and tissue. The man behind him was caught by the shrapnel and went down howling in agony.

David caught sight of Abasi running not far behind him but suddenly he fell to the ground and disappeared from sight. The rest of the squad turned back towards the lodge and started shooting.

The rotors of the other Bell started to turn and the noise of the engine built to a crescendo. The weight was slowly taken off the wheel's suspension and it lifted off the ground. He kept his rifle trained on the spot where Abasi had fallen just in case he tried to make a run for the helicopter. But there was no sign of him. The pitch of the single engine increased steadily as the huge beast climbed, creating a dust storm that enveloped the clearing. After hovering for what seemed like an eternity the Bell turned 180 degrees, tilted forward and thundered away from them.

The cracking sound of automatic weapons being fired resumed once the cloud of dust had settled. Abasi's men regrouped as a single unit, lying on their stomachs firing controlled bursts. David ducked behind the armchair as the lodge was strafed and wood splintered off the window frame.

There was some shouting out in the field. Four of Abasi's men got to their feet and started running towards the buildings. They were taken down in a hail of bullets from the Ranger's inside the huts.

After a couple of minutes the number of shots fired by Abasi's men tapered off until they stopped altogether. Then one of them decided to make a run for it and bolted for the creek that connected the two waterholes. He made it through the line of snares but not the landmines. One of the smaller payloads exploded beneath him and he was thrown in the air. Shock must have stopped the pain, he tried to stand up but both his legs had been severed below the knee. The man toppled over without a sound, blood pumping from the tattered stumps.

Chege and Rashid sent a volley of fire at the GSU officers from their positions in the trees. That was enough for the remaining eight men, rifles raised above their heads they got to their feet. Rashid came out from the trees and started walking towards them and then Chege appeared. David heard one of the doors to the huts being slammed as someone went out.

David didn't wait. He left the lodge and started running towards where he had seen Abasi go down. He reached the clearing and was forced to walk as he navigated his way through the few remaining booby-traps. Billowing smoke from the helicopter and burning grass were making visibility difficult.

He could hear someone whimpering and followed the sound. The smoke cleared for a second and he could see a figure sitting in the grass ahead of him.

Abasi was too busy struggling with the elephant snare to hear him approach, trying to loosen the barbed wire with his fingers. The wire was connected to a stake buried in the ground a few feet away. It had cut through his muscle to the bone. Elephants had no way of removing the wire and would instinctively pull until eventually they collapsed with exhaustion. Or it cut through their leg completely.

David fired a shot into the ground near Abasi's feet to get his attention, "Put your hands where I can see them."

Abasi twisted towards him and glared but did as he was told. That was when David noticed the golden amulet lodged between his chin and his tunic. He took a step forward to get a closer look and a shiver ran down his spine. The two-headed figure from his nightmares glowed in the sunset, just as it had in the headlights the night that his father was murdered.

"You?" the blood seemed to drain from his arms and legs, David was rooted to the spot.

"Of course it's me, you idiot!" the Commander sneered and the scarred side of his face went into spasm.

David's lifted his rifle so that it was pointing at Abasi's chest, "You don't even recognise me do you?"

Abasi frowned, "What do you mean?"

"Five years ago on a small farm outside Kisii you murdered my father and then raped my mother." David struggled with the words, his voice choked up with emotion, "You made us watch when you shot him in the back of the head! You bastard"

"What the hell are you talking about?" The smirk disappeared and David thought that he saw a flicker of comprehension in the Commander's eyes.

"Well, my mother didn't die. When I dragged her out of the fire she was already pregnant with your child. Nine months later she gave birth to your daughter...my sister," his arms trembled with rage. "I'm going to kill you for what you did to my family, and to Caitlyn." David's finger tightened on the trigger but Damo's voice stopped him.

"Wait! Don't do it David...please put the gun down." There was a momentary pause, "He's my brother."

Abasi stared past David in disbelief, "Damo?"

"Yes Maliki it's me. I see that you are more of a disgrace to the family now than ever. I was devastated when you left. I see now that it was a blessing. At least our father died without knowing what kind of a monster you have become. How could you kill so many people? They say it was tens of thousands."

"They were all Kikuyu bastards and they deserved to die, every last one of them!" screamed Abasi. "Our beloved father was the monster! He made me what I am! How can you turn your back on your own son? Send him out into the bush with nothing?"

"Maybe he knew that you were consumed with greed, envy of his title. It was you who insisted on trying to make the passage into manhood early. You were always pushing to be the Chief."

"Damo." David glanced over quickly but kept the gun on Abasi, "What the hell is going on? Why did you call him Maliki?"

"Because that's his real name," Damo nodded towards Abasi. "I'm sorry. I should have spoken to you sooner. When you first told me about the night your father was killed and described the amulet. I knew then it could only be my brother. Only two of them were ever made and I own the other one. They were given to us by our mother."

David turned the gun on Damo. A seed of doubt had been sown in his mind, "You've got thirty seconds to explain why you never told me any of this before. Are you the one who has been supplying information to him?"

Damo shook his head and walked a few steps closer, "You've got to believe me, I didn't know that my brother was Commander Abasi until I spoke to Bernstein and put two and two together. I haven't seen him for over thirty years."

"So why didn't you tell me that you knew who my father's killer was?" David was shouting, "Were you trying to protect him?"

"I was selfishly protecting myself." Damo' voice broke, "Because I knew how you would react. I can see it in your eyes now, the hate...the doubt. I didn't want to lose you as my friend."

At that point in time David didn't trust either of them and wasn't sure who to shoot first. Out of the corner of his eye he saw a blur of movement from Abasi's direction.

"No!" screamed Damo.

Time stood still and he was frozen to the spot. Damo threw himself at David and knocked him sideways. In the same moment there was the deafening sound of a gun being fired twice in quick succession. Abasi had a smoking pistol in his hand and an insane grin on his lop-sided face. The madman started swinging the gun in David's direction. David instinctively reacted and pulled the trigger as his shoulder hit the ground.

The bullet went through Abasi's arm above the elbow and the gun flew from his hand. Then there was the sound of other voices as Chege and Rashid arrived on the scene.

"Cover him, I'll get the Captain," shouted Chege.

"Lie face down on the ground with your hands behind your head," Rashid walked over to Abasi and kicked him in the back, so that he fell forwards. Then he pressed the muzzle of his rifle against the Commander's neck.

"Are you OK," asked Chege, taking hold of David's elbow as he got to his feet.

"I wasn't hit," he looked down at Damo. He was clutching his chest with both hands trying to stem the flow of blood. His machine-gun discarded on the ground next to him and a wide-eyed look on his face.

David glanced up at the sky where a few of the brighter stars were already visible. The light was fading fast and night would soon be upon them.

"Chege, help me bring him inside. Rashid, make sure that the Commander is secured along with the other prisoners," David shouldered the rifle. He grabbed Damo's collar and pulled him to his feet.

Between them Chege and David shepherded him over to the lodge. Abasi's men had been rounded up and were kneeling in the dirt. Half of them with hands on their heads. The other GSU officers' arms had already been zip-tied behind their backs by a Ranger who was working his way down the line. David did a quick head count of the rangers watching over them. By the looks of it Damo was the only casualty they had suffered. Scott and Bernstein walked over to intercept them.

"Where's Commander Abasi?" Bernstein looked past him towards the clearing but David didn't stop walking.

"Rashid's got him," he called over his shoulder. "Go and give him a hand."

They propelled Damo up the rickety steps to the lodge and lowered him onto the wooden floorboards in the lounge.

"Chege, get headquarters on the radio and ask for Deputy Director Tanui, refuse to speak to anyone else. Let me know when you've got hold of him."

"Yes sir," the ranger went over to the desk and started twiddling with the dials of Scott's equipment. The sound of static invaded the room.

"You've got some serious explaining to do when you get better," David knelt down beside his friend and unbuttoned his shirt. One of the bullets had penetrated his lung, pink frothy liquid bubbled out when he exhaled. The other slug's passage was marked by a puckered hole two inches to the left that was spurting bright arterial blood.

David went over to the counter and retrieved the med kit they had left there. He opened it on the floor next to Damo and found a padded bandage.

He put it over the wound and applied pressure, "What the hell did you do that for?"

"I should have told you before that my brother killed your father," Damo's eyes closed for a second and then fluttered open again. His voice was hoarse, little more than a whisper when he spoke.

Tears were running down his cheeks. David had to lean closer in order to hear him, "I'm sorry David."

Imagining Abasi without the scars David realised now why he had looked so familiar the first time he saw him, "Why didn't you ever try to contact him?"

"Maasai tradition forbids it...he was expelled from the tribe for failing the lion hunt." Damo gasped like he was fighting for breath, "Besides he's pure evil, he always has been, ever since he was a child."

Those were Damo's last words, his eyes glazed over and the life went out of him.

EPILOGUE
Nairobi War Cemetery, Ngong Road
August 27th, 1996

A week later nearly all of the Rangers on active duty gathered at Langata Cemetery for Damo's funeral. As his coffin was lowered into the ground David and the rest of the honour guard fired a single shot to mark his friend's passing. The sound reverberated through the gravestones like rolling thunder and then the heavens opened and it started to rain. To David it seemed only fitting that the weather reflected the sombre mood, raindrops ran down from his brow and mixed with the tears.

As the bugler finished his reverie the crowd began to disperse. David instructed the squad to shoulder arms and then dismissed them. Chege, Rashid and Makori embraced him before they left and David hoped that he didn't have to witness so many grown men crying ever again. Everybody he spoke to said the same thing, albeit in different ways. They simply didn't come any better. David was devastated by his death but there was a lot about Damo that he didn't know. He understood now that most of the time people only let you see what they want you to. Both Caitlyn and Damo had taught him that.

David was glad in a way that he wasn't able to go to Caitlyn's funeral. At her mother's request he had made the arrangements for Caitlyn's body to be flown back to Ireland.

Somebody coughed to get his attention and David realised that Deputy Director Tanui was standing right beside him.

"I'm sorry about Damo." They were both staring down at the coffin, "I know that you two were close."

"It's not your fault, sir," David looked over at him, "What's happening with Abasi?"

They seemed to be sticking with 'Peter Abasi' even though they now knew that his real name was Maliki. When the Commander's residence was searched they found enough incriminating evidence in a vault behind his study to put him away for the rest of his life.

"He's being held in Kamiti Maximum Security Prison until a trial date can be fixed," replied Tanui. "The tape recording of Gupta's confession that you sent to your Aunt will be used as evidence. That was good thinking on your part."

David thought it fitting that Abasi was being detained where he had first recruited Gupta all those years ago.

"What about Councillor Wei?"

Tanui sighed and threw some dirt on the coffin, "Diplomatic immunity. The bastard's already left the country and I don't expect that he'll be coming back anytime soon."

"So that's it? He just skips the country and there's nothing we can do about it?" David unclenched his fists. It still hurt when he tensed his shoulder muscles.

"I'm afraid so, it's up to the Chinese authorities to follow up on the report I sent them. But I wouldn't hold your breath. Wei's family is well connected and trading ivory is so embedded in their culture that it isn't really considered to be illegal over there."

David didn't know what to say. The rain started to get heavier and came down in sheets.

Tanui produced a black umbrella and held it above their heads, "Come on, I'll walk you to your car."

They walked between the weeping willows that lined the path of neatly clipped grass. Either side of them, rows of identical white tombstones marked the final resting place for thousands of Kenyan heroes. Soon there would be one more above Damo's grave.

"We did discover something about Abasi's past." Tanui spoke up to be heard above the rain bouncing off the canopy, "His Swahili servant was interviewed, a man called Jozi. He's known Abasi since he was thirteen. They lived together on the streets in Mombasa before a British family called the Masons took Abasi in. Apparently he slit the throats of the parents and two children in their sleep when he turned eighteen. Then he stole a small fortune from their safe and burnt the house down. According to Jozi, Abasi used the money to fund his poaching enterprise. The police in Mombasa are checking with the local school to see if there is any record of a 'Peter Mason'. That's the name he was using then."

David shook his head woefully, like the Maasai God depicted on Abasi's medallion the two brothers had been opposites, good and evil. The world seemed out of balance with Abasi still alive and Damo dead, even though he would probably rot to death in jail. In Kenya life meant life.

"Has the President made a statement yet?"

"No and I don't expect him to." Tanui sucked in his cheeks, "Moi's been seen to campaign against poaching for years, he'll want to distance himself as much as possible from any political backlash."

As David remembered it was Moi who had lit the twelve tonnes of ivory in front of the world's media. Abasi being convicted of smuggling certainly wasn't going to look good for him in the eyes of the public. The lawn walkway ended between some flowered borders next to the gravel car lot. They made a beeline for his LandRover that was parked near the exit.

"Have you got any further finding out who the mole is that was supplying Abasi with information?"

"No, but detectives have been going through Abasi's telephone bills," replied Tanui. "Looking for any numbers that match our records. Hopefully something will turn up."

They reached the battered old LandRover and David found the key for the door. Surprisingly, only the wheels and windscreen wipers needed replacing when he found it outside the supermarket near the airport.

"Thanks," David got in behind the steering wheel and closed the door. He wound the window down a fraction.

"There's something else I wanted to talk to you about." The Deputy Director leant towards the jeep, "I've been offered the job as the new head of the GSU. Minister Kamotho put my name forward at Professor Mutungi's suggestion. When I phoned the Professor he said that it was your idea and I should thank you."

The Professor had come to see him earlier in the week at Headquarters, he was trying to organise a medal or some sort of commendation but David had refused. Being in the public spotlight was the last thing he wanted.

"I just mentioned that you might be the right person for the job." He managed a fleeting smile, "To tell you the truth, I couldn't think of anyone else when he asked me."

"Well thanks anyway." Tanui remained serious, "I'm going to need people that I can trust, people who can think for themselves. I'd like you to come and join me. It would mean a promotion and a significant pay rise."

David was honest with him, "I'm not sure what I want right now. I'm going to spend some time with my family before I decide what to do next."

His mother would be waiting for him with Kiira and Aunty Farisi. David hoped that bringing his father's killer to justice would bring his mother some sort of closure.

Although so far it hadn't worked for him, the recurring nightmares had got worse if anything.

Perhaps it was because of the tremendous guilt he felt. Not just because Caitlyn and Damo had died, but that he had come so close to pulling the trigger and executing Abasi. The line between right and wrong seemed very blurred.

"Promise me that you'll think about it at least?"

"OK," right then David would have said anything to get away. He started the engine. "I'll give it some thought."

Watch out for the other books in this series;

DIVIDED THEY FALL
Part II in the David Nbeke Series

And

SWAHILI SUNSET
Part III in the David Nbeke Series

Printed in Great Britain
by Amazon